Num8ers Guy

By Ping Ha Chi

Published by Ping Ha Chi, LLC www.pinghachi888.com
North Carolina
Copyright © 2016 by Ping Ha Chi, LLC

Num8ers Guy
ISBN-13: 978-0-9984025-0-5 ISBN-10: 0-9984025-0-8

Cover & Book Layout by Joy Klein

Printed in the United States of America

∞

DEDICATION

All that I am or ever hope to be,
I owe to my angel Mother.
--Abraham Lincoln

To my 3 moms – Mom, Carol and Becky. Thank you for your love, support and teaching me how to fly. There is no measuring how much you are missed. Know that you are in my heart, always.

∞

DEDICATION

A friend is one that knows you as you are, understands where you have been, accepts what you have become, and still, gently allows you to grow.
-- William Shakespeare

To my friends. Thank you for all the fond memories.
As we grow older, I smile when I reflect on the
special moments spent with you.

∞

DEDICATION

"What" and "If" are two words as non-threatening as words can be.
But put them together side-by-side and they have the power to haunt
you for the rest of your life: What if? What if? What if?
-- Letters to Juliet

To my Mona Lisa.
I am so fortunate that our paths first crossed
on Okinawa. Thank you for the inspiration
and I will always think of your fondly.

ACKNOWLEDGEMENT

There are so many people to thank who provided ideas, comments, advice and support. I could not have made it this far without all of you. Thank you.

- Dad for planting the seeds early in my life about writing a book. Dad never completed his book project so I felt compelled to publish. Thank you.
- My sister for all your tutoring, support and love during those especially difficult times. Thank you.
- My family for always being there. Thank you.
- Jules for the wonderful coffee to discuss this project in January 2016. Your mentorship in navigating all the stages of writing a novel was priceless. Thank you.
- Joann, Joy, Kelli and Suzy for your commitment to this book and responding to the daily excessive calls and emails. I treasure our friendship, the daily conversations and comments. Thank you.
- Judy, Ron, Ronnie and Sean for enduring the first draft, all the emails, phone calls, subsequent drafts and redlines.
- Becky, Brian, Brittany Qiunn, Cheri, Debs, Kathy, Liz, Randy and Tams for allowing me to bounce ideas off. Thank you.
- Wanda for your valuable insights on the book cover and artwork. Thank you.
- DeeDee for your translation of important words and concepts. Thank you.
- Holly for the amazing photos. Thank you.
- Riena for the wonderful artwork. Thank you.
- Team (Beach, Belt, Mr. Bolisy, Compliance, Improver, Inspiration, SuperWoman and Teacher) for making the Num8ers Guy come to life! Thank you Lindas for listening to me.

CONTENTS

Chapter 1

GSD

September 2007

Ping! I glanced down at my phone…1,888 emails and 88 text
messages stared back at me. Excited, I thought, ah, the number "8"
repeating… lots of 8s appearing means it's going to be a lucky day!
The quantity of emails, combined with the number of texts received,
was often a good indicator of how busy I would be that day. For me,
it was always about the digits and numbers. Digits represent art,
especially the number 8. To the average person it is just a number,
but the figure 8 is much more than that. Two interlocking circles,
gracefully connected, infinitely. For me, the numbers never lie. Got
to give those 12th Century Europeans an "atta boy" for having the
foresight to adopt the Hindu-Arabic Numeral system. Just think, we
could still be using the Roman Numeric system today. I shuddered.
The thought of such nonsense sent a wave of nausea through my
system. I redirected my attention back to my phone. Looking
through my texts, I thought the quantity of emails and texts were a
bit low for noon, but that was okay. I saw a text marked "urgent" and
read it. *"Eight meetings today starting at eight-thirty."* Disgusted, I
growled, "Blasphemous! How could anyone defile numerals—
especially the beautiful number 8—like that?"

I put the phone down, glanced back at the emails and
thought, well, the day is still young.

There was still a high probability that those numbers would
double in the next couple of hours. The number of deals that would
roll across my path on any given week was, at most times, obscene,
but I loved it. Each deal made me feel ecstatic—a high unlike any

I'd ever experienced. As the stakes got higher, I was driven to outdo my previous deals. My name is Sam Rivtoc, and I am a deal junkie.

High-stakes business was the name of my game, and I always found a way to be smack dab in the middle of it. I'd been advising start-up companies for as long as I could remember. In a previous life, I was a Silicon Valley lawyer representing high-tech companies, venture capital (VC) firms and public companies with growth strategies. There were always individuals looking to monetize their equity through an initial public offering (IPO) as well as expand or exit from dabbling in mergers and acquisitions (M&As).

High-stakes business was the perfect environment for a deal junkie like me looking for his next big hit. It was the only way to keep the high going. Seven days a week, 16 hours a day, it didn't matter. I loved the game of negotiation. The adrenaline rush created from finding simple workarounds for challenging issues was my drug of choice. And as with any addict, the drug of choice always came with a price. There was never anything less than $20 million on the line. A child of a results-driven Korean-American Mom, it seemed apropos that I would be nothing but successful. Success can be measured by many sticks and can mean different things. In the gray matter between my ears, success meant one thing and one thing only. Results.

I recalled a $150 million M&A transaction where neither side was willing to budge on a $1 million issue. We'd been negotiating for weeks. The CEOs asked everyone to leave the room. In the hallway, all the advisors were nervously waiting, wondering how the deal was going to play out—deal or no deal. Observing everyone in the hallway reminded me of those days as a child watching game shows with my mom, Tong-Im. She would sit on our military-issue couch with the mustard-yellow upholstery and watch game shows day after day with me at her side, just observing and not asking any questions. I remembered the contestants jumping up and down, excited just to be in the game. It was a curious thing for a child of 5, but I learned early on that everything was about the numbers. I shook off the memories and refocused myself. Back in the hallway, the air was thick with anticipation. Although I may have appeared calm and collected, inside I was jumping around like I was getting ready to embark on the journey of a lifetime. No doubt about it... being a contestant in this game of high-stakes negotiations was the ultimate turn-on.

Every day, for weeks during those negotiations, I would sip coffee for energy and eat a scoop of Dulce de Leche ice cream for relaxation. It was the secret to my late night, high-stress lifestyle. After 5 hours, we still had no deal.

"Damn it!" It was the bottom of the 9th, and I was being paid to close deals. But this hiccup was just that. I had anticipated that this might happen. I was always prepared to expect the unexpected. Running my hands through my hair, I left my spot on the wall and walked into the room, suggesting we flip a coin to settle matters. Addressing everyone, I said, "I recall a time when I flipped a coin and learned a valuable lesson." I reached into my pocket, grabbed my lucky 1888 Morgan Silver Dollar coin that Mom had given to me and looked at the CEOs, hoping my gamble would pay off.

"Heads you pay, tails we pay."

My intuition was intact. Just like that, the deal was done.

I left that deal on top of the world. That coin flip solidified many things in my life. The average partnership track was 8 years. I made it in 5. I was the youngest partner in the 1000-person law firm of Billings, Day and Knight, LLP, billing at $500 an hour, cruising around in a Mercedes Benz S500 and living in an $800,000 restored 3-bedroom Craftsman. I wore only the finest Brioni suits and Robert Graham shirts. On any given night, you could see me dining at premier restaurants, topping the evenings off with Dom and Armand. There were drizzle-makers, rainmakers, but only one, Head Honcho. I was the King of the Hill. Many tried to knock me off, but I was like the Rubber Band Man. I would bounce right back on top. I had the respect of all on my team - 15 lawyers, 7 paralegals and 8 legal assistants. When it came to the deal, I had a knack for closing. My nickname was Gets Shit Done (GSD)! I was trained to believe that everyone deserved representation. The harder the deal, the bigger the adrenaline rush.

I was a deal junkie, always in search of my next fix.

Can you raise capital for a founder with a past bankruptcy? Sure, everyone deserves a 2nd chance. Can you go public with a convicted felon CFO? What felony? I love the challenge. It might be tough, but I'm willing to give it a try. My fix was on. The higher the risk, the higher the high. I was addicted to the thrill of the deal.

Another problem was looming, though. The bigger the deal, the increasing awareness that my body was giving out on me and taking a toll on my overall health. I didn't care. What addict does? Someone wanted results? I was your go-to guy because I got shit done.

I checked my phone again. Sure enough, there were another 308 emails and 78 text messages. That was more like it.

I was the life of the deal party… and a ticking time-bomb to boot, ready to explode at any moment.

Chapter 2
Serving Two Masters

Flashback to September 2006

Ping! 2608 emails, 88 texts, all about the same thing. Business ethics became big news, and regulatory scrutiny started intensifying in 2001. In the beginning, those issues were merely speed bumps to me. By 2006, they had become roadblocks and detours. A real drag on the deal flow. Major headlines showcased the uncovering of big business defrauding investors with creative schemes. It was a sobering wake-up call. Everyone was being affected. The aftermath was crippling. Through Enron alone, over 4,000 employees lost their jobs; investors were defrauded of nearly $60 billion, pension funds were lost, and trust in the American economic system began to spiral downward. These events came at the worst time possible. The findings created new obstacles and put a huge damper on the number of deals flowing my way.

My administrative assistant, Jules, regularly clipped the newspaper articles exposing the many different companies that were suspected of fraud.

"Can you believe Enron followed by Tyco, Adelphia, and every month a new list of companies?" Jules asked almost rhetorically. She shook her head. "Don't any of these companies have any scruples?"

I threw my hands up, knowing that question was almost impossible to answer. It had been a long couple of months watching the house of cards come tumbling down. I sighed inwardly, aware that this could only mean more bad news for everyone.

"Just have Debs keep an eye out for changes in the law due to the Enron scandal. We need to better understand the Sarbanes-

Oxley Act since Congress and the SEC are planning to place more regulatory controls on publicly traded companies." Sarbanes-Oxley, or SOX for short, was enacted by the 107th United States Congress in July of 2002 to regulate public companies in order to protect shareholders and the general public from accounting practices that were not on the up and up.

Jules jotted a note to herself. "Sure, I'll let Debs know. It's a shame, though, all those thousands of dollars lost."

She was right about the money. Still, I didn't think that she fully grasped how far-reaching the impact of these scandals was on everyday people. "Don't forget all the families and folks that invested their hard-earned currency in these companies. Many had been investing not only for their future, but for their kids' futures as well. Their entire investment portfolios were wiped out in a single day. Serving one's own interest can only lead to one thing."

Jules nodded her head in agreement.

Prior to government intervention, legal firms would skirt the issues to serve their own interests. I learned quick ways around legal mumbo jumbo. There were always loopholes that firms would use as workarounds. SOX made it difficult to do anything. I served the interests of many of my clients, as well as my firm, regardless of the ramifications to the average Joe.

I ran through all of my cases in my head. I felt a little nauseated. Was I part of the problem? I received the American Jurisprudence Award for the highest grade in legal ethics during law school, but did I know the true meaning of fiduciary duty?

I could define "ethics," but did I really understand the meaning of that word? Every officer and director owed a duty of care and loyalty not to profit from their relationship unless they had the shareholders' express informed consent. Sounds easy on paper, but it was challenging in real life. The application of fiduciary duty outside the ivory tower had many shades of gray, and prior to SOX, everyone would push the envelope to see how far he or she could go.

After devoting years of representing tens of thousands of companies, I had earned my black belt in the gray areas of business ethics—maneuvering and refining my skills on a daily basis. Yes, I was an expert in counseling CEOs and boards on how to maneuver around the wall instead of hitting it. But what about real life, complex fiduciary duties? How did my knowledge of how the "deal" works impact others? I may have known how to work around the wall, but going through it in sheep's clothing was a much bigger task.

All in all, the unscrupulous dealings of other firms slowed down my action. I needed to find new and creative ways of finding or developing clients that were still in the game of "deals." After all, I wasn't a dull compliance lawyer; I was a deal guy. Mr. GSD. It was challenging, but those needle-in-a-haystack clients were out there. I knew how to find them, but there was always something.

In November 2006, I earned my wings on perhaps my most challenging deal with a wireless start-up. Wireless Towers was a company that built cell towers throughout the South. They hit the market running and grew to a $50 million-valued company in just 2 years. Their Earnings Before Interest, Taxes, Depreciation and Amortization (EBITDA) were $10 million, and they had a valuation of 5-times that. Always in the black, they operated with $15 million cash on hand.

The primary principals involved were Wanda and Keith Jenkins, who owned one-half of the company, while their daughter, Suzy, owned the other half. Wanda and Keith wanted to sell the company for $40 million, and Suzy wanted to continue to grow it. I represented Wireless Towers, which meant I represented the Board, whose only members were Keith and Suzy.

It was 4 days of the Hatfields and McCoys. 4 grueling days that always ended in a deadlock. After hours and days of emotionally charged meetings, we were at a stalemate. Each day, I had consumed a pot of coffee and a pint of Dulce de Leche ice cream to keep me going. This impasse had me caught between a rock and a hard place. Although I was present in the meeting, the family focused atmosphere encouraged my mind to drift to fond memories spent with Mom. The fun arguments and strategies that I used to negotiate how much ice cream I could have. How often she would fall for the *I'm-sick-and-depressed* tactic versus the *I-love-you* approach. It was this place and time that I would escape to when I felt conflicted. I had an excellent relationship with my parents. Floating back to these moments gave me clarity.

As I broke out of my daydream, I asked Wanda if I could speak to her alone. I opened the door and motioned for her to come. We went downstairs and out the door for a walk outside. November in Atlanta was typically mild. The air was crisp, and the city almost seemed magical, just right for a slow stroll. On the corner was a quaint little bakery tucked away below the high-rise buildings, offering a respite from the hustle and bustle of business life. We sat outside.

"Coffee or tea?" I asked.

"Earl Gray, please." Before I could ask, she added, "With cream only."

I walked inside, ordered, and emerged with 2 drinks. The heat from the cups warmed my hands as the aroma of bergamot wafted from Wanda's teacup. I placed the tea in front of Wanda, pulled out a wobbly chair, and sat down across from her. As she was in mid-sip, I asked, "Aren't you proud of Suzy?"

Shocked and bewildered, Wanda looked up at me and glared. "Are you siding with Suzy?"

I laughed. "Of course not. I think she's one tough cookie, no question about it! I'm guessing it has everything to do with a like-mother, like-daughter thing."

Wanda smiled and responded, "Well, yes, I raised her that way. She was always shy growing up. We wanted to raise her to stand up on her own 2 feet and always to shoot for the stars. We're very proud of her." Wanda took a sip of her tea and continued, "But Sam, we want out. And, as you well know, she doesn't."

As a cool breeze passed by, a childhood memory came to light. "This reminds me of a story Mom once told me. Near Korea, on 2 separate islands, there lived the exact same species of bird indigenous to those islands. On one island, there was an abundance of food and the birds no longer flew because all of their nourishment was provided for them locally. On the other island, finding food was an arduous undertaking. Those birds had to fly many miles to forage for food." With childlike optimism, I looked at Wanda, winked, and said, "Don't you think it is time to let Suzy fly?"

Wanda smiled. "What do you suggest?"

"Let me take my legalese hat off and paint you a hypothetical situation."
Wanda put her cup down, tilted her head, and squinted at me as if she was bracing herself for the ace up my sleeve. "Assuming that your house and cars are paid off, if you were to receive $10 million from the cash account and deposit that into a savings account, could you and Keith live off of an annual salary of $600,000 based on the interest?"

Wanda quickly responded, "Well, of course, we could. Who couldn't?" She winked at me and said, "Sam, I'm not that fast with numbers. Please speak English to me and not Finance. What are you getting at?"

Knowing that I had piqued her interest, I broke it down for her. "Sell Suzy your half for $10 million. You guys live on the interest of approximately $600,000 a year. Leave the remaining $5 million in cash for Suzy's operating expenses. In return, you'll receive a promissory note from Suzy for $5 million. Look at it as a $5 million investment in your daughter and a $5 million loan. If she succeeds, you're a proud mother. If she fails, then you get Suzy to realize that you fully supported her. In addition, you have a lifetime of 'I-told-you-so,' which I personally think is priceless."

Wanda laughed. "Let's get back in there. Give me about 30 minutes to work on Keith."

We finished up our drinks and headed back to the building. As we made our way back, I noticed the sky seemed little bluer and, although we walked in tandem at a regular pace, our return trip seemed quicker.

As we walked in, the boardroom was quiet. There was a noticeable chill that overwhelmed us as we reentered. I looked at Suzy and motioned for her to come with me to get some fresh air while her parents mulled things over.

Outside, Suzy quipped, "Wow, you guys were gone for only 30 minutes, but the silence while you were away was deafening. It made it feel like you were gone for hours. You're lucky that you left when you did." Suzy grabbed a pen and wrote the words "Eight million dollars" on a napkin she had in her pocket. "That's a lot of money they want to walk away from."

∞

I cringed as I read the words "Eight million dollars" that Suzy had scribbled onto the napkin. If that visual could be translated into a sound, it would be the sound of someone scraping their nails down a chalkboard. I wondered what ignoramus decided it was a *faux pas* to use digits in formal writing? The figure "8" is such a beautiful number and not merely an "eight." What if the National Football League 49ers were the Forty-Niners? They would be a team with a mid-life crisis and no longer be a football dynasty. I took a deep breath, shrugged off the blasphemous visual, and navigated back to the deal.

I looked Suzy right in the eyes, shook my head and said, "You know what? I would trade $50 million to be able to argue with my parents again. My parents passed away 2 years ago." I knew I had Suzy's attention and continued. "When I was in my teens, I was so angry at Mom for something that was so stupid and childish. I threw her favorite watch against the wall and broke it into a million pieces. What I didn't know was that it was a Cartier given to her by my father the day I was born. She was devastated but forgave me for my actions. It took me nearly 15 years to replace that watch. I bought 1 for me and 1 for her when I turned 30. There's no measurement I can give you to show you how much I miss my parents."

Suzy paused, silently acknowledging what I was trying to tell her.

"Anyway, I want you to know our firm thanks you for the 4 days of billable hours amounting to over $50,000. I thank you for the 4 days because at times I was reminded of the brutal arguments I had with my folks. They loved me and would have died for me. I'm certain that your parents love you, too. So here's what I'm thinking. Why don't you buy out your parents for $20 million?"

I stretched the number to $20 million from the $15 million I told Wanda because I wanted there to be some room to negotiate and felt that $5 million was a safe enough cushion.

"We can structure the deal in such way that you pay them $12 million today and the remaining $8 million in a year or 2. I figure you need approximately $3 million for operating expenses. You're starting your career and can afford to take risks, while they are at the end of their risk-taking days. That way you can have your cake, and your parents can eat it, too."

Suzy, smiling from ear to ear, lunged at me with a grateful hug. "Deal. Let's go in there and wrap up this family feud."

Upon my return, the air in the room seemed lighter. I motioned for everyone to sit down. "My firm appreciates your business. At this rate, you'll likely be paying our firm hundreds of thousands of dollars wastefully. While I've got all the billable time in the world for you, I need to attend a wedding this weekend. Therefore, I have a hard deadline of 3 o'clock tomorrow afternoon." Looking at my calendar, I stated, "I have 2 IPOs that need my attention early next week. We can reconvene next Thursday if we don't come to a meeting of the minds today."

I looked down at my watch to pace myself. "Can we take a 10-minute break?" I did this to manipulate the time for all to consider the points I had discussed with Wanda and Suzy separately. Although I was serving the interest of the board, I knew that this type of manipulation was within the boundaries of my fiduciary duties.

As I headed to the restroom, Jules handed me a note. It said "A-3 for flight to DC. Sorry, Sam, no A-1 again. But only 2 more flights to achieve SWA companion pass!"

As I folded up the note and put it in my pocket, I thought, Well, maybe then I will get the coveted A-1 ticket.

As an ongoing joke, I frequently told people my current place of residence was on a plane. I rarely spent more than a week in a single location, and I always obsessed over how many miles I had traveled each month. It took 1000 one-way flights or 110,000 miles in a single calendar year to achieve an SWA companion pass. It was the end of the 3rd quarter, so once I acquired the companion pass, I could designate anyone I wished to fly with me the rest of the year and the next calendar year for free. The question was… who would that lucky duckling be?

Chapter 3

TSA PreCheck

"Ping!" There were 8 missed calls, 300 more emails, and 24 additional texts. The messages were endless. I needed to focus on the task at hand.

I swung back by my office and logged into Southwest Airlines from my laptop. As I stared down at the screen, I thought, Damn it! Why don't I ever get the A-1 pass? That person must fly all the time!

I prided myself on being a Southwest frequent flier. I like Southwest, as they are well known for their excellent customer service. Once you reach the "A-list," you are automatically pushed into the "primo seat" queue. I was always curious: "Who could be flying more than me?" It was just another aggravation, like TSA screening. I looked back at the screen and saw that I was TSA PreCheck approved. Sweet, I thought. At least the expedition allowed me to shave off about 30 minutes. I didn't have to remove my jacket, laptop, belt, or shoes. Time is money, and at my rate, that would be $500 every time I flew. By my calculations, a hundred flights at $500 per incident equaled $50,000 in billable hours lost. Yeah, yeah, yeah... I know all these precautions are in the name of National security, but that's the way my mind was trained to think. Numbers, numbers, numbers. But I digress.

Noticing the time, I logged out of Southwest Airlines and headed back to the conference room. When I arrived, I turned to Wanda and asked, "Have you had a chance to talk to Keith?"

Keith acknowledged and laughed at my inquiry. "You know, when we started this business, all we expected was that it put food on the table, pay the rent and help our daughter with a job. Never in our wildest dreams did we imagine making $5 million, much less more than $40 million. We've seen a lot of dot.com companies succeed and fail overnight. Our company is solid. Wanda and I are old and ready for retirement. We're ready to head out to Destin, Florida, to break out our beach chairs and begin sipping golden margaritas. Suzy, what if you buy us out for $5 million? Your mom and I can live on $400,000 a year on the interest alone, and you keep the rest. Deal?"

Suzy looked at me and screamed, "Hell, no! No deal!" She had tears in her eyes. "I would not be able to set foot in the office knowing all the sacrifices that you've made for me. I say, $10 million today and a $15 million note payable in 4 years, plus 10 percent interest and not a penny less."

Wanda countered, "I'm your mother, and Mother knows best. It should be $5 million today and a $5 million note payable in 50 years."

In the interest of doing my job, I jumped in. "You do know that you guys are negotiating against your own self-interest? Are you sure that's your final offer, Wanda? Suzy, are you going to counter with a higher offer?"

It was about 8:00 p.m. In earnest victory, I suggested, "Why don't you guys go celebrate over dinner and give me time to draft the closing documents? We can reconvene tomorrow at 10:00 a.m. to go over the documents and sign off by 1:00 p.m."

They agreed, gathered their things, and began to head out the door. Wanda turned to me. "Won't you be joining us, Sam?"

"Thank you, Wanda, but there is much to be done. I'd like to get this knocked out with precision and without any hiccups."

Wanda smiled. "Don't stay up too late, tiger. Mothers know best." She waved and threw a wink my way. It made me nostalgic for those days when Mom would say the same thing.

I summoned Debs to the conference room. Debs was my right-hand gal. Born in mid-western Nebraska, she'd spent the last 8 years of her life at Billings, Day and Knight—5 of those dedicated to taking care of all my scheduling and business needs.

"We need to draft a stock purchase agreement, a promissory note, resolutions and other ancillary documents. Can you work on the first draft? I need to go home and pack for tomorrow."

Debs took down all the information while I grabbed my jacket and phone. As I began to leave, I added, "Would you place the printed drafts on my desk? I will be back at 10:00 p.m. to review them."

Concerned, she glanced up at me. "Have you eaten dinner, Sam?"

I let out a loud "Ha!". "Debs, you know the answer to that question. Can you go out and get me something?"

"What would you like to eat? The usual?"

"Yes, sushi would be awesome."

Debs added "sushi" to her list of to-dos and left my office.

As I drove home, I was pleased that what started as a stalemate of the worst kind ended with a happily ever after. But the deal reminded me to avoid situations where neither party had a larger share than the other. A 50/50 ownership was challenging and required a lot of finessing to break a deadlock. It was true with everything in life, work or love: no single person could serve 2 masters.

Once home, I showered and changed into jeans and a Georgetown Hoya sweatshirt while thinking of all the things that needed to get packed. This was the first Saturday and Sunday I'd taken off in 8 months. I was ready and excited to go to the wedding. My colleagues were shocked that I had finally decided to take a 2-day vacation. What did I need to pack? My Brioni wedding tuxedo, bow tie, cufflinks, 2 shirts in case I spilled something, shoes, 2 boxers, 2 black socks, jeans, Robert Graham shirts, gloves, accessory bag, and last but not least, my sentimental winter cashmere tan overcoat I nick-named Ba-Ba-Ri.

Ah, my coat. About 10 years ago, shortly before the holidays, I asked Mom what she wanted for Christmas. Most years she was quick to say, "Some Coco Chanel or Chanel No 5 would be nice." Mom was a big Chanel fan. She admired Gabrielle Bonheur and how she made a name for herself as a fashion designer and businesswoman. But that year Mom wasn't quick to say what she wanted. She pondered and responded that she would like a Ba-Ba-Ri coat. Not wanting to look stupid, I called my sister, Jean, and asked if she knew what a Ba-Ba-Ri coat was.

Jean responded, "Huh? I have never heard of a Ba-Ba-Ri coat before. Anyway, I don't wear those heavy coats in California, so I wouldn't know. I'm sure if you ask any salesperson at the store, they could help you."

Taking Jean's word for it, I headed to the mall and asked several sales associates if they knew of the coat. Each time, I was told, "Sorry, Sir, but I've never heard of that coat."

The mad Christmas holiday shopping had already begun. Crowds of people stood and waited in long lines. I made an executive decision and purchased Mom a cute red winter coat. She opened the gift, smiled, and thanked me. The following year, I asked her what she wanted for Christmas, and again she replied, "A Ba-Ba-Ri coat."

At that moment, I realized that last year's gift was an "EPIC" fail. I flew to New York City, figuring they would have a larger selection of coats to choose from. Again, each salesperson would stare at me as if I had 3 eyes. I felt like I was in a scene from that movie *Groundhog Day*. I changed tactics. Perhaps Ba-Ba-Ri was a color? I began my search for this idea of the coat.

Again, there were large crowds and long lines. I'm all about time and not much of a shopper. Most times, I know what I want, so I go to the department store, find what I need, pay and exit. Having to stand in line was not my cup of tea. I had places to go and people to see. I made another executive decision. This time I purchased a tan winter overcoat. As she had the year before, Mom opened the gift, smiled, and thanked me.

The next year, I asked Mom what she wanted for Christmas. Same story. "A Ba-Ba-Ri coat." Ugh! My spider senses were off when it came to Mom and this coat. I cringed, knowing that I had spent hours and days in 20 different stores in 2 separate cities.

I called Jean and told her what had happened. I could almost hear her roll her eyes. "Mom doesn't need any more coats. She already has 4. Don't buy her another winter coat!" We laughed and decided on other gifts. Still, Mom was consistent and would always request a Ba-Ba-Ri coat every Christmas until she passed away 2 years ago.

Last October, I was fortunate to negotiate a distribution agreement for a clothing manufacturer with a leading Korean department store. While in Seoul tying up loose ends, I decided to wander through some of the department stores. On a whim, I asked the saleslady, "Do you know what a Ba-Ba-Ri coat is?"

She nodded yes and directed me to the "Burberry" section. I was so overwhelmed with joy that I laughed loudly and struggled to hold back tears. After I had gathered myself together, I explained the whole story to the salesperson and told her I would be back the following day. That night, I asked Jean, "What size coat do you wear?"

"Sam, what are you up to?" she asked.

"Sis. It's a surprise."

I purchased 2 Ba-Ba-Ri coats the next day, 1 for myself and the other for Jean as a Christmas present. This is the reason why I love the winter season so much. It allows me to wear my Ba-Ba-Ri coat and to reminisce about Mom every time I put it on.

When I returned to the office at 9:45 p.m., the Wireless Tower closing documents were neatly organized on my desk along with a sushi dinner, coffee, and a note saying, *Check fridge for ice cream.*

Debs always knew what it took to keep me going. I probably would have starved to death if it weren't for her.

Life was good. I dove into the food and papers in a planned, purposeful, and multi-tasking manner. I'm all about efficiency. When the Wireless Tower closing documents were marked up, I dropped them off at the Word Processing Department around midnight with a notation; *Please turn these documents around by 7:00 a.m.* Satisfied, I grabbed my coat and headed out the door.

I drove over to the financial printers, where my team was working on 2 S-1s, public offering registration statements. We were responding to SEC comments for Silicon Networks, a cyber security company, and SocMedia, a social media company. Each deal was staffed with 3 attorneys from Billings, Day and Knight representing Silicon and SocMedia, 2 attorneys representing the underwriters, or the investment banks, 2 officers from the companies, 3 accountants, and 2 underwriter representatives.

It was 12:45 a.m. During the day, there were normally 10 to 14 people in each of the conference rooms. After dinner, the heavy lifters remained, while the C-level people retired for the day. I snuck into Conference Room A first, confident that the Silicon deal had the least amount of issues attached to it. There were 5 people working like busy bees. I asked if everything was okay and everyone nodded yes. The junior lawyer representing the investment bank responded, "We are in good shape!"

In Conference Room B, I instructed the Billings, Day and Knight lawyers to work with SocMedia and the accountants to flag every page on S-1 that would be affected by this issue. I grabbed the latest version of the SocMedia S-1 and headed to the lounge. By 4:15 a.m., I had reviewed, commented and marked up both the Silicon and SocMedia registration statements, handed them to my team, eaten a scoop of Dulce ice cream, and headed back to the office. As I closed the door, I set the alarm for 7:30 a.m., and placed a notepad and pen next to my head. As I fell asleep on my office sofa, I mumbled... "I have too many masters."

∞

Chapter 4
Looking for the Fool

Ping! I grabbed my phone to check the time. It was 5:55 a.m. I glanced over at my laptop and saw that 88 emails had arrived while I had slept. I needed to get up, but my body begged me to close my eyes again. It seemed like only a couple minutes had passed when there was a knock at my office door. I jumped up off the couch as the mail deliverer entered. "Excuse me, Sir, but here is the document from word processing you requested to be delivered by 7:00 a.m."

I rubbed my eyes. "How many times have I told you not to call me Sir? Sir makes me sound old… like, my father. I'm Sam and thanks for getting this to me on time."

When the courier left, I chuckled to myself. "I am Sam. I should have said, 'I am Sam I am.' Oh well, a missed opportunity."

I reviewed the documents and noticed a few typos along with some edits. I grabbed the notepad I had placed on the stand near the couch the night before. As I began to write, I noticed the words "Get It" written at the top. I continued to leave a message on the paper for Jules, my assistant. It read:

Get It. Please make these changes and send to Debs Foreman. I am resting in the office. Wake me up at 9:00 a.m. Wireless Tower to arrive at 10:00 a.m. No one is to disturb me until then. Thanks.

I lay back down again on the couch and drifted off to sleep.

I've never been a vivid dreamer. The content of my dreams usually consisted of a reenactment of the day that had just passed. Meticulously, I'd go over the details in my mind. The boardroom, Wireless Towers, coffee, Earl Gray tea, bringing a family back together again. All the details down to Wanda's ivory chenille

21

sweater. But wait, who was that sitting in the corner of the room? I heard a knocking in my head, and I began to stir from my slumber.

Another knock. "Good morning, Sam. It's me, Jules, and this is your 9:00 a.m. wake-up call. I brought you a towel, shampoo, toothbrush, toothpaste and gel. Your extra suit, shoes, socks, shirt, and tie are on the chair. Debs wanted you to know that 3 sets of closing documents are upstairs. I'll let her know that you'll meet her up in the conference room by 9:30." I gave her a salute and a 10-4 as I popped up off of the couch. Good Ol' Jules. She was like my 2nd mother. *Wake up... move, move, move.* Without Jules, I would probably drive my staff insane.

I showered, changed and headed to the conference room. Keith, Wanda, and Suzy had already arrived and were reviewing the documents. The smell of coffee penetrated my senses as I wandered over to the coffee station. "Would anyone care for some coffee or tea? Wanda? Keith? Suzy?" All acknowledged that they were fine for the moment. "Please take as much time as needed to review the documents. I am here to answer any questions you may have." I poured a cup of coffee and sat down.

Keith asked, "This transfer of ownership is a straightforward transaction, correct?"

I acknowledged, "There are no hidden elements here. What you see is what you get, no contingencies." By noon, that deal was inked, and 3 sets of originals were signed. A set for Keith and Wanda, a set for Suzy, and the last set for Billings, Day and Knight.

"That's about it." I stood up and stretched. "Shall we celebrate over lunch?"

The 3 were elated. I called Jules and asked her to arrange a town car to drive us downtown for lunch. "Jules, while you are at it, please let FancyFoodie know we want a room off to the side."

∞

We arrived just in time to beat the lunchtime rush hour. "I know it is a little early to start drinking bubbly, but maybe just a little bit is in order to celebrate such a joyous occasion." I motioned for the server to bring us a bottle of their best champagne. The server returned with 4 glasses and poured champagne for us all. "On behalf of Billings, Day and Knight, we would like to congratulate you on your recent *friends and family* buyout. Wanda and Keith, we wish you an enjoyable and fun-filled retirement. Suzy, may you take your mother and father's legacy and shoot it to the moon!" Everyone lifted their glasses and cheered away the afternoon. After the food had arrived and we all settled into a little coffee and light dessert, I leaned over to Suzy and asked, "Was there someone else in the room the other day when we returned from our stroll?"

Suzy shook her head. "No, there were only the 4 of us. Why?"

"Well, usually I spend the evening going through the events of the day to make sure I have not missed anything. I could have sworn I saw someone in the corner sitting quietly."

Suzy smiled. "Sam, it was a long day and sometimes our eyes can play tricks on us. I wouldn't worry about it."

I laughed, "You're right. I think maybe I drank too much coffee." I closed out the bill, and we went back to the firm and parted ways.

The next day, there was a chill in the air. It was Friday afternoon, and I had just come down off my adrenaline rush from closing the Wireless Tower deal. Now it was time to come back down to Earth and maneuver my butt to DC. There was a wedding I needed to attend. Joe Raben was getting married, and there was no way I was going to miss that.

Joe and I became best friends in law school. We were thick as thieves back then. There are many things we participated in, many of which I would most likely plead the 5th on. We were also quite proficient at observing the mundane. While in law school, we spotted an older student at the library berating an undergraduate. Apparently, the undergrad was correcting him and he "didn't want some kid telling him what to do." We were like flies on the wall and found that specific interaction quite amusing. After that day, it became a running joke to throw our chest out spouting those eternal words… "I don't want no kid telling me…." As I reminisced about our peculiarities, it amused me to see how a couple of 35-year-old lawyers could behave in such a juvenile manner.

I landed at Reagan International in my Ba-Ba-Ri coat and was greeted by my best friend, Randi Cruz. Randi gave me a hug and said, "Where have you been hiding? Oh My Gawd! You look like you've gained at least 25 pounds." She poked me in my paunch.

Randi never did beat around the bush. We were solid friends from the day I met her, and I treated her just like family. Randi and I were both products of the military brat culture. Her father was a Major in the Navy while my Dad was a GS-11 working for Civil Services when we met on Kadena Air Base, in Okinawa, Japan. Our friends came from all walks of life—everywhere in the U.S. and internationally. The student body consisted of an amalgamation of every different combination of race and culture. Friendship, respect, and accomplishment were based on merit, not inheritance or rank. Granted, if your dad was the Base Commander, you might have gotten some preferential treatment.

Mom was Korean, and Dad was a civilian architect from Atlanta, Georgia. Randi's mother was from the Philippines, and her father from Hickory, North Carolina. The odds of us meeting on

Okinawa were 1 in a billion. She was new to the school, and my good friend immediately had a crush on her. He was dating someone else at the time but was hedging his bets. If she liked him, he would dump his girlfriend. Everything had to be top secret, so he asked me to run a covert operation because I was reliable and Got Shit Done at an early age.

"Thanks, Randi, for the compliment. I like you, too, but then again I like skid marks on my underwear." I grinned and nodded as we returned to our sophomoric ways. Randi gave me a slight push and laughed. I pulled out my phone. "Hey, give me a sec while I give Joe a call."

I called Joe, and he answered, "Hey, kid, have you landed?"

I replied, "I don't want some kid telling me he's getting married!" I laughed. "So what are we doing tonight? Let's go crazy!"

Joe whispered into the phone, "I can't do that. My wife, I mean fiancée, will kill me if I get drunk and ruin the wedding tomorrow."

I teased him. "I don't want some kid telling me their boss won't let them out. What are you, a skerdy cat or a lap dog? What time is the wedding, and when do I need to be there by?"

Joe warned me, "Don't get too crazy tonight, kid. The wedding party is meeting at 3:00 p.m. in the lobby at the Willard."

"Okay, kid, see you at 3:00."

Randi jabbed me in the side and asked, "Where to, Sam?"

"Let's go to that cigar place in Adam's Morgan."

"Ummmm, I've never smoked a cigar before in my life."

I laughed. "No worries, kid, I can walk you through."

Upon arriving, we ordered 2 double Macallan 25s, neat, and 2 Cohibas. The waitress asked to see my ID, and I looked at her and said, "What about her?" pointing to Randi.

She said, "No, she's fine."

I handed the waitress my ID. Randi rolled her eyes at me, closed them, then whispered, "Wait for it. Wait for it."

As the waitress read my ID, her eyes glazed over, and she looked back at me. "February 1971? Wow, I would have never guessed that. Thank you, Sir. That was 2 double Macallans, neat, and 2 Cohibas?"

Randi turned to me and said, "And there it is."

"Randi, don't be jealous because I have maintained my youthful demeanor and good looks."

"Sam, get a hold of yourself. What are you trying to imply?"

Luckily, the waitress returned with our order just in time. Randi asked while holding up one of the cigars, "What am I supposed to do?"

"You punch the cigar, and I'll light it while you smoke." She took a deep breath and coughed profusely.

"Oh, I forgot to warn you that you shouldn't inhale!"

Randi sarcastically responded by giving me the finger.

After Randi had caught her breath, we waxed nostalgic about our time in Okinawa, Japan.

I exhaled and said, "Ahhh, those were the days."

Randi sat up. "Remember running around stealing toilet paper from the bowling alley and the Kadena Air Terminal to TP our friends' houses?"

"Yes, Randi, but I'm only admitting this now that the statute of limitations has expired."

Randi leaned back in her chair and looked up at the ceiling. "That was fun running around hiding the rolls of TP in our pants and then destroying Tracy's house. Right?"

"A dozen times, right!"

"Remember Homecoming? You were limping around like a wounded biatch and complaining during halftime at the Homecoming game. This Queen wants a do-over. I was robbed! Instead of a handsome and charming King, I got a feeble whining and wounded one."

"Well, I know you felt horrible after you found out the next day that I had actually broken my ankle. I still don't know how I finished playing the game and danced all night long."

"Guilty as charged and sentenced to carrying your books to class for 2 months."

"Yeah, Mom was furious at me for further aggravating my injuries. She grounded me for a month. Cruel and unusual punishment, especially without any ice cream."

"Hey, by the by, didn't you date Caroline Dean?"

I glanced at my watch and noticed that it was 8:32 p.m. "Gosh, Randi, who didn't I date? It was like singing the lyrics from that popular song." Laughing and singing to the tune I spouted ... "a lot of Ann Marie by my side... more of Sarah with a smooth vibe... and a little bit of Susan in my stride."

Randi rolled her eyes again. "Seriously, what happened to Caroline? You had such a puppy crush on her."

"Caroline had that southern charm about her. We went on a double date to Naha at Kona Gardens. She was always so proper whenever I saw her."

"Do you remember gracefully tripping over a bush and tumbling as you said good night to her?"

"That was an epic fall, but I will never forget that first memorable kiss."

"Well, what happened?"

"I plead the 5th, Randi and am so happy that you don't live in Atlanta."

"Objection, non-responsive."

"What? Don't get all lawyerly on me, Randi." I took a puff off of the cigar and continued. "I was at Georgetown, and she was in Austin. Yes, she was there, and I was here. It was impossible to date someone long distance, especially at that age. I compared every relationship I had ever had to her. Is it wrong for me to compare every potential girl to Caroline?"

"By comparing all your relationships to your Sweet Southern Caroline, you are already dooming those relationships. They'll be bittersweet because no one will be as sweet." Randi picked up her single malt and took a swig. "Do you still keep in touch with her?"

"We talked about 2 years ago. She's unhappily married with 2 kids, living in Virginia."

"Wasn't she the one you bought that infinity necklace for?"

The thought of that necklace stirred up a lot of emotions for me. I tried to hold back the sadness I had locked away for so many years about that failed relationship.

"Yeah, I was like a child laborer working at the Naval warehouse near Gate 3. It was a sweatshop! A 90-degree summer heat coupled with 70 percent humidity. I worked the entire summer making $2.76 an hour, diligently saving to buy a used car. Instead, I seized the moment to purchase that infinity necklace. I told her that I would always love her infinitely…. or something dorky like that."

Randi put her glass back down. "Do you think she was the one? Was she the one that got away?"

∞

"I think she could have been the one, but I don't believe there is only one one."

I sighed and glanced at my watch; it was 9:03 p.m. "Obviously, I wasn't the one for her. "Remember Katy, Randi?"

"Oh yeah, you used to talk incessantly about her too and dated her for, wait for it, drum roll, please…. 1 whole long year! Wasn't she the person you dated the longest?"

"Hold on. We need another scotch." I caught the waitress' eye and motioned for her to come over. "She was the 2nd love of my life; ergo, our theory is correct that there isn't just one!"

The waitress came over, and I pointed to the Macallans, signaling for another round.

"What happened?"

"We drifted apart, literally. I went to law school, and she moved back home to Boston." Distance seemed to have been my biggest enemy when it came to relationships.

"I think it's more time for you than distance. You have no time for anything except work. Do you know what Katy's doing now?"

I shrugged my shoulders. "She's either traveling around the world or happily married with a zillion kids waiting for them to graduate from high school so that she can travel around the world again."

I took another puff. "Don't you think it's odd when you break up with someone, and they ask if you're happy?"

"Did you shout, FREEDOM!?"

"Haha, too funny, Randi. I was taken aback, and I think I said something equally stupid like, 'I am excited to be off to law school and happy that our paths crossed. I wish you the very best.'"

"Seriously, who says that?"

29

"Apparently I do."

"Do you still talk to her?"

"No, I haven't spoken to her in over 10 years."

"Frankly, if you could answer that question again what would you say?"

"First of all, I am not Frank, but if I was given a mulligan, I would say, 'Katy, at one time in my life, there was no way to measure how much I loved you. After we split, I experienced a profound sense of loss, but I am happy knowing that you are happy. Please know that I will always remember you fondly.'"

"Stop the presses, I almost believed you for a second, Sam. Is the wedding tomorrow getting you all sentimental and romantic?"

"So to answer your question, Randi, I've been dating someone for approximately 5 years now."

"What? No way! We are BFFs. How did I not know, and why didn't you say something earlier?"

"We met at work. An interoffice liaison of sorts."

"Where is she from, and what does she do?"

The waitress walked up, sat our drinks on the table and asked, "Are you finished with your cigar?"

I motioned to let her know we were fine.

"Sam, I'm feeling very lightheaded right now, but I do want to know more about this person."

I laughed. "I'm engaged to Billings, Day and Knight."

Disappointed, Randi responded, "Haha! You are such a stinker. You had me for a second."

"What about you and Ron? Before you answer that question, let's order a bottle of Opus." I called the waitress back over and asked her what years they had in stock.

"We currently have the '91. According to the winery, it is very 'opulent.'" I nodded, letting the waitress know that it would be fine. She left and returned quickly with two glasses and the bottle. After presenting it over her arm, she uncorked the wine and poured a small amount for me to taste. It was as she stated... 'opulent.' I motioned to her that it was perfect. She poured Randi a glass, added more to mine and left.

Returning my attention to Randi, I asked, "Where were we? Oh yes... What about you and Ron?"

"I really like Ron a lot! He's very fun to be around and a great coach for the kids' baseball teams."

I wanted to get Randi's feathers all ruffled, so I asked, "When is the wedding, BFF?"

"Shut your damn mouth. Not anytime soon." Mission accomplished, but my question brought out some unexpected emotions. "I don't think I will remarry."

"Why not?"

"I don't know."

To lighten things, I said. "I have this theory, Randi. I think there are 3 key categories of attraction: (1) physical, (2) intellectual and (3) emotional. For guys, the initial threshold is physical attraction, with the desirable person ranging from a 7 to 10 in their estimation. Then, it is intellectual attraction, but that could range from 3 to 10, depending on where she falls on the 'hotness' scale. Finally, emotional attraction, with that being a case-by-case determination. For women, on the other hand, the initial threshold is intellectual, ranging from 7 to 10. Then, physical, from a 1 to 10. Finally, emotional. All women look for an emotional connection in the 6 to 10 zone."

Randi tried to divert the attention onto me. "Sam, do you remember that hot/crazy girl matrix that I tagged you on social media?"

"That was fun, and I enjoyed the banter. I believe there is a Unicorn, but let's test my theory out on you, Randi. How do you rate Ron intellectually?"

"I think he's about an 8. Smarter than the average Sam."

"Ouch! Physically?"

"I think he's suaver than the average Sam, so an 8."

"This isn't about bashing your BFF's ratings. Emotionally?"

"I spend lots of time talking to him about my day, and he listens and supports me on the tough days like the anniversary of the passing of Michael. So an 8."

"Wow, Randi! You do realize that's a score of 888! That's some mighty fine feng shui."

"What do you mean? I mean I know what feng shui is but I thought that it only dealt with how to move your furniture around your house."

"Well, it's much more. It encompasses the 5 arts of Chinese metaphysics. I can't believe you don't know what the power of 8 means, much less 888? In Asia, the number 8 looks like an infinity sign and three 8s together signify extreme prosperity. The power of three is extremely significant. You need to marry Ron."

"Sam, you lost your 8, and I have my 888."

"What?"

"Yeah, Caroline with the infinity necklace was your 8. All the others were 666," she says with a cute but goofy drunken smile. Then it hits me.

"Call Ron now, and give me the phone!" Randi dialed the phone and handed it to me. "Hello, Ron, this is Randi's BFF. Listen,

I'm giving you my blessing to marry Randi and live in extreme prosperity so long as you let her be my wingwoman at a wedding I need to go to tomorrow."

Ron sleepily responded, "Excuse me, what time is it? You just woke me up."

I responded matter of factly, "It's 2:30 a.m. Ron, I mean like in 14 hours. Yeah, I think my consent for you to marry my BFF is more valuable than your consent for me to take Randi to a wedding. Okay, deal. Talk to you soon, and I'm shipping your smoky and liquored-up girl home. Try to at least get to 2nd base, please." I hung up before he responded.

I looked at Randi and said, "Randi, I've cleared your calendar for tomorrow. Make sure you wear something conservative." Looking for the waitress, I motioned to her. "Check, please." Randi grabbed her coat. "I'm off to REM. Make sure you get to the Willard by 5:00 p.m."

After I had entered the cab, I turned on my cell phone and saw 112 text messages and 48 missed calls. A bubble of emotion began to well up in my chest. I was happy that Joe and Randi had found the time to connect with such wonderful people, but the feeling was almost bittersweet. I looked back at my phone. The texts and missed calls validated my importance, yet I felt like a fool for being so tethered to my work.

Chapter 5

The Person You Can't Live Without

Ping! Oh my, 204 additional emails and 42 texts. By 7:00 a.m. the next morning, I had almost finished answering all the emails and text messages from the day before. I called the front desk to see if any packages had arrived. The desk clerk affirmed the arrival of a package and asked if she should have it delivered to the George Washington Suite. I responded, "Yes, please deliver them to room 2508."

I was exhausted. My team was still working on the Silicon Networks/ SocMedia, deal. I called the financial printers and asked for Debs Foreman. "Hey, Debs, how are you holding up?"

"Everything is fine with Silicon, but we have an issue with SocMedia. The accountants have raised a question about potential backdating of stock options to some of the key executives." Backdating is when a company grants executives the right to buy stock at a price lower than the market value when the options are granted. SocMedia had issued a couple of the executives the right to buy 1 million shares of SocMedia each, at a price of $4/share instead of the currently proposed IPO price range of $10-$12/share. The question was, when were these actually granted? If they were granted a year ago when the fair market value was $4/share, there would be no issue, and the executives deserved the $6-$8 million benefit. But if they were granted 3 months ago and backdated to 12 months ago, then there was a problem. George Lee, the senior partner on the deal, wanted me to tell SocMedia that he had done that in the past and didn't think this was a problem.

"Everyone wanted to hear from you before proceeding," Debs said.

"You know that backdating rewards the executives without proper disclosure to the shareholders, thus affecting the taxes paid by SocMedia and the executives?" Before Enron, I would have leaned toward George's view, especially in the 90s during the tech bubble, but not in today's environment. "Debs, tell SocMedia and George that there is a high possibility SocMedia will need to restate earnings for costs pertaining to these option grants. Also say there is a high probability there will be a class-action lawsuit from the shareholders and an even greater potential that criminal charges will be filed for misrepresentation. One other thing, let them know that I agree with the accountants. We should follow their lead and properly disclose. We get paid the big bucks so that they don't go down like the Titanic! Hold down the fort for the next 24 hours since I'll be unavailable after this call."

She replied, "No worries. I got your back, boss. Also, I have something important to tell you when you get back."

"Okay, Debs. We'll chat later." I hung up and looked at the time. It was 9:00 a.m. I put the "Do Not Disturb" sign on the handle, requested a 2:00 p.m. wake-up call, and headed to the shower.

After I had brushed my teeth, I prepared my nightstand with my notepad and pen.
I had been studying various ways to manage my time more efficiently. Efficiency at work, efficiency socializing, efficiency eating, and yes, even efficiency while I slept. I generally sleep from 4 to 6 hours and had decided to engage in something called sleep work. By placing a notepad and pen next to my bed, I hoped to improve my sleep and work skills. Practice makes perfect, like brushing my teeth. I'd been religiously doing this for the past 5 months and had noticed some positive trends. By the 3rd month, I could identify the word "get." By the 5th month, the writing was

neater, and the note read, "Get it." Naturally, I was eager to continue with this experiment, wondering what my subconscious was trying to reveal to me.

Around noon, I was rudely awoken by a knock on the door. I opened the door. There were a couple of security personnel standing in the hall. "Mr. Rivtoc, sorry to disturb you, but are you okay?"

Confused, I answered, "Everything is fine."

They looked at each other suspiciously and asked, "Were you having an argument?"

I replied, "No, I was asleep."

"Do you mind if we take a look around?" It was quite evident that I was thoroughly annoyed, but I reluctantly let them in. I had not yet unpacked from my early morning check-in. Other than a liter of water on the nightstand and the yellow notepad on the bed, there was nothing unusual.

"Thank you, Mr. Rivtoc, we are sorry we disturbed you. Some of the guests in the adjoining rooms had reported a disturbance in your room. Everything looks clear. We only request that you keep the noise level down when talking on the phone." The guards left, and I immediately called downstairs and asked to speak with the manager on duty. I was annoyed, and because my status was "Presidential," the top 1 percent of all guests, I knew my complaint would be taken seriously.

The manager answered, "Good afternoon, Mr. Rivtoc. How may we assist you today?" I told him that I had checked in around 3:00 a.m. and posted the "Do not disturb" sign on my door, but was greeted 10 minutes ago by 2 security officers. I grabbed my notepad and asked for his name and for him to explain why they interrupted me when I expressly asked not to be disturbed.

"We do apologize, Mr. Rivtoc, but several guests reported a person yelling the words, 'Get It Done,' 'Get it Done,' 'GET IT DONE!' They notified us, and we immediately sent security officials to investigate. We were only looking out for the best interests of our guests. I hope you understand."

I looked down at my notepad and could see the words "Get It Done" written across the top. Duh, the light bulb blinked on and I became deeply embarrassed. "Oh, I'm sorry. I was on the phone with my contractor for the house and wanted them to get the repairs done. I did not realize that my decibel level was that high. Please let the other guests know I'm sorry." I hung up the phone, excited, knowing that there was progress with my experiment.

I turned on my smartphone. There were 1,424 new emails, 45 text messages, and 24 missed calls. I started to believe that I was the person the firm could not live without. I needed some more "me" time, and I climbed back into bed.

Ring…. Ring…. Ring…. "Hello. Good afternoon, Mr. Rivtoc. This is your 2:00 p.m. wake-up call."

I turned on my phone. 2,602 new emails, 72 text messages, and 38 missed calls. I thought, I don't have time to respond to all this. Let me call Debs.

"Hey, Debs, everything okay?"

"Craig, the CEO of SocMedia, is upset at your suggestion and wants to talk to you. George is afraid to speak to him again. Do you have time?"

"Yes, go find Craig and Bill and put them on the call." I patiently waited and flipped through all the urgent emails Debs and George had sent me.

Craig and Bill were conferenced in. "Hey, Sam, we understand you're at a wedding and appreciate you calling us back, but we are talking about a $12-$14 million issue. We are really upset at those accountants for flagging this."

"Gentlemen, I'm glad they did. Let's step back and look at things from 100,000 feet instead of 10,000 feet. We are looking at a SocMedia valuation of $500 million. You guys own 40 percent or $200 million. You can't spend all that money in this lifetime, correct?"

"Correct."

"Are you willing to risk the $200 million for an additional 7 percent?"

"Hey, Sam, I'm Chinese-American, and Bill's Japanese-American. You aren't speaking Chinese, Japanese or English. Please make it simple so we can understand."

"Okay, gentlemen," I responded. "Let me tell it to you in jail lingo. If you restate the financials, you could go to jail... Do not collect $200... go directly to jail. Is $12-$14 million really worth it to you?"

Craig replied, "No, not really, but we need to evaluate the risks."

"After Enron and Tyco, there is a high possibility that that will happen. Don't you guys have kids?"

"Bill does. As far as myself, I just have my mother."

"What price would you put on your financial stability if the potential worst case scenario materializes? I don't think you need more than $100 million each to live so why risk it all for another $14 million? The risks outweigh the rewards. You need to do what is in the best interest of SocMedia and all its shareholders."

Craig asked, "Sam, can you give us a moment?"

"Sure." I sat and flipped through my emails on my laptop while I waited. Chain mail. Ugh. Note to self, don't give friends my work email.

The 2 returned, and Craig responded, "Okay, okay. We get your point and will forgo the valuation. We don't care about the $14 million."

"Yes. Gentlemen, this was a $14 million 10-minute call, which, if you hadn't listened to me, would probably have been the most expensive phone call you ever made. I'm going to quote *Casablanca* because I love you guys. 'Maybe not today... and maybe not tomorrow, but one day and for the rest of your lives, you will thank the accountants and me.'" I peered down at my watch and announced, "Gentlemen, I've got a wedding to attend. See you tomorrow." I disconnected and logged into SWA to check-in for my next day's flight.

Chapter 6

Mazel Tov

Ping! 118 additional emails, 12 texts of gratitude from SocMedia, and 18 missed calls. I brushed my teeth, shaved, and brushed my teeth again. I had the morning-after-nasty-taste-in-my-mouth syndrome. Tossed a few mints into my mouth, showered, changed and headed down to the lobby in my Brioni wedding tuxedo. Pulling out my phone, I texted my BFF to ping me when she arrived. Randi responded, "What did you do to me last night? I'm still hungover!" I smiled and put the phone back in my pocket.

On the way to the lobby, I ran into Marty, Joe's mother. She proceeded to explain the historical significance of the Willard Hotel lobby. "President Grant frequently consumed brandy and smoked cigars here. People would approach him seeking legislative favors and jobs as he walked through the lobby." Marty explained, "That's how the term 'lobbyist' was coined."

I looked at Marty and said, "That is an old wives' tale." Marty insisted and called over the concierge to back her up. I looked at both of them and noted, "I'm sure you guys tell all the guests the story to make this hotel more of a landmark, but President Grant was in office from 1869 until 1877, and the term lobbyist was commonly used in Britain starting in the 1800s. Go ahead and look it up."

Joe came walking by and said, "Hey, kid, is Marty bothering you again?"

"Actually, Marty was educating me on the origins of the word 'lobbyist.'" I put my arm around him and said, "Hey, Joe, I don't want some kid telling me they are getting married today... Kid."

"Well, I don't want some kid eating all the ice cream at the wedding." We laughed, and Marty handed me a yarmulke with the word 'Ahava' embroidered on it.

I gave Marty a big hug and said, "It is an honor and a pleasure to be an honorary Jew today at your son's wedding."

Marty led us through the schedule and showed me the location of the chuppah. "This is the wedding tent, where the *ketubah*, the marriage contract, will be located." She explained, "The *ketubah* is a written agreement that is supposed to protect the wife. It is sort of a dowry paid by the groom to the parents. If the husband dies or there is a divorce, the wife would have enough money to live on. In the *ketubah*, the husband promises 3 things: food, clothing, and a little wink-wink-nudge-nudge if you catch my drift."

I laughed at Marty's candor.

Marty continued. "*Halakha* states that there must be 2 witnesses when the rings are exchanged. During the ring ceremony, the couple makes a declaration to one another called the *Haray Aht*. The *Haray Aht* is roughly translated as 'With this ring, you are sanctified to me as my beloved' or something close to that."

"So it is pretty much like 'with this ring I thee wed.'"

"Somewhat. The *Haray Aht* is an Aramaic phrase that contains 32 letters, and the number 32 in Hebrew is seen as 'heart.' The symbolism is that both man and wife are pledging their hearts to one another."

"Wow! If I were only Jewish."

Marty winked at me. "It could happen. I have a nice Jewish girl for you."

After a few seconds of silence, we both laughed. I really loved the story behind the ring ceremony. The numbers gave it so much more meaning. "Hey, Marty, by the by, what does *Halakha* mean?"

Marty let out a huge laugh. "Mr. Lawyer doesn't know what *Halakha* means? Jewish law, my good friend. *Halakha* is Jewish law. Everything about Judaism is about Jewish Law."

Marty elaborated a little more about the ceremony. I was pretty impressed since this was my first Jewish wedding.

Joe pulled me away so we could start the rehearsal. We rehearsed several times, and I was excited to experience the breaking of the glass. After the rehearsal, Joe and I had a few minutes to ourselves. So I asked him how he was holding up.

"Hey, kid. Ya got those butterflies rolling around in your belly?"

"Yeah, I'm a little nervous."

"You're so lucky I'm here as your wingman, kid. I did a little online recon of the top 5 things that make kids like you not nervous on their wedding days... 1 and 2, don't go out the night before and have the kid smoke cigars. You stayed home like a nice lapdog. Next, 3, don't get inked up because it could cause blood poisoning. Kid, you don't have a single tattoo on you. Four, don't rush the groom. Seriously, I think the tortoise beat you in the race, kid. You've been dating for centuries! Finally, have your best man, ME, bring mints. Here you go, kid. My checklist is complete. You'll be fine!"

Joe smiled. "Thanks, Sam, I needed that. But I think you need the mints more than I do after those cigars last night." Joe looked at his watch. "It's go time, kid!"

When I walked out with my yarmulke, I was received with a loud burst of laughter and cheers as I noticed Randi seated and waving. The whole ceremony was beautifully orchestrated and moved gracefully. Witnessing the covenant of Joe and Sara was a first for me. As they sealed their marriage with a kiss, my mind gravitated to Caroline and our first kiss. I remembered it like that Humphrey Bogart moment in the movie *In a Lonely Place* when he said, "I was born when she kissed me." My all-encompassing work life had taken a toll on my non-existent relationship life. At that moment, I had clarity and realized something was missing in my life. Perhaps it was time to make some changes and celebrate the other aspects of life. The nuptials had gotten to me. For lack of a better word, and embracing this cultural moment, I got a little *verklempt*. For too long my victories were career-oriented. Was I too late?

I shook myself out of my little reflection and turned my attention back to the wedding. Marty yanked me to the dance floor. "You need to check out the breaking of the glass ceremony! There is a tradition at every Jewish wedding, and it's the breaking of the glass. There are 3 theories on why but I want to share the fairy tale version. When we are born, God breaks a soul into 2 pieces. The mission for each half is to find the other in this world and reconnect."

Randi agreed. "Yeah, Sam, life is short and fragile, like the glass, so when you find your soulmate, you need to seize the moment." As they smashed the glass, I thought maybe I should start to live every day as if it were my last with those that I loved.

The pace of the ceremony moved quickly and soon it was time for my speech as the best man. I grabbed the mic in karaoke fashion. I hadn't prepared for the moment. I figured I would just say what came from my heart. I started with that old cliché, "There comes a time in everyone's life when they meet the one, their soul mate. That day came for Joe when he met me 13 years ago in law school." The guests let out a chuckle. "Ladies and gentleman, my name is Sam, and I am the best man. I met Sara during our first year in law school. She was 'interviewing' folks to join her study group. The questions were things like 'What did you score on your SAT? LSAT? Where did you attend undergraduate and what was your GPA?' Surprisingly, I made the cut and was invited to join her study group. Joe, on the other hand, was rejected. It was at this point that Joe approached me regularly, borderline stalking me so that he could meet Sara someday. One night after a Torts exam, we decided to go to the pub. I invited Joe, and the rest is history. The moral of the story is, Joe's good enough to be her husband but not good enough to be in her study group. That was the beginning of my entry into Joe's circle of friends. In our 3rd year, we decided to take an 'easy' graduate-level history class. That class had zero bearing on our law school class rank. We were never prepared for class and received C's and B's on our papers. The shocker was that we had to write a 50-page paper to pass the course. Blasphemy! This requirement was unacceptable! Right, Joe?" I looked over at the happy couple. Joe was laughing, and Sara was holding on to him with such love. "We needed to negotiate with the professor. I offered the professor a sweetheart deal. Instead of wasting everyone's time, we would receive a letter grade of B+ without having to turn in that 50-page paper. It was at that moment I entered into Joe's circle of family. And today, I am honored to be the best man and an honorary Jew in this wedding circle of thousands for Joe and Sara. I would like everyone to raise their glass and thank Sara for inviting all the really hot bridesmaids today for the multitude of single men out there, including myself. Mazel Tov!"

Everyone cheered "Mazel Tov!" The music began, and I sat down and reveled at how I pulled that off.

I texted Randi, "Tell Ron to dress up and meet us at Willard. Open Bar!"

She replied, "Ron asked if it is okay to crash the wedding."

"Tell him yes and that he's late, so he has a 2-shot penalty for every hour of lateness. I think he's like 3 hours late already and closing on 4."

Champagne, Kamikaze, Goldschlager, Jagermeister, Fireball…. I was hungover from last night, sleep-deprived, and slowly entering into another dimension.

"Do you have Caroline's number?" Randi asked.

"Yeah, right here." I flipped through my contacts and handed her my phone. She dialed Caroline's number, and I instantly grabbed it from her and hung up. "Are you trying to give me a heart attack?"

Randi laughed uncontrollably.

The phone lit up like a Christmas tree, and the name "Caroline" pulsed in bright lights on the faceplate of my cell phone. With mouth agape, I tossed the phone to Randi in a panic.

She grinned at me and answered. "Hey, Caroline, it's me, Randi. Remember me? Yeah, Sam's in town, and he accidentally drunk-dialed you but was too scared to talk to you, so he hung up." Sounds of laughter could be heard coming from the phone. I sat thinking my head was about to implode as I watched Randi chat up a storm with Caroline. "He hasn't changed from that nervous high school guy that tripped over the bush in your front lawn after the 2nd date. Haha, I know, right? We are at the Willard for a wedding. There are thousands of guests here, and my boyfriend will be crashing the party any minute now. What are you doing tonight? Nothing? Can you make it out too?" I heard a response but wasn't sure if she said yes or no. Randi looked at me and choked back a laugh. She turned away quickly and continued her conversation with Caroline.

"Wonderful! Great! See you in an hour. Dress wedding conservative… bye." This seemingly one-sided conversation with Caroline had me anxious.

Randi hands the phone back to me. "Hey, Sam, Sweet Southern Caroooooooliiine's coming!"

"Yeah, right. Stop pulling my leg. I'm tired and drunk, and there's no way she would be able to come out tonight considering she has a husband and kids." I was hopeful but figured the odds on Caroline making an appearance were actually closer to zero. I changed the subject. "Let's dance." The usual wedding songs came up. Every time a song came on, the wedding planners handed out party favors—beads, leis, plastic sunglasses, wine glasses, matches, mints. The golden rule was one needed to dance to receive a party favor, which resulted in hundreds of people dancing. We were loaded down with party favors, Between songs, Randi would torment me with "Caroline's coming!"

When Ron arrived at 7:42 p.m., we moved to the bar, and I sang the "Ron is Thirsty" song. *Ron is thirsty. Yes, he is. Yes, he is. Ron is very thirsty. Ron is very thirsty. Yes, he is.* I proceeded to order 8 shots for him. "Ron, you've heard of the 4 wise men, right? Johnny Walker, Jim Beam, Jack Daniels, and Jose Cuervo. Say hello to their twins too."

Ron looked pale after downing the 8 shots. I felt a tap on my shoulder and heard, "Hey, kid." I turned and saw Joe and Sara. I was busted!

"Heeeeeey!!!! Congratulations, guys! This is the best wedding ever. Oh, let me introduce you to my wedding-crashing friends, Randi and Ron."

"Are you staying here?" Joe asked.

"Yes, they upgraded me to a sweet suite, the George Washington Suite."

"Really? That's like a 2,500-square-foot room."

"2,800 square feet, but who's counting?"

"Awesome! The party stops at midnight, so can we send 4 cases of champagne to your room and continue to celebrate?"

"Absolutely, Joe, I'll take care of it. Go do your wedding duties, and we'll see you after midnight." Joe and Sara cha-cha-ed off to the dance floor.

I anxiously looked at my watch; it was 8:32 p.m. At that moment, I noticed a familiar face smiling in a sea of wedding guests. She waved and approached us. Wearing a satin lapel black dress while holding an LV clutch, as she turned her head, her brunette hair just brushed her shoulder. As she walked up, I could felt those piercing eyes gazing at me. She was stunning. I felt like a deer in the headlights, speechless. And then those words filled my head.... Oh, how sweet that Caroline. Was this a dream? If so, I didn't want it to end.

Randi leaned over. "I told you she would come."

"Yeah, you weren't kidding." I gave Caroline a slow, long hug and whispered, "I can't believe it has been 17 years. I'm so happy to see you again! You look stunningly the same!"

Caroline responded, "Why, thank you. You look healthy, Sam."

Randi laughed. "Yeah, all work, no exercise, and all that ice cream make Sam very healthy." Then Randi looked at me and said, "What about me?"

I laughed and said, "Caroline looks great, and ummmmmm....I really love your Christian Louboutin shoes."

"Ha, ha, very funny." Randi quickly changed the subject. "We are celebrating tonight. A wedding, a reunion. Champagne for everyone, and I won't take no for an answer."

I followed Randi to the bar. On our way, she winked. "Do me a favor. Put your tongue back in your mouth. It is not socially acceptable for a man to drool in front of a married woman."

"A guy can dream, can't he? A little compassion would be nice at this moment. It wasn't that noticeable, was it? What do you do when someone reappears after 17 years—the someone who happened to germinate my seed of love with an unforgettable kiss?"

"You're so dramatic, Sam." Randi nudged me in the arm. "Did you notice the necklace?"

"What necklace?"

"The infinity necklace. She was wearing the infinity necklace you bought her."

"No way! I don't believe you."

The bartender approached. "What's your poison?"

"We would like 4 cases of champagne sent to room 2508 around midnight please, and we would also like 4 glasses now." I turned back to Randi. "What does her wearing the necklace mean?"

"It could mean only 3 things."

"Aaand?"

"One, there is 20 percent chance there might be trouble in paradise at home. Two, which is highly unlikely... I'd say there is a less than 5 percent chance that she thinks that you might have been the one for her too. Three, which is most likely... a 75 percent chance that it's an upgraded Tiffany infinity necklace. But please don't trip over the case of champagne, a table, or a bush, in case it is numbers 1 or 2." With a wink and a smile, Randi grabbed 2 of the glasses.

"Hahaha." We returned, and I proposed a toast. "To loving, dancing and drinking. If you are going to love, love your friends infinitely. If you are going to dance the night away, I say dance it collecting party favors. And if you are going to drink, drink with me. Cheers! Caroline and Ron have a lot of catching up to do in terms of drinking, dancing and collecting party favors. Let's dance!"

Chapter 7

All Good Things Must Come To An End

I turned off my phone. No pings tonight! We all had a blast, but time surely flies when you are celebrating. We reveled for hours. Unlike the glory days of high school and college, I felt winded on the dance floor. Yes, I admit, I was no spring chicken. We danced and danced until we couldn't accept any more party favors, and my dawgs started barking. After setting into some seats, we toasted profusely to anything and everything. That night, we had the time of our lives.

The wedding DJ indicated that he was going to play the last song for the evening, a slow song entitled "Beautiful in My Eyes." There was a clear demarcation between couples and non-couples. All the couples, including Randi and Ron, started smitten dancing. The choices were staying on the floor with the probability of receiving the Heisman rejection or migrating with the other lonely folks. It was that awkward moment, and I had about 5 seconds to decide. The easiest path would have been to exit stage left without any eye contact and head towards one of 2 directions – the bar or the bathroom. I opted to take the road less traveled.

"Caroline, I take thee at thy word, call me to dance, and I'll be newly baptized." Caroline smiled, and we swayed to the Joshua Kadison song, serenading each other and quietly talking.

"You're my only one ... my sweet Southern one... There will only be one Caroline in my life. I can't believe you still have that necklace after all these years. I figured you had gotten rid of it many moons ago."

"I'm glad you noticed, Sam. You know I would never part with this. You were and are very important to me, even though we

∞

seldom communicate. That doesn't mean I don't think of you fondly."

"Really? That might be the sweetest thing anyone's ever said to me. Caroline, you know that you will always be beautiful in my eyes, and we should try to keep in touch regularly." With butterflies in my stomach, I asked, "Do you like me?"

Caroline looked down. "Sam, you know I can't answer that question."

As I finished serenading the rest of the song to her, the lights came up, and the music stopped. Randi and Ron swung by and asked what was next on the agenda. Caroline asked for the time. I responded, "It's late in the evening, and I'm wondering if you could join us for the post-wedding celebration upstairs."

Caroline grimaced, "Oh, I never go out this late. 12:30, 30 more minutes, and I turn into a pumpkin." She then flashed me that award-winning smile of hers and I began to melt. I put my arm out for her to take, and we headed out into the lobby.

About 50 of us proceeded to room 2508 for a more intimate post-wedding celebration. We entered the George Washington Suite to an excellent wine and cheese spread with 48 bottles of Dom neatly arranged on ice. Everyone grabbed a bottle, and each of us offered up a toast. Caroline nudged me and said, "I have to go now." She quietly made her goodbyes to Randi and Ron. I grabbed my champagne bottle and offered to walk her to the front lobby.

As we were walking to the elevators, Caroline and I hit the down button on the elevator simultaneously. Our fingers touched for a brief moment. As I pulled my hand back, I felt her hand delicately move down my arm and towards my fingers. "Thanks for inviting me. That was the most fun I've had in nearly 7 years, and as always, it was wonderful to see you."

Our pinkies clasped for 8 seconds, but it felt like a lifetime. As our eyes locked, I released her finger. Time seemed to rewind, and I felt like it was 17 years ago. Caroline whispered, "Don't think I'm going to let you kiss me tonight like I did back then."

Ping! The elevator opened, and I responded, "I wasn't planning on kissing you at all, but if you want to kiss me, I might let you."

Caroline changed her tone and stopped smiling. "Listen, my marriage is not well, and I'm not sure how much longer we are going to stay together, but I don't think I could respect myself if we did anything more." I could feel the uncertainty: the conflict of loyalty to her children, the desire for the least amount of disruption in their lives, her strong Christian values, the deep pain and hurt from the actions of her husband, and the urge to suppress her feelings toward me. She was married. I knew it was wrong. She wasn't available, but I felt comfortable around her. I couldn't take advantage of Caroline while she was vulnerable, so I backed up and gave her some space.

To break the silence, I proposed an offer. "We will only do what friends do and nothing more. Caroline, I am giving you a dollar bill as consideration."

Caroline smiled again, "You're the lawyer. Is this a binding agreement?"

I softened my gaze. "Yes, Caroline."

Caroline slowly grabbed my hand and asked, "Do friends hold hands like this?"

I held her hand and reluctantly released it. The 3 seconds of intimacy was bittersweet. I wanted to hold her hand longer but needed to protect her from both herself and me. "Of course, friends hold hands, but this gentleman wants to give you his arm and properly escort the elegant and sweet Caroline." Arms clasped, we continued off the elevator through the lobby to the entrance, silently aware of our mutual desire for intimacy. Caroline motioned the valet for her car. She turned around to thank me for a wonderful evening and asked for clarification.

Curious, I asked, "What clarification?"

"Do friends give Eskimo kisses?"

"I'm not sure about that." I noted the distinction between Eskimo kisses and butterfly kisses. "If you asked for a butterfly kiss, I would have had to decline at this time. I haven't Eskimo-kissed anyone since middle school. It's unclear, but if you don't sue me for childish behavior, I won't sue you for breach of contract."

We embraced for a while and gave each other the most tender and, for me, sensual Eskimo kisses. Slowly we parted, and I asked her to text me when she got home safely. She agreed, but waited for me to get to the top of the steps before she yelled out, "I just wanted to make sure you didn't stumble and fall." I blushed, and for a drunk, savvy Asian man like myself, that's hard to notice. But she did. She tilted her head with a smile, turned and entered her car.

I hadn't expected anything like that embrace. I felt like I was back in my wonder years again. My heart pounded, telling me to "Carpe diem" while my brain crooned, "Simmer down, fella." I pulled out my phone and checked for messages. I saw 5,249 new emails and 68 text messages. My focus was not on work. It gravitated toward Caroline. When I returned to my room, the crowd had dwindled to about 8 people. Everyone turned to me and asked, "Well?"

"Well, what?" I mused.

"We want to know more about the girl."

Randi chimed in with her best Sam imitation, "Let me break it down for you in a nutshell. She was the one for him, but he wasn't the one for her back then, and so she got away. Now, I think she might think she made a mistake. But is she still the one for him, and will he make time for her? Also, is this all legal since she might still be unavailable?"

I sat and waited for Randi to finish her spiel. "Now that we are all on the same page, I need to clarify many of the ambiguous points in Randi's summary. Caroline and I have a binding contract. We are friends and nothing more." I knew, as in my usual approximation of good faith, that I had omitted some key points. I gracefully shifted the subject by reminiscing about the highlights of the wedding.

Joe asked, "Between Caroline and ice cream which would you choose?"

"In terms of chemistry, both Caroline and ice cream occupy the same position on the periodic table. I like them equally." We toasted some more, and I broke out my last 5 cigars.

It was 1:32 a.m. when Caroline texted. *"Thanks for a wonderful time. I'm back home safe and sound."*

I texted her back with a thank you and *"BTW, you are missing one heck of a party. Will likely go until about 3 am; come back if you change your mind. Lol. Talk to you soon. Good night."*

Around 2:45 a.m., I told everyone that I was wiped out and calling it a night. We said our goodbyes. I turned to Randi and Ron and said, "All good things must come to an end, but you are more than welcome to crash in the other room."

I contacted the front desk to call me at 11:30 a.m. with a follow-up wake-up call at 2:30 p.m. Check-out time at the hotel was at 4:00 p.m., but my flight departed for Atlanta at 6:00 p.m. I set my reminder alarms for noon and 3:00 p.m. then headed off to bed. I knew I had many work messages, but there was only a single message that mattered. I had no desire to sleepwork. A thousand things ran through my mind that night. What a fool I was for letting go of her hand so quickly. She wanted to hold my hand. What did that mean? Does she, like, like me? It was intimate and felt so right. She's married and vulnerable. Wow, I can't believe it has been 17 years. Tonight was "quaint." Of course, it was "quaint"; numbers don't lie. It had been 17 years, and "Q" is sequentially the 17th letter of the alphabet. Caroline Dean, the one… the one that got away. Why don't I even know her married name? I don't want to know it! Don't tell me because maybe I don't want to believe she's married. All I wanted to do was dream about Caroline as I fell asleep, intimately holding her hand in the elevator. A guy can dream, can't he?

Chapter 8

A Wake-up Call

Ping! The phone rang. I fumbled for the phone. "Good morning, Mr. Rivtoc. The time is 11:30 a.m. Today's high is 57 degrees, with a low of 40."

Crap! I wanted to dream just a little longer, but it was time to face reality. I pounded a liter of water and moved sluggishly to the couch. I hadn't partied like that in years. My body was sore from the lack of sleep, dehydration, dancing, and excessive drinking. Time to break out my trusty go-to for hangovers. I reached for my Absorb spray, a product from a California start-up that I represented. This handy-dandy product saved me on more than one occasion. The glutathione in Absorb was marketed as an antioxidant with properties to prevent aging, cancer, heart disease and Alzheimer's, but was also the charm to curing my typical hangover when I occasionally imbibed a little excessively.

Last night's debauchery had a net negative effect on my system, and I was definitely hungover. After shaking the bottle, I sprayed the glutathione 8 times on my liver area and prayed that I would recover within an hour.

I put the spray bottle on the table while I tried to remember something…. "Oh yeah, the pings." I grabbed the phone to check for any other messages from Caroline. The emails rocketed to 7,402 and 83 text messages. I composed myself and called Debs. "How are things?"

"We're ready to submit all documents tomorrow at 8:00 a.m., but everyone is waiting for you to sign off on Silicon and SocMedia."

"I land around 8:00 p.m. Please arrange car service to pick me up and take me to the printers. I'll review and sign off them tonight."

"Do you want us to order you any dinner?"

"Yes, sushi would be wonderful."

"Sam, please remind me that we need to talk about your sign-off on the two S-1s. Also, Absorb wants to know if you can be in San Francisco on Tuesday to negotiate their Series A Preferred financing."

"Email them and let them know that I will make it. Do you have time to join me, Debs? Please print their term sheet, too. I'll review that over dinner. See you soon. "

I showered, packed my clothes and a few of the party favors from the wedding to share with co-workers. I knocked on Ron and Randi's door. "Do you want me to order room service? What do you want? Coffee, bacon, eggs, French toast?" Randi gratefully agreed with my selection. "Hello, room service? I would like to order a pot of coffee, 3 side orders of bacon, 6 eggs, 2 scrambled, 2 over hard and 2 sunny side up, 1 French Toast and 2 hash browns. Oh, do you have any ice cream? A small scoop of chocolate would be perfect. Utensils for a party of 3, please. Can you please repeat the order for me? It will be here in an hour? Excellent." I knocked on their door and told them, "The food will arrive within an hour, so get ready!" I popped open my laptop and started responding to the emails and text messages.

Touched with a little OCD, I meticulously sifted through the emails, moving and categorizing each mail by client and matter, while disregarding the ones my associates had answered. I flagged a few that required my input, mostly those that related to the firm's budgeting and compensation packages. I was deeply engaged in my correspondence and had lost track of time when, suddenly, there was a knock at the door. I rushed to open it, knowing that room service had arrived. Randi and Ron stumbled out of their room looking disheveled, hungover and famished. We dove into the food. Randi remarked, "Last night was a fun. Why don't you look and feel like we do?"

I explained, "I represent an anti-aging company that has developed a glutathione spray that is supposed to cure hangovers among other things. It is in trial stages. I look and feel marvelous."

Randi perked up. "Shut up! Let me try it out."

"Umm, you might want to wait until after we finish breakfast because it has a noticeably sulfuric smell to it. Wouldn't want you to lose the contents of your stomach with all these goodies in front of us."

Randi got a little miffed. "Fine, keep your anti-aging and hangover secrets to yourself while we commoners suffer."

"Haha."

"When are you going to contact Caroline again?"

"Well, that is a little complicated, don't you think? To answer the question you posed last night, it was a little bit of 1 and 2 and definitely not 3. There are problems in paradise, she thinks of me fondly, and the necklace was the original. I rest my case."

"So are you going to wait another 17 years to see what happens next?"

"No, but you gals have this 3-day rule. If I don't contact her within 3 days, then she thinks I'm probably not interested, right? But I have to balance that with the fact that she's still married, even if unhappily, still living under the same roof. There are probably archaic laws about that in Virginia. Like Section 20-91 of the Virginia Code: *a divorce may be granted based on the fault ground of adultery, or sodomy or buggery committed outside the marriage.*"

"What are you talking about, a 3-day rule?"

"That's all you got out of my last statement?"

"No, Sam, I was paying attention. I just choose not to acknowledge the latter part of your statement. You definitely should limit your text and emails because you might leave incriminating messages down the road."

"Randi you need to stop 'buggering' me, or Ron might have grounds. In common law, 'buggery' included sodomy between a male and an animal."

Randi rolled her eyes and said between her teeth, "Sam, please! No more explanation on buggery. Not while we are eating."

We continued to eat in peace… for a moment. "So what's your goal with Caroline?" Did I forget to mention Randi cannot handle the sound of silence?

"Okay, I guess I won't be eating for a couple of minutes until I satisfy your curiosity. I admit, prior to last night's events, my goals may have been filed categorically in the 'gray area.' After last night's encounter, my new objective is to be emotionally available for her in hopes of reconnecting again. Maybe there will be a relationship; maybe there will only be friendship, maybe mere companionship, or maybe just the dream… the impossible dream." I grabbed a napkin and pen on the tray where the food sat. I continued, "More importantly, I'm going to draft a plan, just like I counsel all my start-ups to do. Yes, a well thought out 5-year Caroline plan describing past problems, new solutions, locking in key dates throughout the year to connect with her. I'll even attach a budget to the Caroline plan. Seriously, though, I think I'm going to create weekly reminders to have fun for 2 hours a day and some monthly reminders to stay in touch with Caroline." I took the pen and napkin and wrote at the top, "5-year Caroline Plan."

"Sam, I'm just shaking my head. Relationships don't operate like a business and aren't so calculated and analytical. I'm so fortunate that I found my Ron who is the exact opposite of you, Sam."

I looked over at Ron, who was sitting quietly, babying his hangover with breakfast. "Hey, Ron, you have been pretty quiet all morning! What say you?"

Ron looked up mid-mouthful. "The Ron needs food!" We stared at him silently as he looked back down at his food and resumed eating.

The telephone rang. "Good afternoon, Mr. Rivtoc, this is your 2:30 p.m. wake-up call." That was perfect timing.

"Hey, guys, I've got to pack and head to Reagan International Airport. It was so wonderful seeing both of you, and Ron, wake up and smell the Randi rose. She's in full bloom, and you have my blessing to marry her." I rapidly finished my breakfast, packed, and bid everyone adieu.

Chapter 9

Don't Fret Little One

Ping! Ping! Ping! My phone lit up like a Christmas tree. I went to the valet. "Taxi, please. Reagan International, Southwest Airlines." Texts were coming in from everyone at the party. Apparently, a great time was had by all.

I checked into SWA. A-1. I whispered to myself in excitement. "Yesssss! Finally, on the 100th check-in this year, I have achieved companion status!" I now had the coveted A-1 boarding pass, which had eluded me all this time. I was batting .010 on the A-1, but I was still excited. I swiftly cleared airport security through the TSA PreCheck line. I was an hour early and checked my phone. There were 328 additional emails and 15 new text messages. As I checked all correspondence from the morning, I wondered if Caroline had messaged me again. All I saw was the text from early morning: *"Thanks for a wonderful time. I'm back home safe and sound."*

I melted and was unmotivated to work. My mind continuously flashed back to our friendly agreement in the elevator that had culminated in the Eskimo kiss. I didn't care what Randi said. I took out my laptop and commenced my 5-year Caroline Plan. I was a pro at editing and building business plans. How difficult could this be? All I had to do was interchange business stuff with "Caroline" stuff. Piece of cake.

Section 1

Problems

I live in Atlanta; she resides in Virginia.

I've seen her twice in 17 years.

We communicate once every 6 months.

I am a workaholic, and she is married.

As I read those words, I thought, Could this relationship even be possible? Reaching for straws, I examined Section 2:

Section 2

Solutions

> I have 500,000 miles saved up and can visit Virginia frequently.
>
> Maybe we can sync up bi-monthly.
>
> I can try to communicate once a month.
>
> I can take more vacations, take time off on the weekends....

I looked at my list. *She's married.* That might be the deal-breaker. Was there light at the end of the tunnel? Maybe we weren't meant to be and should just keep it in the "friend zone," at least for the next 5 years. I plugged into my notifications the 12 days I had committed to contacting Caroline during the year. Saddened, I realized that it was over even before it had begun. A voice announced over the loudspeaker, "Boarding for business class only." It was time to board, and I decided I wasn't going to fall in "like" with someone who was truly unavailable.

I landed in Atlanta around 8:30 p.m. with my driver waiting. We headed over to the financial printers. I called Debs and asked, "Is everything going as planned?"

She responded, "Everything is moving as planned, but there are some issues with Absorb that need to be attended to." That wasn't really what I wanted to hear.

I asked the driver how far out we were. "Traffic is light this evening. We should be there shortly," he said.

I had arrived at the printers at 9:30 p.m. and moved to a private conference room with Debs. Debs revealed, "I have lots of good news and 2 bits of potentially bad news. The good news is that there are no issues with the Silicon deal, and we are electronically filing at 8:00 a.m. tomorrow. Also, good news, all SocMedia issues are resolved. The accountants revised the financials; everyone is fine with the changes, and we are electronically filing that at 8:00 a.m. also." She brought the documents over for me to sign. "Please sign here and here." I wondered where we were on the Absorb venture financing.

Debs got up and poured a glass of water for me while she poured a cup of coffee for herself. "Now with the not-so-good news. The Absorb VC deal is possibly blowing up. The VC group is asking for 2-times liquidation preference."

"Hmmm. VC group wants to get paid first in the event of a liquidation? Do they think there might be a problem like bankruptcy or are they looking to sell off the company?" Absorb's pre-money valuation was $30 million, and the VC group was proposing to invest $10 million. So after the investment, the VC group would own 25 percent of the company with an investment of $10 million on a post-money valuation of $40 million. The issue was with the normal 2-times liquidation preference. "Did you explain the situation to them, Debs?"

"Yes, I explained a hypothetical situation to them. If this were a deal without any liquidation preference, and Absorb sold for $100 million, the VC group would receive $25 million and the other Absorb shareholders would receive $75 million. Under the proposed 2-times liquidation preference, the VC group would instead get paid $20 million first, then share a 4th of the remaining $80 million or another approximately $20 million. The net/net outcome would be $40 million for the VC group and $60 million for the other Absorb shareholders. I told them it was unreasonable to ask for the double liquidation with the type of transaction they are doing."

I agreed. "That's too rich for us. We need to negotiate a more reasonable and appropriate transaction."

Finally, Debs grabbed my glass poured me another glass of water. "Now for the really bad news. I'm leaving the firm."

In mid-swallow, I almost choked. I was shocked! She was the heavy lifter of the group, and I was planning to nominate her for partnership in 2 years. After almost swallowing, I responded, "You are supposed to give me a 2-year notice for any termination to be effective. In 2 years, you would be up for partnership. Partnership is everyone's dream. It is the crème de la crème. To put things in perspective, only the top 15 percent of law students are interviewed by Billings, Day and Knight. Of the 5,000 or so applications, we only select about 150 to be vetted through our summer associate program. Of those, only 50 receive an offer to join our firm as associates. Of those 50, only 20 make it past the first 5 years. Of those 20, only 2 are extended partnership. Those percentages are far worse than the 1 percent chance of getting an A-1 boarding pass. I'm telling you today that you are in that small circle. I will go to bat for you in 2 years, and let's agree that this conversation never happened. I reject your notice."

Debs started to cry. I felt like a heel. She said, "I need a life. My life has been all work. I've enjoyed every moment and appreciate your mentorship. But my parents are getting older. They live in Northern California, and I want to be closer to them and spend more time with them."

I would have traded anything to be near my parents. I had no words. I knew deep down that she was right. I would do the same thing in her shoes. But in bad faith, I grasped at my last straw. "Can't you just move them out to Atlanta?"

"I'm sorry, Sam, I need a life too. I am getting older and would like to have a family someday. I'm thinking of giving my 2-week notice tomorrow and leaving by December 1."

I thought quickly. "Debs, I'm not going to accept that deal. You've worked way too long and especially hard this year to leave your year-end bonus. To get your bonus you have to be an employee on December 31. For you, I am talking about $25,000. You should give your notice effective the first week of January. Use up all your vacation days moving out to California and overlapping with the holidays. For all intents and purposes, you'll be working about a week in December. Don't fret, little one, I've got your back!"

After a few moments, Deb accepted the deal. "Thanks, Sam, for all your support and understanding." I had used up my last "Hail Mary" with her. I knew it would be almost impossible to find the perfect person to take over Debs' position. She was definitely a star, in a class of her own. I am a difficult person to work for, but she seemed to go with the flow and rise to every single occasion without complaining. I don't like to micromanage. If there was a way to get something done, she found it. To reward her dedication, I wanted to make sure she was taken care of, even if she was leaving the firm.

Chapter 10
Pigs Get Slaughtered

Ping! I returned to the office and evaluated all the talent on my team to determine who could replace Debs as my new legal rock star. The only way for our practice group to grow was to retain key talent, train new talent, and bring in new clients while efficiently working on projects. Retention was the name of the game. My book of business was slightly under $10 million in 2005. The average billing rate was $400 an hour for the 16 attorneys (including myself), with billable hours averaging 1,920, and non-billable hours averaging 300. Collections were maxing out at around 80 percent. All of that added up to something just below $10 million. Debs was an integral part of the money and efficiency train. In addition, she would switch hats to bring the junior associates up to par. With Debs leaving the group, I had to have a contingency plan. My goal was to grow the practice to over $12 million in the next fiscal year, but now I was concerned that it might shrink to $8 million instead. I prepared a practice group plan to reflect a downturn in our revenues for 2006. I decided to focus on increasing collections from 80 percent to 90 percent to offset an approximate $1 million in lowered revenues due to Debs' departure. I looked at the time. It was midnight, and I was exhausted. I decided to head home and pack for my Tuesday trip to San Francisco.

The alarm went off at 7:00 a.m., and I started my regular efficiency routine. I checked my notepad, showered, changed, and packed for the 2-day trip to California. Into the carryon went 2 Robert Graham shirts, 2 sweaters, a pair of khakis, a pair of trusted Levi 501s, 1 Brioni suit with my good luck red Hermes tie, cufflinks, 2 dress shirts, socks, and boxer shorts. I arrived at the office by 8:30 a.m. and asked Jules to contact SWA and reschedule my flight to the 3:30 p.m. flight. This would allow me to land in Oakland around 7:30 p.m. Jules called SWA and was placed on hold. I had almost forgotten about my new status with SWA. With childlike enthusiasm, I blurted out, "Hey, Jules, I finally achieved companion status."

Jules looked at me and laughed. "You look like a little kid who got the big chocolate bunny for Easter." I had to admit that I was a little too excited about the achievement.

"Jules, do me a favor and add Debs as my companion and have her join me on the flight to San Francisco. Let her know to pack for 2 days. Also, make 2 reservations for 2 nights at the Mark Hopkins San Francisco and ask Mary and Mandy at Absorb to meet us in the lobby at 9:30 p.m. for drinks."

I went to my desk and was surprised when I saw a 125-page document there. The document was from a reputable New York law firm. The cover letter read, "In connection with the proposed Series A financing of Absorb, enclosed are our comments on the transaction document. These are subject to further comment from our client, CalBio Ventures." I knew then that I had just been New Yorkized. Most of my VC deals were done with California law firms. There was an unwritten rule that early-stage transactions could be completed with 20- to 30-page documents. We had sent the first draft to Absorb and CalBio that was 25 pages. The term sheet indicated that Absorb would pay up to $50,000 of CalBio's legal fees. In non-legal mumbo jumbo, a term sheet was a non-binding document outlining the material terms to a business agreement. After the term sheet is executed, it guides all parties involved, including the lawyers, in how to prepare the final agreement. I skimmed over it and realized there were 3 areas where we did not see eye to eye on the business and legal terms. We had offered a 1-time liquidation preference, and they had countered with 2-times. Assuming there would be a $30 million pre-money valuation, with an investment of $10 million, the old shareholders would own 75 percent of the company and the new investors 25 percent. However, with a liquidation preference of 1-time and, assuming a sales price of $100 million exists, then the first $10 million would go to the investors. The rest of the $90 million would then be split 75 percent/25 percent. So the new investors would make an additional $22.5 million, totaling $32.5 million, while the old investors would keep $67.5MM. With 2-times liquidation preference, the investors would get the first $20 million. The remaining $80 million would be split 75 percent/25 percent. So the new investors would make $40 million, and the old investors $60 million. They had also revised the legal fees from $50,000 to $100,000, and legal terms were modified from standard Atlanta representations and warranties for similar transactions to standard New York reps and warranties. As a result, we had a proposed 125-page legal document instead of the original 25-page document. I didn't appreciate the last-minute tactic of sending major revisions, much less the revisions they had made. They had over a week to comment but elected to send everything on Monday morning. I was not amused.

I called Debs at 9:00 a.m. regarding the 2 S-1 filings. "No issues and everything was filed 5 minutes ago."

"Go home, pack, and meet me back at the office by noon."

Jules came in and said, "Mark Burns is on the phone."

"Okay. Who is he?"

"He is the lawyer for CalBio."

"Tell him I'm busy until after noon." I was more concerned about how we would operate once Debs departed. I skimmed Mark's document and was appalled. Without tailoring their comments to this transaction, they had cut and pasted representations and warranties that didn't apply to Absorb. Absorb was an emerging cosmeceutical company started by Mary Kim and Mandy Chen. Mary and Mandy were 2 California do-gooders with PhDs in biology and chemistry. They initially developed Absorb as a cosmetic line but began claiming that the products had medicinal qualities.

The plan was to raise this round of funding to develop their packaging, marketing, and compliance so that the product could be sold across state lines. I was annoyed by the numerous unnecessary comments from Mark, including the product and product liability claim reps and warranties.

At half past 11, Mary and Mandy called. I sensed a concern in their voices. Apparently, they too received Mark's document. "Are you going to be able to resolve all the issues in their 125-page document?" I explained the problems and asked them to consider the liquidation preferences business issue, allowing me to handle the quasi-legal and legal issues.

"Please arrange a conference call with CalBio, Mark, and our firm for 1:00 p.m. EST."

My phone rang again at noon. "Jules, who is that?"

"It's Mark Burns."

"Tell him I'm sorry, but I cannot talk to him at the moment."

He called again at 12:30 p.m. I gave Jules the same response.

At 1:00 p.m., Debs entered my office, and we dialed into the conference call number. I opened with, "I didn't realize that this morning was Christmas. I was surprised to receive a 125-page document and revisions to the term sheet. You guys had over a week to comment but waited until this morning to send this gem to us. In all my years of legal practice, this is a first."

Mark apologized for the last-minute circulation but said, "We wanted to do a thorough job."

"A thorough job? Let's cut to the chase. On the business point, we agree to valuation. The only issue is liquidation preference. We aren't that far apart, but we would like to meet with you face to face tomorrow to discuss. We are far apart on the increase in legal fees from $50,000 to $100,000 as well as the additional 100 pages of legal issues."

Mark objected. "We need to do our jobs thoroughly and believe that $100,000 is a reasonable amount to charge for this deal."

At that point, my displeasure became evident in my voice. I asked Mark if he understood the current status of Absorb. Naturally, he replied that he did. I then asked if he had read the 125-page document thoroughly. Again, he affirmed. I asked if everything in their document made sense and was important for the deal. Promptly and defensively, he responded, "Of course."

I drew his attention to the product representation and warranty and stated, "Why is it important that Absorb has not sold, or received written notice of any product or group of products, defective or nonconforming, to their warranties, or contractual requirements made by the company to their customers? Absorb doesn't have any products and hasn't sold anything yet. Let's look at another. The product liability claims. To Absorb's knowledge, they are not subject to any known claims for liability due to products sold or services rendered. We don't have time to go over a hundred pages of irrelevant or immaterial sections. Although our firm would enjoy the incremental revenue, I believe in value-added legal service. Frankly, I think legal fees of potentially $150,000 would be better spent developing a quality product for sale in the near future. I'm sure Absorb and CalBio would agree. CalBio does lots of Series A financings in California. Have you ever seen such a thing before? I don't believe we have the time or resources to be New Yorkized. We would agree to 5 more pages. You guys decide what is important."

CalBio chimed in and said, "We agree. Thirty pages and limit the fees to $50,000."

"So we are now down to the liquidation preference and the 5 additional pages, right?"

"Correct. See you in San Francisco tomorrow." I abruptly disconnected and shook off the near New York man-handling.

"Jules, who is that?"

"It's Mary and Mandy."

"Hello! Great job, Sam. We appreciate your advice and counsel. What next?"

"Mary and Mandy, focus on the liquidation preference issue. Perhaps offer them a 1.5-times deal that goes away in the event of a sale of the company or an IPO in excess of $200 million. Think about it. We need to head to the airport, or we will miss our fights. See you tonight!" I hung up and asked Jules to get us car service to the airport. Debs met me in the lobby, and we headed to the airport to catch our flights.

SWA had given me an A-4 boarding pass, and I zipped through airport security and again at the TSA PreCheck. Debs, on the other hand, with her C-15 boarding pass, had to go through the regular line. "Sorry, Debs, I'll meet you at the gate and reserve you a seat." I boarded and proceeded to the emergency aisle, placing my briefcase on the aisle seat and sitting in the window seat. The flight attendant smiled, and I struck up a conversation with her while I waited. It had been a very event-filled day, and I was feeling a little frisky. "May I ask you a question?"

"Sure," she responded.

"Do you have to be beautiful to work here?"

She blushed and said, "No, you just need to have a great attitude, be smart, and avoid pick-up lines like that." We laughed until Debs finally boarded the plane.

"Window or aisle, Debs?"

"I'll take the aisle, thank you."

Upon seeing Debs, the flight attendant looked at me with a flat smile, got up and walked away.

After Debs had settled in, I turned to her and asked, "What are your plans when you leave the firm? Are you going to continue practicing law?"

She let out a long sigh. "I'm not sure at the moment. If I do, I will need to take the California Bar."

I nodded my head. "That exam is no walk in the park."

"I'm certainly not going to join another firm. I want a life, to spend time with my family, and to focus on the possibility of a relationship. If I stay in the legal profession, I'll look for a position as in-house counsel somewhere. I'm also thinking about going back into nursing. I have a bachelor's degree in nursing. Who knows? I have 2 months to figure things out. In the meantime, I have to get myself from Point A to Point B."

"Debs, can I ask you a question?"

"I might regret this, but sure, Sam."

"This would be covered under attorney-client privilege. I'm retaining you as my legal counsel related to relationships. Here is $5. Consider that my retainer. So, I met with a past love recently, and it was bittersweet. Threshold question, do you think I would be a difficult person to date?"

"Yes! Oh, sorry, did I answer that too fast? Please let me restate. Honestly, I would have to say yes, Sam."

∞

"Oh boy." I leaned back in my chair and said, "Lay it on me."

Debs locked her hands together and then pushed her palms outward for a good stretch as if she was getting ready to do shot put. "First off, you work all the time. You are a compulsive workaholic. I get emails and texts from you after midnight regularly. That would require a really understanding and tolerant person. Second of all, you work all the time. You believe that you are on a vacation when you take Saturday and Sunday off. Finally, you work all the time. Every conversation over lunch or dinner revolves around a deal or work. I'm certain that any woman you were involved with would get bored of the subject matter after a few meals. How do I know this to be true? Sam, you are my mentor. Although I have not mastered the art of workaholic-ism, I am slowly noticing this evolution. If this were martial arts, I would consider myself a brown belt. All my friends tell me that I work too much; my parents tell me I work too much, and everyone I date tells me I work too much. My only defense is that I don't work as much as you, Sam. Did I mention you work too much?"

"Debs, I have this theory about attraction – physical, intellectual and emotional. With women, it starts with intellectual."

"You are lucky then, Sam because most women would find you to be intellectually attractive. I would give you a 9 because I'm a Soviet judge."

"Haha. Then I think it migrates to physical attraction."

"Now, she's got to be saintly, Sam. You are 30 pounds overweight. At the present moment, I would give you a 3, but there is hope. You can work on that component and drop some of that excess weight and move up to a possible 6 or 7."

"Haha. Then let's talk emotional attraction."

"I'm actually surprised, Sam. Prior to my giving you notice, I figured you to be unemotional. But whenever you talk about your mom, I get a true understanding of your sensitivity. Your solution for me also was absolutely sweet. I cried for an hour after you left. It still makes me cry knowing you really care. You are a closet 8, but to the world, you project a 3. Girls like emotionally available guys. Maybe you can bifurcate your emotions, projecting a 3 to guys and an 8 to girls. You can call it an emotional multiple personality disorder. But you are skirting the issue. You work too much to have a relationship. Who is this person who has you asking me for counsel?"

"Oh, you don't know her. She's unhappily married."

"In that case, I would move very slowly and tread cautiously. Divorced women or about to be divorced women are complicated. They need time to get the death of the marriage out of their system. Typically confused and all over the place for a good 1 to 2 years. Just imagine that she has a 'no trespassing' sign on the electrical fence that surrounds her bodice."

"Thanks for your honesty, Debs. With that, I need to rest my eyes for the next couple of hours." Although I tried to sleep, I was content with replaying the elevator scene followed by our Eskimo kiss. Debs' comments had sobered me, but not by much.

The hours flew by. We landed at Oakland and made our way to the Powell Street exit, caught a taxi to Mark Hopkins, and checked in. The woman at the front desk wore a white blouse, and her hair was straight and neat. I looked at her name tag and addressed her. "Good evening, Jenny. I have 2 reservations for Sam Rivtoc."

"Yes, Mr. Rivtoc. I think you will be pleased to know that we have upgraded you to the Suite, Room 422. May I have your phone number, please?"

My face deadpan, voice calm, I said, "Umm…8,6,7,5,3, ooooh." I paused. "I can't have a room on the 4th floor."

The attendant and I stared at each other for a moment as if she was waiting for an explanation. After what seemed like forever, she looked back down at her computer and began typing. "Hold on a second…. would the Presidential Suite, room 1702, be okay?"

"Jenny, someday I will make you as happy as you just did me." The others at the front desk laughed. She gave me my keys, and I started to walk away. Just then Jenny said, "I'm not that girl." We all laughed as I headed towards the elevators.

On the way to our rooms, I texted Mary and Mandy to meet us in the hotel restaurant, the Top of the Mark, at 9:30 p.m. instead of in the lobby. Debs and I parted ways, and I went to settle into my room. After what seemed like only 30 minutes, Debs knocked on my door, and we proceeded up to the 19th floor. Mary and Mandy were already there. We ordered a bottle of wine and discussed the next day's strategies. Mary and Mandy agreed we were prepared to cave on the 2-times liquidation preference only if it went away upon the sale of the company or an IPO with a valuation of over $200 million.

"That is reasonable, but allow me to be the 'bad cop' so we may negotiate the best deal possible. Debs, this is Mary and Mandy from Absorb. Ladies, Debs was my legal rock star."

"Why so gloomy, Sam? Wait? Was?"

"I am so sad and need to drown my sorrows." I said it in a playful way, but I was legitimately sad. I needed to drown my sorrows because Debs would be leaving the firm soon and moving to California. "She wants to be close to her parents. They live in the

Bay Area. I can't blame her for that, but she will be extremely missed."

Mary asked Debs, "Are you planning to stay in the Bay Area?"

"Yes. I have a medical background and am not sure if I want to pursue that or practice law as an in-house counsel."

Mary asked, "Are you familiar with the glutathione product?"

Debs nodded. "Sort of. I understand that glutathione exists in both GSH (reduced) and GSSG (oxidized) states. Your product is in the GSH stage, and you are using a unique nano-based delivery system so that people can absorb higher levels of glutathione than from other creams or sprays."

I proudly expressed, "See, Mary and Mandy, she knows her shit!"

Both Mary and Mandy looked at each other. "What if we offered you a job as General Counsel to Absorb? We have budgeted approximately $160,000 for this position and will grant you 1 percent in stock options at the current fair market value. Granted, this offer would be contingent on the successful closing of a certain Series A financing."

Noticing that this was totally off of Deb's radar, I quickly responded to give Deb time to process this Godsend.

"Debs needs to take the California Bar to be licensed to practice law in that state," I noted.

Mary addressed Debs. "If you agree to come aboard, we'll agree to give you a year to pass the California bar."

I turned my attention back to Debs and said, "I'd hate to see you leave, but this is an excellent opportunity for you. You'd be part of a great team and awesome product, and it fits your plans for the future. Hurry up and accept the offer so that I can draft the agreement." I smiled and added, "It's all about the upselling of legal services."

Debs looked overwhelmed and at a loss for words. I knew if Debs accepted the offer and started working for Absorb full-time, our legal services would diminish significantly. Still, it was all for the best and I was happy to close any deal that would benefit Debs.

We chatted a little more casually until I looked at my watch. Catching the "not so subtle" hint, Mandy asked, "What time does our meeting start tomorrow?"

"At 10:00 a.m., your office," I said, "I have a lot to do before I turn in." I looked for the waiter and motioned for the check. "Debs, let's meet in my room for breakfast at 8:30 a.m." After I had addressed Debs, I looked over at Mary and Mandy. "I must bid you, ladies, a good night, but please stay and enjoy yourselves. That includes you too, Debs. We will see you at 10:00 a.m." After I paid the check and made my exit, I went upstairs and performed my usual nighttime ritual.

The next morning I awoke at 7:30 a.m., checked my notepad, showered and grabbed my laptop. There were 424 emails and 15 text messages, but nothing from Caroline. It had been 2 days since the wedding. Even with the married risk factor, I felt compelled to text her. *"Hey, Caroline. In SF. Trust all is well."* Delete. *"Caroline, it's me. Hope all is well."* Delete. *"In SF, how are you?"* Delete. Seriously, I was spending 20 minutes on this seemingly simple text. Finally, *"Hi, Caroline. Friends text weekly. Still hungover from the wedding party? In SF. Will send pictures shortly."* Sent. Uploaded picture of the Bay and sent. There was a knock on the door. It was room service.

Minutes later, Debs emerged in the doorway. "Wow wow wow! I looove your room, Sam! Breakfast looks wonderful. Thank you so much. Mary and Mandy are awesome. I get to utilize both of my passions at Absorb, medicine and law on top of being close to my parents. I owe you big time, Sam. You planned that all along, didn't you?" I smiled.

Ping! I checked my phone. It was Caroline. She responded to my text. *"Wow, SF is gorgeous. Hate to ask you for a favor."* I responded, *"What?"* *"Can you get me a magnet of the Golden Gate Bridge? I've always wanted to visit there and Napa. If it is too much trouble, don't worry about it."*

I texted back, *"No worries. Your wish is my command."*

Debs looked at her watch. "We better head out to Absorb. They are down on Embarcadero, right?"

"Right." We arrived at Absorb by 9:45 a.m. and were greeted by Mark Burns and Alex Enzer, the managing director of CalBio. Mary and Mandy joined us shortly after. Alex started things off. "We appreciate your time and the conference call yesterday. Mark has limited his comments to an additional 5 pages. For us, the important business term is the liquidation preference issue. What are your views on our proposal?"

"Assuming we sell Absorb at $100 million, the difference between our 2 positions is about $7.5 million," Mark said. "But the difference increases as the valuation increases. Will you be willing to agree to terminate the liquidation preference if the Absorb reaches a valuation of $200 million either via an IPO or the sale of the company?"

Alex paused. "Of course we would."

Mary turned to Alex. "Can we also split the difference from our 1-time and your 2-times to 1 and a half times liquidation preference?"

Alex grinned. "Yes."

I addressed the group. "I'm glad there aren't any pigs in this room because I've been told bulls make money, bears make money, but pigs get slaughtered. I guess I'm done, and the rest is all legal mumbo jumbo. Before we get to the documents, I wanted you to know that I tried the spray after an all-nighter of a wedding." I mentioned the quantity of alcohol consumed. "When I woke up, I applied 8 spritzes of the spray to my liver area, and within the hour, I had completely recovered from the drunk fest, whereas my friends were still hungover when we met for breakfast." We all laughed and silently agreed that Absorb was going to be huge.

Alex mentioned the sulfurous odor. I explained that I was single and didn't have to worry about smelling bad. Mary approached the issue from a more technical angle. "If it doesn't smell like sulfur, it doesn't have sufficient glutathione. The smell only lasts 15 to 20 minutes."

"Alex, why don't you, Mary, and Mandy go tour the company while Mark, Debs, and I stay here and work on the documents? Mark, do you believe we can move quickly on the 5 pages and be ready around 2:00 pm?"

Mark nodded, "I don't see why not."

During our negotiations, I got to know Mark. He had been a senior lawyer or Of Counsel with the same firm for 15 years, working 14 hours a day and billing 3,000 hours annually. I was impressed with his loyalty and in-depth legal analysis. "I apologize if I came across rudely on the call yesterday."

Mark apologized, "Sorry for the last-minute document submission, but you remember those days when you had to report to a partner. It was sitting on the partner's desk for a week. I understand why you would be annoyed. The partner wanted to include an extra 100 pages. Unfortunately, I ended up being the messenger. Fortunately, you intervened, and we were close to finishing the deal."

Mark was the type of lawyer I was looking for to properly layer our practice with seasoned senior attorneys, especially with the imminent departure of Debs. As noon approached, we all decided to grab dim sum at the famous Yang Sing restaurant. Peking duck, Shanghai dumplings, cha siu bao, shumai, jiaozi, and xiao long bao. Oh, and green tea ice cream. We finished lunch and headed back to the office to wrap up the Series A financing. By 4:00 p.m., the deal was closed, and Absorb had $10 million to continue their business plan.

The mood was festive, another deal done.

Beaming, Mary walked over to thank me as I was saying my goodbyes. "Sam, you have to join us later for dinner to celebrate!" I was back in the city, close to where Jean lived and close to where our parents were buried. I was hoping to call my sister and see if she was available. Not wanting to offend Mary, I pulled her aside and said, "I think it might be better if I excuse myself tonight. This way, you, Mandy and Debs can get to know each other better. I don't want to be the 4th wheel." Mary smiled and thanked me for my sensitivity.

As I walked out the office, I texted Jean to let her know I was in town. She responded, *"You're in town? Wow –Thanks for the advance notice!"*

I replied, *"I'll be at Walnut Creek Bart Station at 5:30. I want to visit our parents' graves & grab dinner."*

Jean responded, *"Let me change my schedule around just for YOU! You're lucky I don't have kids tonight & I'm such a WONDERFUL sister. CU at 5:30."* It was time to visit my sister.

Chapter 11

That Smiling Face

Ping! I texted Jean back, *"I'll be wearing my Ba-Ba-Ri coat."* I walked to the Embarcadero Bart Station heading toward Walnut Creek. Jean was waiting for me at the passenger pick-up area. We went to the Asian supermarket around the corner to pick up some tangerines, melons, and Korean duk cakes. Walking to our parents' gravesite, I felt nostalgia creeping in. "Thanks for meeting me, Jean. I've been meaning to visit here for a while. Mom's lessons keep coming back to me. I feel like she really instilled the 'never quit, I can overcome anything' attitude in me. Remember when she had her knee surgery?"

"Oh yes, double reconstructive surgery was rough. Didn't you bribe her with a trip to Korea with Dad?"

"I did. I came to visit her at the hospital early one day. She didn't see me, but I saw her. It was so painful to watch her sitting dejected in that wheelchair. Of course, when she noticed me, she put on her brave face. She was so determined to walk again, and I just wanted to give her something to look forward to."

"Sam, the nurses were all so surprised when Mom was walking just a month and a half after her surgery! I know Mom and Dad treasured the time they spent visiting family and friends in Korea."

I could see their headstone just ahead and slowed down a bit to get my last thoughts out. "I hope one day to be as strong as she was. Sometimes I think of my work as a kind of battle, but I can't even imagine what it would have been like to survive the Japanese occupation, the Korean War, immigrating to the U.S., her reconstructive knee surgery, and then finally Parkinson's disease."

"Mom was pretty remarkable. Look how beautiful she looks with Dad," Jean said softly, staring at the photo engraved on their headstone.

That engraved photo, a snapshot of a lifetime of smiles, a lifetime of companionship, and the courage to embrace destiny and death together.

Jean began, "Hi, Mom and Dad. Sam dropped by today, so we decided to come visit. We brought you some of your favorite treats! Guess what? Sam finally decoded the *Ba-Ba-Ri* coat mystery! Do you like them?" Jean twirled around to give Mom a better look.

"Hi, Mom and Dad, it's me, Sam. Guess what; I'm single. I know, I've been such a horrible son. You know I had this theory, Mom, that you would always be alive, harassing me and holding on until I settled down. So I played my part by staying single. If I ever do date seriously, get engaged or get married, I promise to introduce her to you!" I paused a moment to steady myself. "Mom, I was talking with Jean on the way over here, and I want you to know that you were the strongest person I have ever known. I really do appreciate all the life lessons you tried to teach me." I paused to assuage my guilty feelings and continued, "I'm still learning. Through college and even after law school, we only saw each other during the major holidays and telephoned every now and then. Whenever I came home, you always had my favorite ice cream available and made the best meals. I remember once you were blasting my old CDs loudly, and I said that was one of my favorite songs in high school and you always told me to turn down the stereo. You said, 'I know.' Thanks, Mom, for always being motherly towards me."

I sighed then looked at my father. "Hi, Dad. You were such an avid photographer. I remember the final months when you ordered us to take so many pictures of the 2 of you. I didn't understand. But now, every time I look at those pictures, I notice something different that reminds me of you. And in all the pictures, you have a certain smile, one of contentment and peace, knowing that your time together was coming to an end."

Thinking about their smiles, I flashed back to a terrible rendition of the Mona Lisa I had painted in high school. The original was full of tiny details in the background, but I had painted bold colors, basically deleting all detail. I was no artist and didn't have the time or skill to incorporate them in my copy. Everyone has his own reasons for appreciating Da Vinci's masterpiece. It wasn't Mona Lisa's clothing, hair or eyes that I found intriguing; it was her smile. I thought Da Vinci had captured the essence of this unknown woman, Mona Lisa. When I looked at the pictures of my parents, I noticed something similar. I remembered those last few months. I studied their smiling faces in the photos that Dad took and realized that he had found his Mona Lisa in Mom.

Returning from my memories, I focused again on the headstone. "Mom, look at your smiling face. Don't worry. I'm still working on finding my Mona Lisa. If not in this lifetime, I'm sure you guys are already searching for her in my next. Thank you for everything. We will be back soon!"

I turned to Jean and said, "Let's go to that sushi restaurant in Walnut Creek."

"Sure. What Mona Lisa are you talking about? That terrible painting you painted? Never mind. My boys are wondering when they are going to be able to see their crazy uncle again. What are you doing for Thanksgiving?"

"I'm not sure. I need to check my schedule. Jean, I am not going to lie, I will most likely be working."

"Oh come on, Sam! You work all the time. It's Thanksgiving, and the boys keep talking about that crazy Thanksgiving rock, paper, scissors thing you started 2 years ago."

"Yeah, I remember. That was brutal. I got destroyed." I had come up with this crazy game for the boys to play. After our Thanksgiving dinner, we would arrange 5 plates of leftover food, including turkey, mashed potatoes, pumpkin pie, pasta salad and corn on the cob. Aaron, Nathan and I each picked a plate and played rock, paper, and scissors. The loser had to finish that plate within 5 minutes. Two years ago, I lost all 5 times and wanted to stick a fork in myself and die.

"Yes, to this day, the boys still talk about you lapsing into a turkey coma by the end of the evening."

Those were some wonderful memories. Jean and her boys were my only connection to anything family since Mom and Dad had passed away. It made me think about Caroline and what my life would have been like if we had gotten back together earlier before she had married. "Okay, I'll make a good faith effort, but make sure you warn the boys that I've been practicing my rock, paper, scissors skills. What time is it?"

"It is 10:00 p.m."

"Oh, I need to get back to the hotel and pack. I have an early flight back to Atlanta."

Jean was noticeably saddened by my need to make a quick departure. "Dumping and running, Sam?"

I knew what she was talking about. Since Mom and Dad's passing, I had found it difficult to deal with the emotional part of their death. Maybe it was because of the amount of sorrow I felt about losing them. I had this big hole in me that needed to be filled.

"Jean, don't be like that. I am dealing with it the best way I can. I did come, didn't I?"

"I'm sorry, Sam. We just don't see you very much. I was hoping since we only have each other left, that you would be around more often. Maybe I should have been nicer to you when we were kids."

I put my hands on her shoulders and then gave her a hug. "Jean, don't worry. I will make a huge effort to come this Thanksgiving to see you and the boys. And yes… you should have been nicer to me when we were kids."

Jean playfully hit me in the middle of my back. "At least you are a *somebody*. Go on, Sam… I know you have to run!"

I waved and then took off quickly. In mid stride, I pulled out my phone to check for any messages. An additional 444 emails and 62 texts. I sensed something bad might be happening in business because of the three "4s." As proof of my business acuity, they were there, evidence of my value. As I swiped though the numbers I felt the familiar rush of adrenaline. Familial obligations completed, deal junkie mode was back in full force.

As I was coming around the corner, something passed in front of me while I was looking at my phone. I looked around for it but couldn't find it. I must be tired, I thought. Maybe Jean was right. My visits to see Mom and Dad always happened at the spur of the moment, without any warning. I came to the realization I'd been working to fill that empty void. I shook it off and started thinking about Caroline and her warm smile.

Chapter 12

Carpe Diem

Ping! I received a text from my BFF. "*Hey, Sam, Ron loves you. We had so much fun. Thx!*"

"*Hi, Randi, don't get jealous on me now. Yes, that was a blast.*"

"*Free this Friday for dinner?*"

"*Asking me out on a date, BFF?*"

"*Yes, we are. Coming to ATL. 8:00 p.m. work? Pick a sushi restaurant.*"

I checked my smartphone and had 642 emails and 14 text messages. I wondered why there were so many 4s. I read Debs' text. "*What time are we leaving tomorrow?*"

"*Meet in lobby 6:00 a.m. Flight leaves SFO 8:00 a.m.-ish.*"

I responded, "*Can't do 8:00, but am free at 7:55.*"

Randi did not respond immediately, but when she did, all I got was a "*?*"

"*8:00 is reserved for Sweet Southern Caroline.*" I could almost see her eyes rolling to the back of her head.

I arrived in my room, and my message light was on. "Mr. Rivtoc, please contact the front desk. There is a message from Mark Burns and a package for you at the front desk."

I rang the front desk and asked that the package be delivered and to connect me to Mark Burns' room. "Hi, Mark. Sorry, I was out visiting my parents."

"How are they?"

"Well, they passed away 2 years ago, but the visit was awesome."

"Oh, I'm sorry to hear that. Are you available to meet for drinks at the Top of the Mark?"

"Sure, give me about 30 minutes. I'm waiting for a package to be delivered." The doorbell rang, and I slid over to the door to answer it. The courier handed me my package. "Thank you," I replied and handed him a tip.

Attached to the parcel was a note. I read it out loud:

Thank you, Sam, for your excellent counsel. We thought you might need some more glutathione sprays after your wedding story. Best, Mary and Mandy.

There were four 30-oz sprays and a brand new Montblanc Meisterstuck Platinum rollerball pen.

I got online and sent Mary and Mandy an email:

Thanks for the lovely surprise. Absorb is awesome, and y'all are the best. Looking forward to many more financings and a massive exit soon. Best. Sam.

I headed upstairs with an inclination that I might have hooked Mark. The deal was done! No conflicts of interest... time to put on my recruiting hat and GSD.

I texted Debs and asked her to join us *"Upstairs at Top of Mark. See you in 45 minutes. Put on your best-recruiting hat."*

At the entrance of the Top of the Mark, I spotted Mark. "Hi, Mark. Thanks to your leadership, that was one of my easiest closings. I appreciate it." He thanked our team but was noticeably uneasy. I sensed why he had asked for this meeting; he wanted to learn more about our firm, my practices, my book of business, partnership track and the possibility of interviewing with us. I eased in with the history of the firm and how I was recruited to join 5 years ago. Casually I explained that I was the youngest partner in the office and managed a team of 15 lawyers and that Debs was leaving the firm to join Absorb as General Counsel next year. "I am saddened because Debs was on track for partnership in 2 years."

Mark smiled, "Isn't she going to be an 8th year?"

I smiled and nodded. I knew that he liked that answer because he was in his 15th year and was uncertain as to whether he would make partner anytime soon… if ever. "Hypothetically, if you decided to move to Atlanta and join us, you would likely be on a 2-year track. Frankly, since our deal is done, I don't see any conflict of interest recruiting you."

Mark was a seasoned lawyer and mentioned his $2 million book of business. In my eyes, that was a respectable book of business, especially in Atlanta where most junior partners barely managed a $1 million book of business. I then dropped the bomb and said, "My book of business was averaging $10 million, but I'm afraid it might dip to $9 million with the departure of Debs."

Mark gave a huge sigh of relief because partners with a $10 million book of legal business are almost unheard of. I told him, "Our salaries run about 2/3 of New York salaries. However, the Atlanta housing market is approximately 50 percent lower than that of New York. To top it off, the average CPI in Atlanta is 30 percent lower than in New York. I expected you to make around $200,000 plus bonuses. If you maintain a $2 million book of business, I can't see why you wouldn't make $300,000 in Atlanta."

At that moment, Debs appeared. "What do you want to drink, Debs?"

"I would like coffee."

"Would you care for anything else, Mark?"

Mark was in deep thought and shook himself out of it, "No, thank you. I'm good."

"Okay, I'm going to go and close out the tab. Debs, you talk frankly and honestly with Mark about the firm, the practice and me. Congratulations again on your new job offer, General Counsel. Good night, folks. I'll see you at 6:00 a.m. in the lobby."

I returned to my room, and my nightly ritual commenced. I scheduled a 5:00 a.m. wake-up call, placed my notepad on the table next to the bed, and turned the phone off to prevent any disruptions in my sleep cycle.

I was asleep before my head hit the pillow that night. Dreamscapes moved in and out of my brain, mostly echoing my travels. San Francisco, Atlanta, New Orleans—the list goes on and on. Each location meant something to me. All the traveling that I had done was encapsulated within the confines of my dream world. I had completed so much in a short period. I remember I heard something ring as I dreamt of a dark figure passing by. The ringing got louder. I stirred from my slumber.

"Good morning, Mr. Rivtoc. This is your 5:00 a.m. wake-up call." My OCD kicked in. I checked the notepad. Nothing new. I showered, packed, and turned on my smartphone. There were 324 new emails, 15 new text messages. I logged into SWA and got my boarding pass: A-6 and TSA PreCheck. I looked through the drawers and found a postcard of the iconic Mark Hopkins. I grabbed it and placed it in my briefcase with a note to self for Caroline. I breezed through the airport security and told Debs to meet me at the gate. Instead of my usual, break out the laptop, responding to email routine, I meandered off in search of magnets and postcards. I found and purchased one of the Golden Gate Bridge and Coit Tower.

Inspired by my dream, I came up with a new plan. I wasn't sure if it was brilliant or even feasible. I thought about creating a photo album of postcards with messages and dates. After I had

∞

acquired a sufficient quantity, I would present the album and magnets from the cities I had visited to Caroline on her birthday in May.

Postcard #1, November 2006. I wrote:

Golden Gate, Napa and introducing you to my family! The 3 things I would like to share with you. Love, Sam.

I drew the infinity symbol.

I waved at Debs at the boarding gate and yelled, "Hi, Debs, you made it through airport security. I'll grab us a seat." I dashed toward the emergency exit seats and was greeted by another friendly flight attendant. It was my A-list preferred ritual to flirt with the flight attendants and man the emergency exits. I told this one, "You know what? With my IQ and your personality, our kids would be super smart and sweet."

She responded, "My personality is awful. You couldn't handle super smart and awful."

"Ah, ha ha." I reply winking and shooting the finger gun at her. She smiled and continued on down the aisle.

Debs boarded, and I asked her if she wanted the window or aisle.

She shook her head and questioned, "Why do you keep asking me? I always pick aisle."

After we had sat, I asked Debs for a recap of her meeting with Mark. She responded, "I know he's pretty much sold on joining the firm. Naturally, he wants to wait until the year-end bonuses are complete."

I was curious. "Did you like him?"

"Yes, I think he would be a good fit. *Carpe diem.*"

"Good. I'm tired and plan to sleep the entire flight. Is there anything urgent I need to know about?"

"No, Sam. All is quiet on the Atlanta front."

"Great, good night." I closed my eyes and instantly dozed off.

We landed in Atlanta at 4:30 p.m. EST. Not wanting to neglect my new task, I stated, "Give me 10 minutes. I need to stop by the store and pick up a magnet and postcard."

Debs yelled out as I dashed off to a gift shop, "Sam, are we heading to the office?"

I stopped and turned around. "No, I'm going to drop you off at home and head home myself."

Debs was shocked. Eyeing me, she asked, "Are you under the weather?"

"No, I'm just exhausted and don't want to get sick, so I'm going to the store to pick up a photo album, hit the foot reflexology place and head home." After dropping Debs off, I headed to the mall in search of a music box to store all the magnets and a unique photo album for the post cards. Mission accomplished.

I entered the foot reflexology store. "How much for a 90-minute massage?"

A tired-looking hostess said, "$50."

"I like really strong massages. Who is the strongest massage person you have?" She motioned me to follow her. The masseuse asked me to take off my shoes and socks and to roll up my pants. As I soaked my feet in the very warm water, she started pressing on my temples and worked her way to my shoulders. Twenty minutes later, she removed my feet from the warm water and proceeded to work on my feet for 20 minutes. Then my legs for 20 minutes. As I relaxed, the stress was fleeing from my body with every hard press. I slipped in and out of sleep and found myself in a deep meditative state. She asked me to roll over and then worked out the knots in my back for the final 30 minutes. I was in heaven and could have fallen asleep there but realized that it was time to leave. I tipped her, guzzled a liter of water, and headed out into the world, refreshed and somewhat renewed.

At home, I placed the 2 magnets in the music box and thought about what to write on the Atlanta postcard.

November 2006. Walking Stone Mountain, visiting the Martin Luther King Museum, and touring Jimmy Carter Presidential Library are the things that I would like to share with you. Love, Sam. I drew the infinity symbol.

Chapter 13

Dinner with Ron

Ping! The rest of that week consisted of calm and normal law days, just maintaining and managing the deal flow in the office. I looked forward to syncing up with Randi and Ron on Friday.

When Friday finally came around, I scheduled a foot reflexology before dinner. Afterward, I was refreshed. I arrived at Sakana, a small sushi bar north of Midtown. As usual, I was 15 minutes early. Ron and Randi were already seated. They had reserved a private room for us.

"What have I done to deserve 2 encounters with my favorite couple in the same month?"

Randi flashed her left hand, and I noticed a 3-carat diamond that shimmered on her finger. I screamed like we were at a football game and my 49ers had scored the winning touchdown. I needed to capture the moment. "Sit over there, guys, and let me take a picture."

I noticed their smiling faces and realized that Ron had found his Mona Lisa. In all the excitement, I heard my stomach grumble. Then suddenly and without warning, I felt an intense and compelling need to locate a restroom. I forgot that reflexology does wonders for my body, but would unpredictably improve my plumbing. At first, I thought, Am I nervous about the engagement? No… it had to be the foot massage. I felt delirious. All I could think was, Please don't have an accident, not at Sakana. I went to the back of the restaurant and rushed to the restroom. Of course, the door was locked. I knocked politely. My legs were crossed as I prayed.

As the sweat rolled profusely down my face, I started pounding on the door, and the guy yelled, "It's going to be a little while longer!" Imagine me with the deer in the headlights look. I really couldn't wait any longer. My survival instincts kicked into 5th gear, and I slowly moved sideways and entered the women's restroom. Quickly, I locked the door and sat with a huge sigh of relief. In my most grateful inner voice, I said, "Thank you, Lord, for saving me." Probably not God's idea of "saving," but I was willing to show any appreciation at that moment. I finished my business, but I worried about how to sneak out of the women's restroom undetected. I peeked out the door to see if the coast was clear. The odds were in my favor. The coast was clear. I thanked my lucky little stars and headed back to the room.

Randi looked at me with a curious grin. "Oh my God, Sam, you okay? You seem a little sweaty."

I deflected the inquiry and said, "Remind me later to explain, but for now give me the scoop, Randi. How did Ron propose to you?"

With her eyebrow risen, she responded, "Actually, Ron was planning to propose to me the night of Joe's wedding, but you rudely girl-napped me to the wedding. He was such a good sport canceling the entire engagement plan until Sunday. He didn't want to upset my BFF. We went back to the restaurant where we had our first date."

I was elated. "How sweet and sappy... I love it!" Like a little girl, I squealed, "Was it at the 1789 Restaurant?"

"Yes. I was on high alert, but Ron didn't ask me there. He wanted to walk off the meal. We walked around the campus at Georgetown and talked about the history of this building, the filming of *The Exorcist*, the history of that building. Then, we got to Healy Tower, and he started to explain the meaning of Hoya Saxa. It's Latin for 'What Rock?' He asked me to chant Hoya Saxa with him. I was embarrassed, as undergraduates were following us in the Hoya Saxa chant." Randi glanced at Ron for a quick moment to make sure he was okay with her rendition of the events. He smiled. Randi continued. "Then, he went down on his knees and said, 'Randi, this 3-carat rock symbolizes my love for you. You are the solid foundation to our relationship, and I can't imagine a day… an hour… a minute without you in my life.'"

In my usual sophomoric way, I stated, "That's beautiful, but I'm about to be sick. Where's a paper bag? Did you say yes immediately? I can't imagine you did. I think you said something like 'Ron, I have 3 conditions before I say yes. 1. Sam will always be my BFF. 2. If you ever cheat on me, you are dead. 3. I wear the pants in the relationship.'"

Randi tightened one side of her mouth, gave me the stink eye, and grimaced. "Haha."

I countered, "You look so enchanting whenever you make that face. Are the kids excited about the news?"

Randi responded, "They are absolutely thrilled!"

I turned to Ron and said, "That proposal was very creative. Kudos to you. When is the big day?"

In unison, they responded, "September 15, 2007." Randi smiled like she had another bonus to reveal. "And we would like you to be our Man of Honor."

I sat back and put my big boy pants back on. "What? What the hell is that?"

Randi explained, "Well, you know what a bridesmaid is, right? You will be walking down the aisle in the ceremony in place of the Maid of Honor."

Not fully aware of how this was to play out, I answered, "Okay, but I draw the line at wearing a dress."

We needed to celebrate this fantastic news. I ordered 3 bottles of Kamotsuru Tokusei Gold sake, a rare and excellent sake generally reserved for very special occasions. We didn't have time to think about what to order off the menu. I motioned to the sushi chef to just keep sending the sushi and sake. Our conversation drifted between the details about the wedding, the proposal itself, and reminiscing about the past.

"Ron, did Randi ever tell you about her purple purse?"

"No, what purple purse?"

With my most terrified look, I stated, "I'm advising you to purge the purple purse while you have a chance." Leaning in towards Ron, I clenched my hands together and responded, "According to Randi's son, 2 years ago while carrying the notorious purple purse; Randi was approached by a 14-year-old young man at a baseball game. And I use the word 'man' loosely since it was a Little League game. The 14-year-old man-boy asked if she was 'seeing' anyone. The man-boy sat next to Randi and asked if he could touch her boots." Leaning back, I continued, "I actually think the man-boy had a speech impediment and meant boobs.... breasteses... mammaries. I'd like to replace the "t" with a "b" please. I was laughing hysterically because the 14-year-old was hitting on Randi in front of her son. Later that same day, Randi and her son decided to take a walk in the park when a married man with a spouse exclaimed 'WOW!' Randi's son responded with 'Wow, what?' The man said, 'WOW HER'! Randi's son firmly believed that the cause of all the commotion was due to the purple purse. You need to do a search and destroy mission on that purple purse, Ron."

Randi rolled her eyes and pushed my arm. "Oh hush, Sam!"

Satisfied by the rise I got out of Randi, I continued, "While we are on the subject of boots, let me tell you the boot joke." I turned and addressed Ron. "There once was this guy who was totally obsessed with women's boots. He ran around society yelling, 'boots… boots… boots.' Society decided to lock him up. After 2-years, the powers that be felt bad about his issues with boots. They went out and hired a shrink to see if he could cure him. The shrink told the patient that they were going to play a word relationship game. 'When I say a word, please tell me what that word reminds you of. Okay?' The patient agreed. First word… 'Watermelons?' The patient opened his eyes really wide and exclaimed 'OMG, big, big, gigantic boots!' The shrink told him to relax. Next word was 'oranges.' The patient responded, 'Boots. Boots. Boots. Small, firm boots.' The shrink pondered a bit, trying to think of something that did not remind this person of boots. 'Windshield wipers?' 'Boots. Boots. Boots.' With an eyebrow raised, he asked the patient, "How do windshield wipers remind you of boots?" The patient said, 'Now move your head from left to right and make that kissing smacking sound.'"

"Ron, have you noticed Randi's boots?"

"Don't worry, Sam," Randi said. "I'll make sure to turn on Ron's wipers tonight!"

I was elated for Randi and Ron. What a wonderful and special engagement party they made me a part of. The night was winding down, and we had consumed enough sushi and sake to feed a party of 5. "Hey guys, I got a foot massage the other day, and it felt absolutely wonderful. They are to die for. Do you want to join me tomorrow at 9:00 am? My treat!" They eagerly accepted my offer as we hugged goodbye.

Chapter 14
A Fearless Cook Indeed

<u>Ping</u>! The alarm went off at 8 a.m.

"What?" I double-checked the alarm. I never sleep more than 6 hours, ever. Checked the notepad. Nothing. Had I taken 3 steps backwards and neglected my sleep work? I looked at my smartphone. Several messages from Billings, Day and Knight appeared. I put the phone down and shook my head. "I'll respond to them after the massage."

I jumped up, showered, and headed out the door. On the way, I called the spa and reserved three 2-hour massages. I wanted to evaluate the difference between the 90- and 120-minute versions. I asked for 3 of their strongest personnel and offered to tip extra if they made either Ron or Randi cry.

We all met at the reflexology place. I laughed throughout the massage. I could hear Randi wince and send out a random "ouch" between deep breaths. Ron, on the other hand, fell into deep REM. He snored throughout most of the massage. Three similar massages and 3 different results. I laughed, Randi cried, and Ron slept. Afterwards, I chirped, "Let's grab some coffee."

We went around to the corner to a local coffee shop. "Man of Honor" was a concept I could not get my head around. I was new to this role and needed some insight. We finished chatting about my duties and delved into some decadent cheesecake. After the last bite had been eaten and the last drop of coffee drunk, it was time to bid the happy couple *adieu*. With a sigh, I got up and announced, "Well, I have to get back to work. Thanks for coming down to Atlanta to share the news. Kudos again on the engagement. By the way, make sure you stay close to restrooms today… reflexology tends to improve the plumbing."

Ron stood up and offered his hand out for a shake. "Thank you for taking the time to see us, for the wonderful massages, and agreeing to be a part of the wedding party. Honestly, I figured you would say NO, but apparently, Randi was correct, as she always is."

"Ron, that sounds like a challenge. I accept!" I pulled him in for a hug and told him, "Take care of this little bird." Ron smiled with acknowledgment. "Safe travels, you 2, and we'll see you again real soon. And definitely at the wedding!" I hugged Randi like I always did, and we set off in opposite directions.

I was on cloud 9 and called my sister Jean. It went straight to voice mail. "Hey, it's me, Sam. Great seeing you last week. I cleared my schedule to come out for Thanksgiving! I'm taking the last flight out on Wednesday night. I'll be there on Thursday, November 24, and leave Sunday morning. Give my best to the boys and warn them about the upcoming rock, paper, scissors event." I hung up and put the phone away.

It was tough growing up with Jean. She was 5 years older than me and set the bar really high. I think she received only one B+ from kindergarten through high school. Imagine going to class and your teacher saying, "Oh, you are Jean's little brother. Jean was my favorite student ever. She was top of the class. What happened to you? Were you adopted?"

Mom was alarmed that I was performing poorly academically. Mom couldn't handle anyone with merely five A's and two B's in light of her other child's squeaky-clean, straight-A record. She had to intervene and hired none other than Jean to tutor me. "Jean, you take Ron and show him!"

She got paid $5 an hour, and I was tortured 20 hours weekly. Jean started with my 4th-grade lesson plans in math and English. I wasn't a marginal student. I was in the top 10 percent of my 4th-grade class. I was arrogant and told Mom, "I think you are wasting your money on Jean."

Jean loved to shop, and I was cutting into her funding for fashion. For math, we went from multiplication in Lesson 1 to algebra in Lesson 2. "What is x?"

"Is this a trick question? I don't know what x is."

Jean turned to Mom and said, "I'm concerned. I knew what x was in 3rd grade, and look at Sam. He's totally lost. I have an imbecile for a brother who may end up becoming a *nobody* in life." Then Jean started my English tutoring lessons. "Spell the word 'amalgamation' and use it in a sentence."

"Amalgamation? I've never heard of the word."

"Mom, Sam doesn't speak English at an elementary level." Jean had no mercy for me. I sometimes thought she was the devil in disguise. Because of her antics, Mom placed me on restriction for 2 weeks. "No more baseball, football or friends."

Public school and torturous tutor sessions were endured for 4 years, but I was patient, knowing that freedom was near once Jean graduated from high school. I must admit that middle school and high school were a walk in the park since they were refresher courses compared to Jean. Regardless of how much she tortured me, I still love her.

I had planned on catching the 8:00 p.m. flight on Wednesday to San Francisco but was delayed due to SEC comments on the SocMedia IPO. The team huddled and strategized on our response on Monday. Since I was going to California, I wanted to meet with the other 3 members of the Billings, Day and Knight/SocMedia team to go over our schedule. "I want a first draft to be circulated internally to the team by Wednesday. Debs, you are the project manager for that. Thursday is Thanksgiving. Who is volunteering to come in tomorrow?" Naturally, those gunning for partnership or wanting to impress would be the first to raise their hand, but surprisingly, all 3 hands went up. "Okay, Debs, you take the lead. Control the documents and circulate to the accountants and SocMedia on Thursday. Ask for comments by close of business Friday. I want another draft circulated to everybody, including the investment bank and their counsel, by Saturday morning. Ask for comments by Sunday noon. We will reconvene at the financial printers at 3:00 p.m. I land at 7:00 p.m. and will meet you guys by 8:30 p.m. Happy Thanksgiving, guys." I rescheduled my flight to the 5:00 a.m. flight on Thanksgiving Day. *"Landing 10:00 a.m., will rent car. See you by noon."*

Jean texted back, *"Okay, won't start without you. Best behavior required. Aaron inviting girlfriend."*

I headed to the airport at 3:00 a.m. and checked into SWA. A-1 and TSA PreCheck. SWEET! The worst day to travel; I couldn't believe people were moving around that early in the morning. Onboard, a late 20s flight attendant stared while I was grinning at a funny SocMedia posting. She politely asked, "Do you live in San Francisco? Whatcha laughing about?"

I looked up at her; she had caught me off guard. "I live in Atlanta and am off to see my sister and nephews. Are you hitting on me?"

With a little grin, she responded, "You can call it that if you want to."

"You're not supposed to be hitting on me. I'm the initiator. Didn't you get the memo? I'm expected to flirt with you. Not the

∞

other way around." The tables were turned. I was blushing and unprepared.

"Well, I noticed your shirt, and I love your responses. My name is Amy, and here's my number." I took the piece of paper, smiled, and sat down. Yes, that was totally flattering, but my mind gravitated toward Caroline. I turned on my smartphone, pulled up my sweet Caroline's number and texted, *"Ping, off to SF. Happy Thanksgiving."*

I arrived at Jean's by noon. Aaron was dressed noticeably differently. "What, no NBA shirt? Your hair is brushed, impeccably dressed. Are you going on a date?"

He blushed and said, "A friend is coming over for Thanksgiving lunch at 1:00 p.m."

Aaron yelled to Nathan, "You need to dress appropriately and not disrespect Melissa!"

Saluting, Nathan barked, "Yes, Sir!" We all succumbed to Aaron's wishes and changed to more formal attire. Jean had been cooking since the day before. I smelled the turkey, ham, corn, mashed potatoes, pumpkin pie in the air and saw the homemade strawberry cheesecake. I will say it again… Strawberry cheesecake baby! Music to my stomach." As the clock approached one, I sensed more nervous energy from Aaron. I wondered if Melissa would be early, on time, or fashionably late. First impressions are crucial, and that would help me decipher the type of girl she was. At 12:50, the doorbell rang. Aaron answered the door. "Oh, Nathan! You-know-who is here!" Jean, Nathan, and I introduced ourselves to Melissa. Melissa was a junior in high school and 2 years older than Aaron.

Jean yelled, "Lunch is ready!" We took our places at the table, and Aaron blessed the food and opened a bottle of celebratory sparkling cider. He filled his glass to the top. Nathan, in turn, poured

∞

himself a full glass. Nathan and I stared at Aaron after we noticed that there was only a little of the sparkly left for Melissa. As Jean glared at him, I sensed panic in Aaron.

After a deep breath, he recovered nicely. "Hey, Melissa, please take my glass, and I'll take yours." No, chivalry was not dead in this family. My heart fluttered, and my thoughts gravitated back to Caroline, my first love in high school.

I broke out of the "Dream Weaver" sequence and focused my attention back on Jean. "Hey, sis, we've been smelling the food for over 30 minutes now, patiently waiting to dig in like a pack of hungry lions." Based on past feastings, Aaron was the pace car. He generally devoured his food at a much faster rate than Nathan or I did. That is, with the exception of today. Nathan and I were done with our first round. Aaron had mentioned earlier that Melissa usually ate very slowly. What? Aaron was at 25 percent and Melissa at 15 percent? My heart fluttered again. Ahhhh, young love. Nathan and I looked at each other and decided to slow down in preparation for the main event. Aaron was so distracted by the presence of Melissa that he probably forgot about rock, paper, scissors. When the moment presented itself, I explained to Melissa our Thanksgiving tradition, and she agreed to participate. Jean, always so clever, said as she excused herself, "I have to clean up this mess and can't join you for all the fun."

Aaron volunteered to assemble the 5 plates of leftovers and placed them on the table with an exaggerated flourish. We commenced with the chant, "Let the games begin!" Round 1, turkey. Melissa lost and ate 1/3 of the plate, but Aaron came to her rescue and finished. Round 2, two pieces of corn on the cob. Aaron lost and finished the plate. Round 3, mashed potatoes. Nathan lost and looked distraught after finishing the plate. During the break, I proudly exclaimed that 2 years ago, I lost all 5 rounds and wanted to die. Both Aaron and Nathan couldn't stop laughing. Melissa laughed, too, but I think she was torn between laughing at me and feeling sorry for me.

I warned everyone, "I've been practicing my rock, paper, scissor skills and today, I'm gonna win!" Round 4, potato salad. Melissa lost. Melissa sensed Aaron's pain and finished half the potato salad. Aaron was caught between a rock and a hard place. His stomach couldn't take any more abuse, but his heart forced him to move forward.

Aaron finished the remaining half. I'm sure Nathan was thinking, "What a fool." In 5th grade, I asked Nathan and his best friend about girls and girlfriends. They both replied, "Let us make this crystal clear, WE DO NOT like girls like that!"

Round 5, pumpkin pie. Before this round, Aaron looked to Melissa and said, "I cannot eat any more food. We cannot lose, or we are doomed." Unbelievably, Melissa lost again. Melissa took a bite and with a squeaky voice said, "Aaron, help me please." Aaron summoned all his energies and finished the pumpkin pie. At that moment, I was reminded that love truly conquers all.

I had such a wonderful visit with Jean and her boys. The Thanksgiving lunch was very memorable. As I was eating my peach cobbler topped with ice cream and a side of strawberry cheesecake, my takeaway on Melissa was 4-fold. Number 1, she was considerate about time management, arriving 10 minutes early instead of being fashionably late. I am sure she wanted to leave a great impression on all. Number 2, she was on her best behavior, watching and waiting, pacing her food intake to match Aaron's. Number 3, she was highly intelligent, well mannered and well spoken. Finally, she brought her camera to capture the moment, and I'm certain that there was that

Mona Lisa smile throughout. Jean had been quoting Julia Child about being a fearless cook: "Try out new ideas and new recipes." I looked for a message from Caroline and was saddened when I saw none. Perhaps that also applied to dating. Be a fearless dater! Try out new candidates.

Chapter 15

Baby Steps

Ping! My calendar pinged me. That dreaded day had finally come. It was January 1, 2007. It was a somber day for me. Debs was leaving the firm. She was loyal, competent and trustworthy at work and in all my private matters. I was going to miss our daily interactions— but I was elated for her. I was also feeling a little melancholy because of Caroline's non-responsiveness. For me, a new year initiates new beginnings, and I had not heard from her since before my last text over Thanksgiving. Perhaps she was trying to salvage her marriage and work things out. I was sad for me but happy for her. I needed to divert my attention from these thoughts. With no deals in motion, I decided to call Mark Burns about Debs' old position.

"Hi, Mark, this is Sam Rivtoc. Happy New Year!"

"Hello, Sam! Happy New Year to you too! To what do I owe this pleasure?"

"Is this a good time to talk?"

"Sure. What have you got on your mind?"

"Well, I wanted to personally call you to let you know that we have an *Of Counsel* position opening in our corporate and securities practice group. The pay is $220,000 annually, plus bonuses and relocation. I can personally assure you that you will be on a 2-year partnership track if not sooner. You'll need to visit our offices and meet some of the other folks. I don't want to pressure you, but I need to know your interest level."

Mark answered with, "Thanks, Sam. Yes, I am very interested."

∞

"When can you come down?

"When do you need me to come down?"

"Is next week possible?"

Mark quickly responded with an emphatic, "Sure! I have been taking some vacation time, so I am free all of next week."

I continued my conversation with Mark. "Great. I'll ask Jules to coordinate everything. Text me your personal email address, and we'll talk soon."

With that out of the way, I felt I was off to a good start, but thoughts of Caroline flooded into the crevices of my mind. I scrambled, looking for the paper that Amy, the flight attendant, had given me. "Ahhhh, there it is." I pulled out the paper with the name *Amy Hunter* on it. A 936 area code. Houston, Texas. I dialed the number, and it went straight to voicemail. "Hi, Amy, this is Sam. Happy New Year! Today is your lucky day. I'm that cute Asian guy with the rocking shirt that flew with you to SF during Thanksgiving. You loved our playful banter, so you gave me your number. Call me back."

I received a text message back. *"Hey, you... you remember me?"*

I responded, *"Hi, Amy Hunter. Of course, I remember you. Traveling to NYC."*

Amy switched gears. *"Three months go by, and you expect me to remember you?"*

"Haha. A guy can dream, can't he? Busy holidays – just surfaced for air... and it's 3 months, not three months. Huge difference!"

"Huh? What difference? Where are you?"

"I'm in Atlanta."

∞

"Ping me when you pass through Houston. We can grab drinks/dinner – maybe breakfast if you're lucky."

"Sure, baby steps! Let me know if you are ever in ATL. See you soon." That little banter brought me back to reality. New ideas and new recipes but in moderation, right? While Caroline was seemingly no longer available, Amy seemed Ms. Right for now. Surely I didn't like to be hit on, but since I reached out to her and not vice versa, I considered it a non-breach of my rules.

∞

Chapter 16

Groundhog Day

Ping! Only a few messages were rolling in. The rest of January was pretty quiet. No deals were in the works. Amy and I quietly bantered back and forth by text. It was a relationship of convenience. No real commitment. Just a lot of talk and no action. Mark had already come down and signed with the firm. He officially started the first week in February and transitioned well. I liked him. He was knowledgeable, organized, handled the clients well, and actively trained junior lawyers. We made the right call in hiring him. I did miss Debs, though. She checked in periodically to catch up. I knew she was happy. Absorb was happy. But was I happy?

Today was my 36th birthday, but I'd been adamant since I turned 30 that I didn't celebrate birthdays. I'd be 30-something for the rest of my life. I received an email from Suzy to meet her at a KaraokeKing with a private room at 7:30 p.m. Reservations were under her name. She wanted to go over details of a potential acquisition. Suzy loved to sing. It was her means of relieving stress.

Later that afternoon I was pleasantly surprised to receive a text from Amy. *"Flying into ATL. Landing 7ish. Free tonight?"* I texted back and said, *"Client meeting @ 8. Late dinner? 9:30?"* Part of me wanted to see her and celebrate, but part of me was afraid of what might happen if she said yes.

Amy replied, *"Sure! The company better be good!"*

A couple of hours passed. Jules came into my office and asked, "Sam, you have any plans for the evening?"

I looked up from my calendar and responded, "Yes, with Suzy from Wireless Tower. She wants to meet me about a deal at a KaraokeKing."

Jules leaned halfway in and out of the doorway. "Well, Debs, Randi, Joe and Ron and a bunch of clients called to wish you a 'Happy Day!' I am leaving in 30 minutes and wanted to wish you a 'Happy Day!' too."

I looked at the clock. Time seemed to be moving swiftly. It was already 5:30 p.m. "Thanks, Jules, for remembering... for remembering to delete the word 'birth.'" Jules rolled her eyes, waved goodbye, and left the office.

My mind drifted back to other matters. The market was pulling back a little in 2007. The Wireless Tower owners were like family to me, and I was concerned that Suzy was contemplating an aggressive acquisition in the bear market. I called Mark. "Mark, any plans for the evening? No? Good. I'm meeting with the CEO of Wireless Tower at a KaraokeKing at 7:30. It'd be nice if you could join us, so I can properly introduce you guys. By the way, can you hold a tune?"

Mark crooned, "Sam, I'm an old school Sinatra kind of guy."

This made me giddy. I loved karaoke. It was great that Mark was willing to play ball. Like a little kid who found a shiny quarter on the ground, I responded, "Awesome! See you there at 7:30."

At 7:00 p.m., I received a call from Wanda. "Hi, Sam, I'm concerned Suzy is thinking about buying another company for $25 million. She told me you guys are meeting tonight. Please talk some sense into her. Also, can you send me our agreements again before you leave?"

"Absolutely, Wanda!" I was frantic because KaraokeKing was 30 minutes away. I made it a point always to be 10 minutes early for any meeting. I texted Mark to let him know I was running about 15 minutes behind. Relieved, I searched for the documents Wanda was requesting and sent them off. I arrived at KaraokeKing at roughly quarter to 8, texted Suzy to let her know that I had arrived and apologized for being late. I entered the private room and was greeted with "SURPRISE!" All the Billings, Day and Knight corporate team members were there, including Jules, Mandy, Mary and Debs from Absorb along with Keith, Wanda, and Suzy from Wireless Tower.

"Okay, nice conspiracy. You all got me. Nice setup. There is no deal, right? Right!" The room sang "Happy Birthday." We toasted and then the music, singing, and dancing commenced. The night progressed, and I noticed I had 2 text messages. My heart jumped. Caroline's text… I had to open it since it was her first message in 3 months. "*Happy Birthday!*" She remembered. I can't believe she remembered. Cloud 9 hit me like a ton of bricks.

The other text came from Amy. "*Just landed… where shall we meet?*"

I responded to Caroline first. "*I guess I should warn you, I don't celebrate birthdays. Haven't since I turned 30, but thanks for the message. Sweet of you to remember.*"

She responded, "*Wish I could be there to celebrate with you. Maybe next time.*"

I waited a few more minutes to see if Caroline had finished responding. When I was certain she had finished, I replied to Amy. "*Celebrating a birthday at KaraokeKing. Join us. Be prepared to sing!*" Country and western songs, pop songs, rap, rock and roll, ballads, duets. You name it, our group sang it. A case of beer, 4 bottles of Johnny Walker Blue label, 12 cokes, 24 bottled waters, 2 bottles of vodka, 2 bottles of cranberry and orange juice, a platter full of fruit, a boatload of sushi. All the celebrating a non-birthday celebrator could handle. This was the most fun our office had had together in months.

"*I'm here. Which room?*" Amy texted.

"*The room is under Suzy Jenkins.*" Amy coyly entered the room. The music stopped, and there was dead silence. Suzy had the mic and said, "Hello, and you are?"

"I'm Amy. Sam invited me to a birthday party?"

I grabbed the mic and introduced Amy to everyone. "Ladies and gents! Located near the front door stands the lovely Amy Hunter, my date for the evening. Amy Hunter, meet the gang! Please give her a round of applause." The look of shock on everyone's face was to die for, but they complied and clapped to welcome her.

The air filled with a multitude of questions and more questions. I heard them all. "When does Sam have time to date?" "Is that who Sam's dating?" "How did we not know?" "Let's go talk to her and get the 411." "I thought we knew everything about him." "Is she a vampire and they date between midnight and 6 am?" "She's got to be the most understanding person in the world to date Sam." I chuckled to myself. The uncertainty that I just created by inviting Amy to my party was probably the best gift I could have given myself. Was it a good idea to invite her from my perspective, or was it a good idea from her perspective? At this point, it didn't matter. The night was young. I would only turn 36 once. I thought, Tonight, I am going to let loose and just go with the flow.

Suzy had reserved the room until 2:00 a.m. By 1:30, the crowd had dwindled to about 9 of us... including the hardcore karaoke fans: Suzy, Amy, Mark, and myself. We punched in our last song selections and continued to sing and dance the night away. I sang to my friends, "You were totally wonderful toooooonight." I called the designated driver number to take my car and me home and offered to pay for the other 7 people in our party.

Amy mentioned that a friend dropped her off and wondered if she could get a ride with me. I wasn't driving and quickly answered "Absolutely!" We got in my car, and Amy held my hand. "Where are we taking you, Amy?"

She gave my hand a squeeze, looked me in the eyes in a way that would've been very seductive had I not overindulged and said in a sultry voice, "Where do you want to take me?"

I started laughing. I was quick on my toes and sung a silly line. "Stop right there. I wanna know now!"

The driver, Amy and I laughed for a few minutes. She told the driver she was staying at the Plaza Hotel next to the airport. As we headed out, she leaned into me and said, "You are such a funny Teddy Bear. Do you want to cuddle with me tonight?" I paused and had a flashback. I remembered liking someone in middle school for years. She asked me to Homecoming. I was shocked and declined. I'm the hunter and feel awkward when I'm being chased. Amy nudged me and said, "Well?"

"You barely know me. We are intoxicated and tired. I don't want you to wake up tomorrow wondering what the hell did we do? I'll probably regret not saying yes, but I'm no hare. I would like to finish the race." I bowed out gracefully, or so I thought.

Amy paused and said, "Wow, you're different. I like that!" She leaned in to kiss me. She placed her hand on my chest, then my thigh. My body was a wanderland as she explored with precision its finer parts. My body reacted accordingly, but my mind was still on guard. We arrived at the Plaza. I walked her to the entrance. The driver asked if I had had a change of heart. I laughed and said no. Amy and I kissed good night at the front. She pouted and said, "You do realize what you are going to miss tonight?" as she grabbed my hands and moved them to her chest.

I didn't resist and answered, "I'm going to miss your boots and the windshield wipers." She looked confused, and I proceeded to move my head from left to right with a smacking kissing noise and motion. We laughed, and I said, "I will certainly take a rain check, though."

She handed me a key to her room and said, "Just in case you change your mind."

I got back into my car and told him to take me home. As we left, the designated driver said, "Um, excuse me for saying this, but I would have brought my bat and knocked that out of the park! Trust me. I'm 50, and opportunities like that don't happen every day. In fact, they don't happen every year. Maybe every 8 years. You need to praise God when that happens and just go with it. Are you sure you don't want me to turn this car around?" I had stopped paying attention to the driver and was glued to Caroline's text. A few seconds lapsed, and I shook myself out of my Caroline trance. "I'm sorry, what did you say?"

The driver shook his head and whispered, "I don't understand young folks these days." A few minutes later, he dropped me off. As I was about to fall asleep, I noticed a missed text from Amy. It was a picture of her in her lingerie. *"Happy birthday, Sam! THIS is what you missed out on tonight."*

I laughed and responded, *"Got the visual. I'll try not to make the same mistake again. Tortoise out."*

Chapter 17
Little Lies, Big Lies, and Pinky Promises

Ping! Amy was texting back pretty regularly. I was slowly working on a relationship with her, but business was crashing quickly. By May of 2007, the capital markets were pulling back. The SEC had investigated more than 100 companies for backdating stock options, resulting in the firing or resignation of more than 50 executives. Broadcom, Comverse, Altera, and even UnitedHealth were being hit. Every day it seemed like another company and another executive. Shortly afterward, I had Jules send Hank and Bill from SocMedia the newspaper clippings of corporations and executives that were in trouble due to the backdating options issues. It was a little rub in their face. I asked Jules to send a note with it. "Aren't you glad you listened to me on that $14 million phone call day?"

Jules walked into my office and asked, Do you have time to meet with Craig and Bill?"

"Of course, send them in." They walked in with a team of movers and presented me with a SocMedia phone booth. It was painted with dollar bills and a massive $14 million sign. Inside the booth were pictures of Craig's parents and Bill's family with a note. ***Our families thank you!*** I was floored and laughed hysterically.

Craig and Bill said, "We keep receiving emails and newspaper clippings about the backdating issues. We figured you would continue to harass us. This is our preemptive strike! We have engaged lawyers to file a cease and desist on you." Everyone got a good laugh out of the spectacle. "Actually, we really appreciate your sound counsel. Thank you." I became a little emotional. I knew I had wonderful clients, but never expected that.

∞

Caroline was turning 34 in April. I had been collecting postcards and magnets as a present for her birthday. I wasn't quite certain about her recent developments or her "status quo." I had only received 2 texts from her since the Eskimo kiss and thought it would be awkward to give her such a personal gift.

I called Randi and asked, "If you were a girl, and you are a girl, what would be a good gift to give someone that isn't too personal?"

"First of all, Sam, thank you for acknowledging that I am a girl. No jewelry. How about a wallet?"

I shook my head, "Nope... boring."

"How about a nice handbag?"

"Knowing that I am not a girl and that I am not aware of 'girly stuff,' what are some nice brands that aren't too cheap but at the same time not too outrageous? Don't roll your eyes at me. I can sense it."

Randi asked, "Too late, I already did. Who is this for, Sam? Wait, let me guess. Amy?"

"Nope."

"Last but not least... sweet Southern Caroline?"

"Yes."

"She was carrying a Louie V clutch at the wedding. She's classy and simple. Get her a Louie V handbag or purse, but don't spend more than $1,500. You can also get your BFF one too while you are at it. Or at least talk to Ron. He's all about gadgets and technology. Girls are about fashion. Please talk to him, especially 2 months before my birthday so that you can condition him. I would greatly appreciate that."

"Louie V might be over the top, Randi. What about a spa package? If you were a girl, and you are one, would you like that?"

"Don't make me fly down there and slap you around, Sam. Who wouldn't like that?"

I messaged Jules, "Please find a high-end spa around Pentagon City and get me 1 gift certificate for $200 made out to Caroline Dean and 1 for $100 for Randi Cruz. I need them by Saturday morning."

I texted Caroline, *"Happy early birthday! Do you have time for lunch this weekend?"*

She responded, *"I can't believe you remembered, Sam. Will you be in DC?"*

"Yes, Friday on business. Does Saturday at 1:00 p.m. work?"

"Yes."

"Meet me at Pentagon City mall, and we will go from there. See you on Saturday."

I texted Randi, *"Flying in this weekend. Cubbies game on Saturday night! Bring Ron."*

I was in a fun mood, so I sent Amy a text. *"Guess which city I will be in this weekend?"*

She quickly responded, *"No... not Houston. Darn, I'll be in DC this weekend."*

I smiled. *"Wanna go to a Cubs game?"* Amy was a huge sports fan, much like myself. Baseball, football, and basketball primarily. Amy and I had been dating, platonically; in baseball lingo, singles and doubles.

Amy replied, *"Love to play ball. Patiently waiting for you to score some runs."*

"Amy, those curves are hard to hit! Need a few more at-bats."

After my breakfast meeting, I headed over to Pentagon City to go shopping. I located the RelaxationSpa and picked up my gift

∞

certificates for Caroline and Randi. I had 2 hours to kill before Caroline arrived, so I found a sporting goods store and grabbed a Cubs hat and a jersey for Amy. As I walked inside Neiman's, I noticed some really cute pajamas and decided… perhaps I might up our game tonight. I texted Amy, *"Picking up my game. Cuddle date afterward? Willard Hotel. Proper attire required."*

She texted back, *"What is a cuddle date? Darn, I didn't bring my cute lingerie."*

I responded, *"I got you covered. You are a size 2, right?"* *"How did you know?"*

"See you @ Willard at 6:30. Let's head to ballpark together."

I found a new pair of boxers and an X-large T-shirt and purchased a set of Three J NYC Coco silk pajamas for Amy. "That is one of the hottest items," winked the Neiman sales representative. "Women love it. Absolutely adorable."

Caroline texted me, *"Where shall we meet? Let's have lunch at the Ritz. Meet you in the lobby."* I walked in with 2 shopping bags full of stuff.

"Sam, what did you buy?"

"I'm going to the Nats game tonight and wanted to dress accordingly." We ordered mimosas and started to talk about her. Caroline was silent at first. She placed her hand on my leg under the table discreetly, giggled, stared at me and said, "Thank you for remembering my birthday."

I looked down at her hand and said, "Do friends do that?" We laughed, and the 6-month ice was broken. Caroline wanted to know about me first. We ordered brunch, and I continued to talk about some of the places I'd visited and some of the emerging companies I was representing.

Then she asked, "Are you dating anyone?"

I paused and replied, "I'm dating lots of people, but I'm just not 'date dating' anyone at the moment." If this were a deal, such a representation would be accurate at the time of this lunch, but I would have probably breached a representation about omitting to disclose the material fact that I was planning to escalate with Amy that evening.

Relieved, Caroline said, "You should get out more often and smell the roses."

I turned to her and asked, "What's new since November?"

"Not much new in my life."

"How are things with your husband?"

"Oh, okay."

Objection, non-responsive. "Weren't there some issues back in November?"

"Yes." She sighed and began to cry tears of pain and regret.

"I'm sorry. I'm just a cruel old man making you cry on your birthday. We don't have to talk about it anymore."

She looked up and said, "No, I want to. He is such a jerk. We have been married for 10 years now, and I caught him cheating on me 3 years ago. He promised he wouldn't do it again, and then I found out in September he was with another person." She began to wring her hands. "Over Christmas, he promised that would be the last time. I'm still furious with him about the past 2 times. I don't love him at all. I'm just staying in the marriage because of the kids. The oldest goes to college this year, and I still have 5 years before the youngest graduates high school. We live in the same house, but for all intents and purposes, we aren't married. I think he's dating another girl now. I just don't care anymore. My life is on hold, and I can't wait until Chris graduates from high school so I can move forward. I was such a fool." She leaned back in her seat. "I should have listened to everyone. Once a player, always a player. He's so selfish. A liar and a cheater." Tears continued to roll down her face. I hadn't expected this.

"Caroline, I'm your friend, always have been and always will be. As your true friend, I will call a spade a spade. Your honesty is courageous. Please know that there are silver linings to all this madness and let me highlight 2." I touched her hand. "First, you now know with every fiber, cell, and breath in your body the truth. Knowing this truth today versus tomorrow is a tremendous blessing. Second, you know that song from *Les Mis*, 'My Life Has Killed a Dream I Dreamed'? Well, you are at the midpoint of your book. Back then, folks only lived into their 40s and 50s. You have a 2nd chance to dream another dream. On hold for another 5 years, but still, you have another 40 to look forward to. I promise to be there to support you."

Caroline wiped her face. "Oh, Sam, I need to freshen up. Please excuse me."

Caroline returned and apologized for being such a mess. I waved it off. "Today is your birthday, and you get a pass to do whatever you want today. If you want to cry all day, you can!"

We reminisced about the camping trip she had planned at Okuma, Japan. I told most of the story. There were 6 of us. It was supposed to be a romantic evening by the campfire, cooking marshmallows, fishing, drinking beer and making out. At about 2:00 a.m., I was freezing and being attacked by swarms of mosquitos. It was too much to bear. I told Caroline and the group, "I have had had enough and am heading back to the resort housing!" I reached over and touched Caroline's hand, "I was wrong. I should have never left you. If I could have a do-over, I would have stayed out there in the freezing cold, and I would have kissed you."

Caroline slowly pulled her hand back. "I was really mad at you for leaving us. Around 4:00 a.m., the entire crew came knocking on the door. The tide was coming in, and we all got drenched. You knew, didn't you, Sam? There's always 1 smart person in the group. Right?"

"Speaking of smart, happy birthday, Caroline. I think you could really use this." I handed her the RelaxationSpa gift certificate.

Caroline exclaimed, "Just what the doctor ordered! I might go visit them right after lunch. What time is the game tonight?"

"7:00 p.m."

"I want to go, Sam! Can I join you?"

I had never lied to Caroline, but I had already committed to Amy. I paused and said, "I would love for you to join us," which was true, "but this is sort of a business meeting, and the tickets were arranged by my client."

"I understand, Sam. It would have been nice. Have fun." She stood up to leave. Being raised correctly, I rose too. Caroline smiled. "Pinky promise me that we will always be friends and that you will not buy anyone else an infinity anything? The infinity is reserved for only me." I smiled back at her in acknowledgment.

Caroline pulled out a card that I had written to her after our first kiss. "Do you remember this?"

"How could I not? I wrote the card."

Caroline read "*Roses are red, violets are blue, whenever I go to bed, I dream of you.* That was so sweet, Sam."

I turned bright red and said, "We need to sign a confidentiality agreement to cover that card."

∞

"Promise to write to me, Sam." It was awkward. I wanted to be with Caroline, but she was unavailable. We weren't dating and had agreed to be friends, but when we parted, I felt guilty. It had been 18 years, and the corresponding letter in the alphabet was "R." I had "reconnected" with Caroline but left with "regrets."

Chapter 18

To Date or Not To Date

Ping! Randi sent me a text saying that she was on her way up. The Willard folks had checked me into the same room, 2508, just like last November. Ron and Randi knocked on my door around 5:30 p.m. "Hey Strangers! Can I get you a beer?" We drank, and I gave them a summary of my lunch with Caroline, as well as the 411 on Amy.

I asked, "Hey, Randi, do me a solid and vet Amy for me tonight. I value your opinion, and it is important to me."

Ping! Amy sent me a text letting me know she was running behind, so I handed Randi and Ron their tickets, shrugged my shoulders and said, "We will meet you at the game."

Amy arrived around 6:40 p.m., and I asked her to come up to my room. "I got you a little something-something for the game." She looked at me suspiciously. I retrieved the bag and handed her the jersey and cap.

She squealed, "I love them! Give me about 5 minutes to change." We arrived at the ballpark around 7:30 p.m., and it was already the 3rd inning. Making my usual dramatic entrance, I introduced everyone to Amy, ordered the beers, hot dogs, and peanuts. Randi and Amy talked throughout the entire game. Everyone seemed to be getting along famously.

During the 7th inning stretch, Randi nudged me. "Hey, walk me to the ladies room." We got up and traveled down the corridor. "How well do you know Amy?"

"I don't know her at all. We have chatted online and been on 5 dates max."

∞

"Here's my initial read. Positives. She's cute, funny, talkative and witty. Negatives. I think I heard her phone go off a hundred times during the game. Are you sure she's single? Also, your biggest pet peeve is tardiness. She was close to an hour late. I know you—that shit drives you crazy."

"It's not like we are getting married. We haven't even made out! Amy might not be 'Ms. Right,' but she might be 'Ms. Right Now.' She's independent and not all clingy. I work crazy hours. This could work. Companionship on an as-needed basis."

"Sam, I realize that you have needs. Just be careful. I still can't put my finger on it, but I sense something. The way she stares at you. I would understand if you were a supermodel, but you are not."

"Gee, Randi, thanks for the little boost of confidence."

"You know what I mean. Also, she just kept talking about the 4 Asian guys nearby. Like she was obsessed. You heard the old saying about Asian girls. I think she is applying the same concept to Asian guys."

"Randi, that might be a bonus. I typically like girls with Southern charm, and whenever I hear that distinctively Southern accent, it just makes me melt."

Randi nodded. "I understand. Still, Sam, be aware."

"Thank you, Randi, you have done your job thoroughly. I owe you 2 scoops of your choice of ice cream."

Randi and I headed back to our seats. The game was a blowout, and Ron and Randi decided to head home early. I turned to Amy, "Ready for our cuddle date?"

"Well, I've never been on one. I'm intrigued."

I proceeded to explain. "Well, a cuddle date occurs in the early stages of a relationship. It is a slight escalation from a casual

125

date without any expectation of sex." Once in the room, I presented Amy with her cuddle-date attire. She held it up and looked at it adoringly. It had been unusually hot at the ball game, and I directed her to the other restroom where she could shower.

While Amy was in the shower, I called room service and ordered. "Dom, 2 glasses, please. I'll be in the shower, so set it in the master bedroom." We met in the living room. Amy looked adorable in her new evening wear. I went over the rules of engagement. Hugging is fine, kissing is fine, caressing fine. "No hitting below the belt. I'm the referee. So let the games begin."

We toasted to our first cuddle date. A long conversation ensued about what we were looking for in a partner. A few hugs and a few kisses later, we started talking about past relationships, the good and the ugly. Amy told me she dated a lot and was not looking to settle down for a while. I admired her free-spirited attitude, her desire to travel the world, experience new things, and not feel tied down. With my most serious face, I said, "… what are your feelings about ice cream?"

"I love ice cream!"

"Whew, I don't think I could trust anyone that doesn't like ice cream." As the evening progressed, our conversation moved to the likes and dislikes of sexual acts.

"I am not too keen on women being too aggressive. I prefer to be the aggressor. Of course, I would like to know what your preferences are. How about you, Amy? What do you like or dislike?"

Amy proclaimed, "I don't like to go down on guys."

"Well that was straight and to the point," I responded. "I'm glad you disclosed that today because that would be a deal-breaker for me." We laughed, and she pointed to her chest and asked, "Will you be cashing in on that rain check from February?"

∞

I pretended that I was thinking it over, but when she feigned sadness, I firmly pulled her near me to let her know in no uncertain terms that cashing in on my rain check would be a great transaction. My hands moved to caress her, and she flinched. I called her out. "Now that's a balk. Runner advances." Before daybreak came, we fell asleep in spooning position. It was a wonderful little cuddle date.

Chapter 19

The Floor is Not the Floor

Ping! Amy sent me a message. *"When are we going to have another one of those cuddle dates? XOXO."* I thought it was so cute how she would send me sweet little texts here and there.

I responded with a quick message. *"Soon, my little Belle."*

Between these little flights of fancy, by September 2007, the capital markets had pulled backed significantly. Major SEC investigations also had a chilling effect on the economy. Those were minor compared to the housing bubble, the subprime mortgage and credit issues, and increased foreclosures with homeowners. Everyone was nervous that the housing bubble would burst, resulting in a recession and perhaps even a depression. Billings, Day and Knight, was not immune to the market conditions. Our billings and collections were down. At the beginning of the year, I had forecasted my books to be close to $9 million. With the current economic outlook, the reality was that my numbers would be closer to $6 million. That was 1/3 less. I knew what the management committee thought. The management committee were the partners within Billings, Day and Knight who had the largest stake but were the least profitable from a legal production perspective. Their strategy was to keep compensation the same for our group and to reduce compensation package for the non-management committee partners as well as other staff. Perhaps even cut staff.

We had a great team of loyal and competent lawyers and staff. I figured they would ask me to cut my legal team by 5 lawyers, 2 paralegals, and 3 legal assistants. I had heard stories in the early 2000s of large, reputable firms imploding overnight with thousands of people searching for jobs chaotically. Brobeck, for example, had over 1,100 lawyers and support staff in 14 cities. They were heavily dependent on the early dot.com technology boom. When the dot.com bubble burst, they filed for bankruptcy protection and shut down. I was not going to let my team down and planned to proactively find them jobs before the December ax fell. Part of the plan was to call all my clients to determine their need for in-house counsel and support staff. I knew how much work we had, and I tried to ascertain our needs to get us to the end of October. This would give my team sufficient time to land softly.

Suzy wanted to meet with me in New Orleans. She had received an offer from OldCable, a publicly traded company, to buy Wireless Tower for $45 million. "Jules, get Mark and see if he can meet me in New Orleans. He needs to be there by tomorrow or ask another attorney who is available."

I landed around noon and had 6 hours to spare. I had always heard stories about New Orleans. Mardi Gras. Beads. Jazz Fest. Cajun food. As I wandered down Bourbon Street, I came across a storefront called Hope of Life. Curiosity got the best of me, and I decided to walk inside. As I entered, I smelled the distinct aroma of sandalwood and felt an immediate calming sensation. I looked around to get a better understanding of where I was. There were crystals and spiritual trinkets for sale. It became apparent that I was in a New Age shop of some sort. Next to the register sat a menu that read, "One-hour Joyful session, $50." I thought, Was this for a reading? I was skeptical about participating in such things. Three years prior, my client Craig, of SocMedia, had devised a plan to solidify the love of his life. He was madly pursuing a girl who was into spirituality. The day before his date, he visited a palm-reader and paid the lady $100. He advised her that he would be back with his girlfriend the following day. Craig's girlfriend wanted a reading of her love life, and the $100 was a prepayment for a positive reading related to matters of the heart for her vis-à-vis... him. Craig returned the next day as planned. The reader told the young woman that the 2 were very compatible. He was the one for her, but this destiny could be realized only if they each purchased a truth candle for $500. She declined and Craig was out $200. The relationship eventually fizzled out. To this day, he is single, and they never saw each other again.

Despite my skepticism, I was bored and had 5 hours to kill. Plus, $50 seemed immaterial. So I moved forward and decided on the hour session. The space was a bit eclectic but open and inviting. I saw a figure move at the far end of the room. Elegant and demure, she quietly emerged from a corner of the building. She introduced herself. "Hello, I am Hope. Please come inside so I can see you in the light." Hope was a lovely lady with straight, caramel-colored hair. Now, I had grown up a military brat and had encountered people from all walks of life. Hope had an unusual multicultural look and feel about her. A mixture of European, Asian, Latin and Native American would have been my best guess. She motioned for me to sit and asked if I required a beverage. I gestured no, and she sat across from me with 1 leg dangling from the chair and the other in a half lotus position. I thought, This is going to be interesting. She closed her eyes and asked, "What is your name?"

"I am Sam Rivtoc."

"Why are you here?"

"I'm in New Orleans for work."

She opened her eyes, smiled and asked again with eyebrows raised, "No, why are you HERE? What is it that you would like answers to?"

"Oh, I don't know. I was just curious, so I dropped in."

Hope sat back opened her eyes. "Your dime, your time. Ask me questions about things you want to know."

She seemed nice, and I had a warm, pleasant feeling, but, of course, I was still skeptical. So I asked her how many women I had loved so far. Hope began having an internal dialogue with herself and swayed left to right. She stopped the conversation and responded, "Four. You have loved 4 people in this life."

Aha, she was wrong because I knew I had only loved 2. I asked, "Who are they?"

"Your mom. You loved your mom dearly, even though she was very strict with you growing up. You loved her immensely. I'm sorry she passed away, what was it... almost 3 years ago." Hope now had my attention. Mom had passed away 2 years and 10 months ago. There was no way she could have known that.

"The other 3 people?"

Hope tilted her head to the side and looked slightly right. "Your sister, a person about 20 years ago, and another 10 years ago. They are unavailable at the moment, except your sister. She is always available. At least, within the bounds of her schedule." Her gaze came back to me.

I was shocked. "How is Mom?"

"She is good, but I see her yelling at you."

"About what?"

"She is laughing and telling you to hurry up and get married." Maybe Hope was good at guessing or just knew the right emotional things to lure people in.

"What about Amy?"

Hope stuck out her lower lip then brought it back to a normal position. "Nothing serious right now."

"Are we compatible?"

"Define compatible."

"Can I marry her?"

"No."

"Why?"

"Active. Very active."

"I'm confused."

"It will reveal itself in due course."

Desperate for more information, as well as to take up the rest of the hour, my questioning shifted toward business. "Do I like my job?"

She looked at me and gave out a little laugh. "Do you like your job?" She shook her head in a disapproving way. "Of course, you like your job. You work too much. You are very good at what you do. Negotiating is your thing, but I sense some nervousness. Something about a deal."

"Should we do this deal?"

"What deal? You have many."

"Wireless Tower."

Hope raised her eyebrows, looked around, and continued her insightful reading. "You are close to the family. They trust you. I see a basement. Better safe than sorry."

"What do you mean by basement?"

"All I can say is I see a basement. I don't ask for clarification. You will know the meaning when the right time comes."

"Will I be a lawyer for the rest of my life?"

"No."

"Can you elaborate?"

"Sure." After a couple of minutes of looking around and tilting her head left to right, she continued. "I see a field of tall

∞

plants... a crop of some sort, some farm animals and technology. Thank you, Sam, your time is up."

Like a junkie coming down from a high, I wanted more. "Wait, I would like another hour please."

Hope acknowledged my need for answers. "Why are you really here, Sam?"

"I want to know about Caroline."

"Caroline is the same. Nothing will change until she sets sail."

"Do you see a relationship between us?"

"Of course. You have one with her now. I see a dollar bill and a necklace."

"I mean romantically.... will we have a romantic relationship?"

"Caroline has to set sail, and you must let it take its course."

"What about my life in the next 5 years?"

"I see a lot of changes, a phoenix rising, paralysis... You will begin to hide from certain people. The number 108 is important. She will set sail, too."

"Okay. Is there anything else I need to know?"

"Yes, a message from Mom."

"What... what message?"

"Do you understand Korean?"

"A little."

Hope leaned in and gestured with her hands. "What is Young-so-eh-o?"

"I don't know that word. Can you please repeat that?"

"Yongseo."

"Yes. Yongseo. It means forgiveness."

She sat back in her chair again. "Your Mom is using that word with…. Ba-Ba-Ri coat?"

I was overcome with emotion as I started crying and laughing at the same time. Hope patted me on the back, comforting me in a strange and calming way. As I left, Hope said, "Here is my card. Call me if you need additional information. My rate for a phone reading for YOU will be $75."

I was a bit shocked and asked, "Why is your rate in person cheaper than your phone session?"

She smiled and said, "Because you will require me to work a little harder and faster in the future. Oh yeah, one other thing; I'm sorry, but we don't sell $500 candles." I sat there with my jaw on the floor. I knew, at that moment, that she was the real deal. I left and frantically tried to dial Jean. I wanted her to know that Mom was there during our November visit and that she forgave us for the Ba-Ba-Ri coat failures. As I headed down the street, Hope yelled out, "I am glad I passed your test. Next time have a little faith in people."

After my little detour, I headed back to the hotel to shower and change. Before heading up, I slid by the front desk to check for messages at the front desk. "Anything for Sam Rivtoc?" They handed me a note. I thanked them and began opening it as I walked to the elevator.

"Meet us at the Nola Restaurant 7:45 pm," it read. I was glad we were meeting on a Friday night after the market had closed. Hopefully, we would consummate this transaction over the weekend before the stock market reopened to avoid insider trading issues. If someone bought OldCable stock while in possession of the non-public Wireless Tower transaction, it would have been a violation of law. I reviewed the OldCable term sheet and everything seemed standard and normal. The key negotiating points would be the price and the role Suzy would play following the transaction. I ordered the crab cakes and fried chicken while Mark described to Suzy the overall market conditions with an emphasis on the wireless sector.

After thinking it over, Suzy said, "This is a fair deal, but I wonder if this is the floor to my sector."

I remembered Hope's warning about a basement. I wanted her to realize our pain in light of the downturn in the market, so I explained about our firm. "Suzy, I have been reviewing our team's numbers. I'm concerned about a 1/3 drop in revenues this year. I'm concerned about the drag the real estate sector is having on the markets." I explained if her sector was to hit the floor, a recession, we could live with it. But if there was a basement or a depression, could she live with or bear the risk?

"My parents would forgive me, but I wouldn't be able to forgive myself. What about the legal stuff?"

I turned to Mark, and he said, "It's normal."

Suzy gestured. "Let me call my folks and tell them we are going to sell the company this weekend."

At that point, I threw out a hypothetical. "If we can get an offer greater than $46 million, could we split the difference 50/50?"

Suzy looked at me. "More money in both our pockets? We can agree to those terms."

We decided to meet on Saturday at 10:00 a.m. at the OldCable headquarters. They had amassed an army of people: 4 lawyers, 2 accountants, 2 bankers and the VP of Business Development. Our team consisted of the 3 of us. Suzy was happy with the $45 million. We were shooting for $46 million to cover all her legal and other fees. Wireless Tower would net more than they had expected. It was time to wheel and deal. We started with valuation and asked, "How did you arrive at the $45 million number?" Their bankers provided us with a detailed spreadsheet analysis with a conclusion that a price between $42-$54 million would be appropriate for a deal like this. I noted, "$42-$54 million? The midpoint would be $48 million and not $45 million. Gentleman, I think you need to recalculate." Then the bankers grumbled and argued about the market conditions. We countered with "OldCable is a great company, but they aren't getting the right valuation because Wall Street perceives them to be in the legacy business. They need transactions like Wireless Tower for the market to recognize a meaningful change in their business. At the end of the day, perception is reality." The room was getting stuffy. "Let's take a break." This little break was strategic. It would allow time for their bankers to convince OldCable that a higher deal was reasonable. After all, they got paid on a percentage of the deal. The higher the dollar amount, the more they made. As they were leaving the room, I pulled the investment banker aside and said, "I want you to know that we have received similar offers in the past year and rejected them even though they were reasonable. Suzy is young and talented. She believes this company is worth at least $50 million and can grow it even bigger."

We took a break for an hour. They returned around noon with a $50 million counter. I didn't want them to have buyer's remorse and think they paid too much. I wanted everyone to feel as if they were at the low end of a potential deal. I felt a need to discuss this with Suzy, Wanda, and Keith. "Can we break for 2 to 3 hours? Mark, please stay here and go over the rest of the term sheet and definitive agreement." I pulled Mark aside and said, "You know we have a deal since they are paying more than they originally wanted. They are going to try to New Yorkize us. We need to engage the other party for hours to ensure that this deal closes on Sunday." I warned Suzy not to say a word until we left the building and got back to the hotel. Keith and Wanda were elated by the news.

Suzy victoriously stated, "Aren't you glad we waited!"

It was 12:30 p.m. We grabbed a quick lunch. "Suzy, we shouldn't go back there too soon. Let's leave here around 2:45 p.m. to give them the impression that we are still trying to convince you to do this deal." I had an hour and a half, and I was still bewildered by my recent visit to Hope. I proceeded to Bourbon Street in search of more answers. I walked into the shop and smelled the sweet smell of sandalwood again. Hope approached and motioned me to sit again. "Welcome back, Mr. Rivtoc. Why have you returned so quickly?"

"I guess because I have faith in you. I would like an hour please."

Hope laughed and sat opposite of me with a cup of tea in her hand. "Can I offer you a beverage?" I motioned no, but she replied, "I think a nice cup of tea will calm your nerves… help you to think clearer." Hope got up and went to the counter to grab an empty cup and a pot of tea.

I was antsy and thought, I don't have the patience for a cup of tea.

Within a split second of that thought, Hope looked over her shoulder and said, "Try and find the patience." I slumped down in my seat like a scolded child. She handed me the cup and motioned me to drink. I sipped the tea as I tried to "find patience."

"Wireless Tower is close to a deal today. Is it a good deal? The floor is not the floor. There is a basement."

"Breathe, Sam. This is a good deal for Wireless Tower."

"Will I be at Billings, Day and Knight next year?"

∞

"Yes and no."

"What does that mean?"

Hope dropped both feet to the ground then crossed her legs. "You will be, and then you won't be."

"Will I be dating Amy?"

"Define dating. Are we talking status quo? If so, yes."

"Will that be a good thing?"

"Physically, yes. Intellectually, no."

"Okay. I have business to finish up." I got up to go. I had no further questions at the moment.

I returned to the hotel, picked up Suzy, and together we headed to OldCable. "Let's get this deal done in 2 days." Suzy asked if we should counter with $52 million. I turned to her and said, "The floor is not the floor. There is a great significant that there is a basement. We should either be a bull or a bear and make money. However, let's avoid being the pig and getting slaughtered. They are expecting a counter from us. There might not be much room left to negotiate. Let's surprise them with an acceptance and close this deal as quickly as possible. I don't want OldCable to get cold feet." Another $1 million to Suzy was immaterial in the big-picture scheme of things.

We returned to OldCable and said that Suzy had an announcement. The OldCable folks were anxiously waiting. "I have good news and bad news. The good news is we are going to accept the $50 million offer. The bad news is that we need to finish this by this Sunday." A loud roar of applause and elation erupted. I turned to Mark, and he said he was getting New Yorkized but was used to it and would be here the rest of the day. I asked if we should fly another associate down to help out.

Mark agreed, "I would appreciate another set of eyes, Sam."

"Suzy, why don't you get some rest and enjoy New Orleans while we keep plugging away? Can you ask your assistant to confirm the disclosure schedules? Also, it would be good if she could fly down tonight just in case we need her tomorrow. Check in with me in the morning on our status." We began going through a 100-plus page definitive agreement, requesting qualifiers like "materially" and "knowledge" throughout the document. We contacted Suzy's assistant at Wireless Tower to confirm that the disclosure schedules were true and accurate and that she would be joining us tomorrow in New Orleans. I had all confidence in Mark's legal skills to protect Wireless Tower reasonably. We weren't billing by the hour anymore. We had just made Billings, Day and Knight $2 million in 3 days.

Time was flying by. We were about 80 percent complete with the closing documents when we retired at 3:00 a.m. Sunday morning. I figured diminishing returns were setting in and suggested that we reconvene at 9:00 a.m. Suzy called me at 10:00 a.m. and wondered when we would be ready to sign. "We have 1 outstanding issue, Suzy. They would like a 4-year non-compete." A non-compete is a standard agreement that Suzy, Keith, and Wanda would not start a similar business in competition with Wireless Tower or OldCable. "The previous drafts were for 2 years. Keith and Wanda are planning to retire, but I wanted to make sure you didn't object to the 4 years. That is the last major outstanding item." Suzy asked for my opinion.

"Consider the extra $2 million as payment for the non-compete, or them paying you $500,000 a year to do something different."

"I can live with that."

"With the 4-year non-compete out of the way, I estimate the time of signing to be around 2:00 p.m." I disconnected with Suzy.

We continued to comb through the documents in search of typos. Finally, both sides agreed to the final execution documents. Suzy joined us. Mark reviewed all the agreements with Suzy, and the signing began. We agreed to the transfer of the $50 million, dispersed in the amount of $21 million to Keith and Wanda, $27 million to Suzy, and $2 million to Billings, Day and Knight by 9:00 a.m. on Monday. A celebration was in order. We met over dinner at August in the Central Business District of NOLA. Suzy pulled me aside and wondered what she was going to do next.

"I don't know too many 30-something folks with $27 million. Go get your MBA while the market is down. It might take the market 2 to 3 years to reach the basement. In the meantime, you can add value to your existing skill sets. Oh, by the way, this is for you." I bought Suzy a Louis V business card holder with my business card inside. "It has been an honor representing you and your parents, and when you are ready to get back into the business world, call me. You guys will be missed."

Suzy winked. "You haven't seen the last of us yet." We hugged and said our goodbyes. Mark and I walked back to the hotel. He had been waiting to talk to me about the stability of our firm and our practice group ever since I mentioned that we would most likely miss our mark by 1/3. He was a true professional and thought in law before business. I told him, "Before today, I thought we would be off by about $3 million. We pulled a rabbit out of a hat, and now we are short about $1 million. We have 3 months to make up the difference. I'm counting on you to close the gap." I didn't tell Mark, but I knew Wireless Tower was a one-time deal. More importantly, we would lose their legal business next year after the sale to OldCable. The market had more room to fall, and I was planning to resize our group by helping 9 of my team members find jobs elsewhere. I had to strike while the iron was hot. After January, I predicted the floor would fall out from under us.

∞

Chapter 20

Man of Honor

Ping! My calendar was reminding me that the day of reckoning had come. I was unfamiliar with the job duties of a Man of Honor, so I researched and inquired with friends who were of the fairer sex to create a checklist:

- Organize a bachelorette party
- Keep a record of the wedding gifts
- Attend gown-shopping excursions
- Coordinate bridesmaid duties
- Be the bride's right-hand "man" and prepare a toast

We were 2 weeks out, and so far, I had been a horrible Man of Honor. I wasn't present for the gown-shopping excursions and was MIA when it came to recording the bridal activities. Of those 5 tasks, I was qualified to do maybe 2… the bachelorette party and the toast. The weekend before the wedding, 7 ladies and I flew to Austin for Randi's bachelorette party. Amy was staying in Houston and decided to drive down for the weekend. Friday night was flagged as a welcoming party and time to go over Saturday's schedule. Once the ladies were all assembled, I began reading my list of activities for the day.

"OMG, we will all meet at Driskell's piano lounge for a few drinks and brunch at 11:00 a.m. Food and mimosas?" I looked up and said emphatically, "Yes, I'm in." I looked down at my list and continued, "Mani and pedi at 12:45 p.m." I looked up at the ladies and said, "I'm not a huge mani-pedi guy, but I'll take 1 for the team."

I continued with the list and my commentaries in between. "At 2:00 p.m., we will meet for hair and make-up appointments. I'll

be there pouring champagne, but I'll pass on the hair and make-up,"
I said with a smile and chuckle. "At 5:00 p.m., we have massages
scheduled." Enthusiastically, I agreed, "Yes, please! Dinner, 7:45
pm. Check. Pub crawl, 9:30 pm-midnight. I'll be the designated
security. God help us all." Finally, a few of the ladies laugh.

"Midnight – 1:30 a.m., live, exotic male entertainment at the
hotel. Note to self: figure out a way to skip that event." I looked at
my list and the back of it. "Wait, aren't we missing something really
crucial?"

"No, Sam, I think that we've covered all the bases."

"What, Sam?"

"Ice cream!"

Randi pulled me to the side and said, "We need to talk." We
excused ourselves and walked around 6th Street, as loud music filled
the air and the place bustled with people. "I think I might have made
a mistake saying yes to Ron too soon."

"What do you mean by THAT, Randi?" And why now? Just
after I've gone over the list of today's activities?" I poked fun at her,
but I could tell that she was in no mood for it.

In a near frantic pace she exclaims, "I'm young and have lots
to see, things to do… I have too much on my plate at work. And the
kids? How can I find the time to please another person in this life?
I'm feeling suffocated and need my space."

"Space? Randi, you guys have been living together for more
than 3 years now. In South Carolina, you guys would be deemed
married based on the amount of time you have lived together.
Fortunately, Virginia does not allow for common-law marriage. But I
want to address your space concerns." I saw a vacant table and
gestured for Randi to sit. "I've been in your shoes before. Randi, can
I be frank with you?"

∞

Randi crossed her legs and smirked. "First of all, your name is Sam. Second, since when have you had to ask my permission to speak openly?"

"Noted! Let me go through the list: You have designated the master bedroom's walk-in closet and 2 closets in adjoining rooms as your own; Ron must walk down the hallway in order to get to the 1 closet you have assigned to him. He's not allowed in the kitchen. The refrigerator is 99 percent full of healthy stuff. He gets to put 2 beers in the fridge at a time. And he rents a storage space for his surfing stuff because you don't like it in or near the house. Space? You have 99 percent of the space, and he accommodates all your wishes and desires. I'm sure if you wanted to decorate with Hello Kitty throughout the house, he would consent. I don't think there is another person alive, man or woman, that would sacrifice so much to make you happy. He's a keeper and probably surfing today since you aren't home."

Randi took a deep breath. "Haha. May I explain?" I nod my head in approval. "What if we get divorced? I don't want to get divorced."

"Nobody plans for a divorce, but you can't not get married for fear of a divorce. There is always that possibility. It's very remote, but you do have great lawyer friends just in case." Randi rolled her eyes and pushed me.

"Hahaha." I looked at my watch and suggested we head back.

By the time we returned, most of the wedding party had left. Amy was sitting with Kathleen, a bridesmaid, as we walked in. "Where did everyone go?" asked Randi.

Kathleen turned around quickly and almost stumbled over. "They got hungry and headed out."

∞

The 4 of us sat around and talked about what qualities we preferred in the opposite sex. Randi started by saying, "I like really smart, slim guys with blonde hair. The nerdier and geekier they are, the better."

I chimed in, "That is not true. On a geeky scale ranging from 1 to 10, Ron hits a 5. That's why I get along with him. If he were any higher, I would have objected to the wedding."

Kathleen said, "My type is the smart, brown-haired, muscular man in a uniform. You know, the type that is in the military, law enforcement or a firefighter. I find a man in uniform to be very sexy."

Amy said, "Ever since I did a study abroad trip in China, I've only dated Asian guys. Yes, I have 'Asian Fever.' You can call me an Asianphile!" We laughed, but I was curious to learn more.

"I have some Asian blood in me. Does that count?" I stood up with my arms open wide.

"Well, I'm here, and didn't I already give you my number?" I sat down quickly, knowing I might have opened my mouth too quickly.

"Wait a minute… why Asian guys?" I inquired.

Amy laughingly interjected, "Because they think differently. They care about their parents' opinions and consult with them on key decisions, like marriage and career choices. They aren't as self-centered, and they always grab the check."

I sat back and wrapped my hands around the back of my head and began to reveal my preferences in women. "Haha. I'm the UN Ambassador for hot women. European, African, Asian, Middle Eastern, Latin, American. I like them all! They have to be on the low end of the crazy meter, but I will take a 5 or 6 on the cray cray scale if she is smoking hot."

Randi interjected, "That's my Sam, never serious about women. He will be single for the rest of his life. He has never been serious." I turned to the waitress and said, "Give them the bill," pointing to Amy and Kathleen, "because I'm only part Asian and my non-Asian side is dominant tonight." The girls laughed and then ignored the statement.

Amy and I said our goodbyes to Randi and Kathleen and headed towards the Intercontinental. "My bags are downstairs, and I was hoping I could stay with you."

"I'm sure if a full-blooded Asian guy appeared, you would break in that direction," I said, laughing.

Amy replied, "Sam, you are my number 1." Unlike the cuddle date encounter, this time there was much more intensity between us. The kisses were longer and more passionate. For years, I had been reluctant to have full-blown sexual relationships with anyone. After a night of intercourse, the relationship would no longer be deemed casual. I always found myself caught between a rock and a hard place when that line was crossed. Even if both partners agreed that the relationship would remain casual, things had to evolve. It seemed to be the unwritten rule. There was going to be no escalation without representation. I needed to feel comfortable about dating. Amy caught me off guard. She slowly moved down my body, kissing my neck, my chest, my stomach. Internally, I was screaming in fear. Externally, well, let us just say my body had its own opinion. She smiled and said, "It is true that whatever goes up must go down."

I said, "Amy, I think you have some Korean in you."

To which she replied, "No, no, I am Irish with a little German in me."

I responded in my sophomoric ways, "Well, you will tonight."

At that moment, we reached a meeting of the minds. A deal was closed; we were now dating.

The next day, Amy and I were openly holding hands and being affectionate. Randi teased us, "My spider senses detect something a little different." I winked at her, acknowledging her perception was right on the nose. We drank champagne through each of the Saturday bachelorette events. I didn't want to be a party pooper, so I participated in the mani and pedi, minus the fake nails and the polish. I indulged in a haircut and passed on the make-up. The day was full of celebration, toasting, conversations, hugs and tears. I knew what it meant to be pampered. I typically requested a deep-tissue massage, but we had booked a relaxing Swedish session. The champagne and last night's activity had made me tired. I fell asleep and caught myself snoring during the session. I emerged refreshed and ready to keep the party moving. At dinner, we presented Randi with a "10 things Randi has to do before midnight" list.

- Kiss a girl
- Drink a shot of 4 wise men
- Dance with someone 50 or older
- Flash a group of strangers
- Take a picture with 10 guys
- Get a stranger to buy her a drink
- Flirt with a bald guy for 10 minutes
- Sing karaoke
- Dance on a table
- Finish a tequila body shot

Custom T-shirts were handed out to the entire crew. Randi wasn't much of a drinker, and I was certain that issue would soon arise. Things were becoming out of control, but we managed to check off the items without getting arrested. Amy and I, meanwhile, were on full public display. Randi noticed a bald 50-something person sitting in the corner with a biker jacket and said, "Get ready to check off another item." About 15 minutes later, Randi hadn't returned. She was borderline drunk, and the guy was interested. Time for me to take off my Man of Honor hat and put on my Man of Security hat.

I walked over to him and said, "Everything okay, Randi?"

She looked at me with her head tilted back upside-down and replied, "I think I drank too much. I'm a little drunk, Sam."

I reached out my hand to her and said, "Okay, Randi, let's go."

Mr. 50-something motioned me away and said sternly, "She's fine. Can't you see we are having a conversation? Why are you bothering us? You have your own girl over there; let me have mine." He grabbed Randi by the arm. I lunged forward, and time slowed. I remembered the words of the designated driver. This guy was 50, and opportunities didn't arise for him every day. In fact, they didn't ever arise. He was thinking of his own bat. As I grabbed Randi, I felt a bottle shatter over my right eye. I dropped like a mic at the end of a "your momma is so ugly" contest. I remember a lot of commotion happening around me. I wasn't hurt too badly, but I was definitely down for the count. After I had revived, they put me in a cab and sent Amy and me back to the hotel. I was a little embarrassed but happy that Randi was safe. The bonus of being knocked out was that I now had a good excuse to miss the live exotic dancer. As we went to the hotel, I began to think of ways to explain my black eye to my co-workers. Could I cover it up with sunglasses? I could say that I made 1 too many cracks about Randi's bridezilla antics and she whacked me…. Naw, no one would believe that. My night as a bachelorette was over.

Upon returning to the office, I was the HOT topic of the day. "Did you hear how Sam brought in $2 million in 3 days?" The partners envied me, and the associates lined up like fans meeting a legal rock star chanting "GSD… GSD… GSD!" Jules entered. "Wow! You are the talk of the firm! The Wireless Tower closing was amazing, and now this. What is this?" She pointed her finger at my black eye. I grabbed her hand to lower it.

"Thank you for noticing."

"Sam, you never wear sunglasses in the office, and your face is absolutely swollen. What happened?" I walked into my office and sat down. "I was coming to the aid of my BFF during her bachelorette party when some guy blindsided me."

Jules mimicked my voice, "That's boring. I would tell them you signed up for an MMA class. Tell them 'I look bad, but you should see the other guy.'" Jules always knew how to put a smile on my face and spin the right story.

"I'm a little slow this week, Jules. Can you make sure I meet with our entire team?"

"Why?"

I motioned for her to close the door. "The Wireless Tower deal saved our team, but I'm concerned about the market. It's bad, but I think we haven't seen the worst yet."

"What are you thinking of doing, Sam?"

I turned around in my chair and got up. My evening of being one of the girls had left me with cotton mouth, so I grabbed a glass and filled it with water. After finishing off 2 glasses, I continued my conversation. "Last year we were close to $10 million. This year, we should be around $6 million, but since we pulled the Wireless Tower deal, it jockeyed us up to $8 million. I think next year will be closer to $5 million." Jules looked at me with surprise, but she knew what I was thinking. "How many people?"

"My plan is for everyone to receive their year-end bonus. After NOLA, we can reduce the cutting to about 4 lawyers, 2 paralegals and 2 legal assistants. We should help them find new jobs in November and December, commencing the next year. Please start scheduling meetings for mid-October." Jules sighed, acknowledged my requests and left. Not the way I like to start the day off, but it had to be done.

It took nearly 5 days for the swelling to come down. During the week, I picked out a larger pair of Jackie Kennedy sunglasses to wear to the wedding. I packed up my Man of Honor attire and headed toward the airport. Upon arrival, I checked into SWA and… boom! I got the A-1 slot. After such a hard week, I needed something like that to lift me up. I texted Caroline to let her know that I was coming to town for Randi's wedding.

"Need a last-minute date again, Sam?"

I responded, *"Man of Honor duties. Busy running around with my head cut off. Never been Man of Honor. Dooooooooooomed."*

I didn't answer Caroline's text directly because I was dating Amy, and she was going to accompany me as my date. After what had just occurred, I didn't want to hurt anyone's feelings. I checked Amy's itinerary. She wasn't landing until later in the evening. We had agreed to specific rules of engagement. We'd see each other twice a month over the weekends, picking random cities to visit. Nashville, NYC, Charleston, or Miami. Needy behavior and excessive texting were absolutely banned. That way it would always be the honeymoon stage of our dating adventure. Visiting new places, exploring new restaurants, and living out of 5-star hotels kept us engaged. We never argued or fought. She didn't know anything about the stresses or the challenges that I faced. Nor did I know hers. Dating Amy was fun, exciting and easy. I was able to see her on my schedule. There was no emotional baggage, and we satisfied each other's physical needs.

At 7:44 p.m., Amy arrived at the Willard. She always looked so refreshed. I stood up, and she gave me a fresh squeeze on the tush. "Hiiiii, Babe!" I was no longer Sam but Babe. We grabbed a quick dinner and raced back to the room to greet each other more appropriately. "Seventh-inning stretch, Amy, I'm up." "I'll throw you a slow curve ball, Sam, hope you knock it out of the park!" It was such a relief knowing how physically compatible we were and how we knew exactly what we wanted.

Chapter 21
Tears Cleanse Our Soul

Ping! Time to be dutiful and take care of the bride. I can recall crying 4 times before this year. Once when my father passed away, once when Mom passed, and 2 other times in my youth. When Amy and I arrived for the wedding, I walked over to the bridal room. "Just checking in! Randi, you need anything?" She had been crying tears of joy with her mom, sharing and acknowledging her 2nd time around. Recognizing this private moment and feeling a little uncomfortable, I backed away, hoping that she hadn't heard me.

The rest of the bridal party arrived. They all embraced and shed more tears. I'm not an overly emotional guy, and the constant crying began to take a toll. It became awkward, so I left the room in search of tissues and water. Intentionally, I waited an extra 5 minutes to return, hoping that the crying had ceased. Around the corner, I saw another group of friends and family members enter the room, adding more water to the already overflowing fountain of tears. I felt so uncomfortable on the bridal side of the dressing room that I walked over to check out the groom. Everyone was laughing, fist-bumping and drinking. That was more like it. I joined in on the festivities.

Ron asked, "What is going on over there? Did they kick you out because they were changing?"

"Let me break it down for you. The ladies have been crying for hours, and I don't think you guys ordered enough tissues." Ron smiled, but obviously concerned, asked if Randi was okay. I acknowledged that she was and that they were nervous albeit happy tears. "I'm better off on this side of the pond. At the moment, I need a beer. I'll go back over there to check up on Randi in a moment."

∞

As I was leaving, I ran into Craig from SocMedia. He and Randi had dated 10 years ago and had remained friends.

"Thanks again for that amazing phone booth gift, Craig."

"My pleasure. Are there any single cute bridesmaids, Sam?"

"Yeah, all of them."

"Did you see that girl over there?" He pointed to Amy. "She's smokin' hot."

Casually, I said, "Craig, that's Amy, and we are dating."

Craig's jaw dropped in disbelief. "What? When do YOU have time to date?"

"Ha-ha." I chuckled. I knew he was right, but that was the old me.

"Let me know if you ever break up." Craig looked back over at Amy. "Wow. She's smokin'!" It was all about the physical attraction for Craig. She could be the meanest, dumbest person on the planet, but if she looked like a model, he didn't care.

Two years prior, we had had a meeting about SocMedia's IPO. Craig was about to make $200 million, but he didn't care. He wasn't focused on the business meeting. Craig kept asking me if we were finished because he had a hot date. "Hey, Sam, do you want to join me on my date tonight?"

I thought it would be weird to have your attorney tagging along on a date. "Craig, she might think I was there to draft a prenuptial."

"I'm meeting her at work."

I was confused. "Where does she work, Craig?"

"She's an exotic dancer. Her stage name is Sparkle."

"That is not a date, Craig, and this conversation has gone beyond absurd." They had "dated" for 4 months before he moved onto other spoils.

I introduced Craig to Amy and headed back to the bridal party section. Other than the occasional tear, Randi's wedding was beautiful and flawless. Relieved, we all headed over to the reception to party.

With all the commotion, time flew by quickly, and it was time for the Man of Honor toast. I stood up and began. "Randi and I met in high school in Okinawa, Japan. My friend had a crush on her, but he was dating someone else. He wanted me to talk to her about going out with him. That Cyrano scene did not work at all for her. She would say, 'Hell, no, I won't go out with him. He needs to break up and ask me out. If he can't do that by the end of the week, I'm not interested and will never go out with him.' Randi was new to Kadena High School, and I liked her honesty and confidence." I looked over at her and continued. "We became friends, thanks to my scared friend. Randi was once called a "tomboy," but now we just call her awesome. She played soccer, and all the girls were afraid of her. Legend has it that she actually beat up girls. I knew I needed Randi to be my BFF. If any girl cheated on me or broke my heart, she would kick her butt. My dating life got easier. I didn't realize until last weekend that the roles were reciprocal. Hence the shades and my black eye today. As Randi's lawyer, I can assure you that Ron and Randi will have the best marriage. She has the entire walk-in closet and 2 adjoining rooms' closets, while he has the outside coat closet. She gets the kitchen and refrigerator, while he uses one of those small college fridges in the garage to keep a 6-pack cold. She decorates the house, and he rents a storage unit to keep his surfboard and guy things in. Don't make me kick your ass, Ron. But seriously, I'm not always invited to be the Man of Honor, so raise your glasses to 2 of my favorite people in the whole wide world. May all your ups and downs be under the sheets. Cheers." Everyone toasted, and the music began. For a moment, I was daydreaming. Was it the flashback to Okinawa or the context of weddings that had triggered fond memories of Caroline?

∞

Chapter 22

Changing of the Guards

Ping! The projections for year-end had come in as expected. We had
increased our collections from 80 percent to 90 percent and netted
$8.5 million. Just $500,000 under budget. The Wireless Tower
transaction saved our team from the panic and micro-management of
the management committee. I had discussed my concerns with all
the associates, paralegals, and legal assistants. Everyone received
their year-end bonuses, and the notices and departures commenced
as anticipated. One by one, the attorneys, paralegals and legal
assistants were re-housed. I was happy that they had safe landings
but was unsure about the future of my practice and the rest of our
group. The emerging growth sector was in renewable energy. This
was a new frontier, and we needed to develop expertise quickly if we
were going to compete. I needed an advantage and a roadmap to
start the year, so I decided to fly down to New Orleans to visit Hope
during the New Year celebrations I had planned with Amy. Only
Jean knew about my sessions with Hope. The situation was
mysterious and intriguing at the same time. Jean was as curious
about Hope's ability as I was, so I asked her to provide me a list of
questions for her. I also started to rough out my own questions. Amy
was arriving after 10:00 p.m., so I headed to Bourbon Street in
search of Hope of Life. With all the questions Jean and I had, I
booked a 2-hour session for 5:00 p.m. I arrived, and Hope locked the
door and put the closed sign in the window. She motioned me to sit
and joined me after she grabbed a cup of tea. As always, she offered
me a beverage. I figured I should just go ahead and accept the
beverage. Hope handed me a hot chocolate this time.

"Thought you might need a change."

"Thank you." The hot chocolate had itty bitty marshmallow stars floating around in it. It was warm and soothing.

Hope sat back down with her tea and commenced the session. "Why are you here?"

"My sister, Jean, has questions. Number 1. Is she at the right job?"

"Yes and no."

"What do you mean?"

"Everybody likes working with her. Good leader and very reliable. Her boss is the issue."

"Why is she an issue?"

"Her boss wants to retire in 3 years and doesn't want to make waves or changes. Too easy. Wants to skate until she retires."

I went to the next question. "Her son Aaron... will he go to medical school?"

"He will be fine. On the path to be a doctor but many choices to make and too early to decide." I smile with pride.

"How about Jean's other son, Nathan?"

"He will have more than 1 star."

"What does that mean?"

Hope touches her fingertips with her thumb. Looking down at them, she answered, "He has many, many talents." Okay, I was beaming now, so I continued with my questions.

"Will I be at my firm in the 2 years?"

"No."

"Will I be practicing at another firm?"

"No."

"What will I be doing?"

"I see significant changes. Field, animals, fire and ashes."

"Will things be better or worse?"

"Yes and no. It is good that you retire from law. It is good what you do next. I see fire and ashes." Hope put her cup down and made herself more comfortable.

"Do I love Amy?"

"Hmm, define love."

"Am I attracted to her?"

She looked at me like I was kidding. "Physically, yes. Emotionally, no."

"Will I be marrying her?"

"Maybe."

I begin to go off script. "Are there challenges?"

"Oh, I see many challenges. She is active. Has many people she sees." I become intrigued.

"Is she dating other people?"

"Because it deals with other people, I do not have permission. I am not allowed to know."

"Is she doing things with them like she is with me?"

"I am not allowed to know."

I changed the subject. "How is Caroline?"

"She is good."

"Has she set sail yet?"

"No."

"Do I love Caroline?"

Hope chuckled and said, "Define love."

"Am I attracted to her?"

"Physically, yes. Emotionally, yes."

"Will I be marrying her?"

"Maybe."

"Are there challenges?"

∞

"Many challenges." I continued to ask similar questions, but in a different format.

Hope smiled. "Please stop asking the same question expecting a different outcome. These matters do not change in a split second. Now that you are aware of the answers, everything goes into flux."

"What do you mean flux?"

Hope put down her cup to elaborate. "Knowledge produces a type of butterfly effect. Having inside knowledge of an issue may change the outcome, especially if you change your patterns based on the knowledge." Hope sat back in her seat. "Thus, everything goes into flux, affecting the outcome of other systems or things."

I was curious. "Will this speed up the outcome?"

"That is difficult to say. The probability is high that it will stay the course, but if you change your patterns, it may slow it down or speed it up. Be careful of the things you wish for. Most times you will get what you ask for, just not the way you wanted."

My head was whirling from the added information. "How am I to proceed?"

"Don't change the way you do anything. Knowledge is healing and can give you peace of mind, but don't put any energy behind it." I was thoroughly confused, but I let it go. The hour was waning. I wanted to end the session on Mom.

"How is Mom?"

"She's fine but still screaming at you."

"About what now?"

"Stop eating so much ice cream and start focusing on getting married." I rolled my eyes.

Leaving Hope, I became puzzled about life. The more questions I asked, the more questions I had. Maybe it would have been better not knowing anything. As I walked back to the hotel, I wondered how I would present my newly discovered information to Amy. We typically consumed our meals relatively quickly so that we could rush back to the hotel. I wanted to enjoy my meal but also wanted to have a conversation in a quasi-public forum in case things went awry. After dinner, I ordered a latte. As we waited, I asked, "What are your thoughts about this relationship?"

Amy looked at me and responded, "I love our relationship. We have fun all the time, and there is no drama between us. You aren't obsessive and needy."

I nodded my head in agreement. "Are we dating?"

Amy sat up and adjusted the ends of her blouse. "Of course, we're dating."

I continued. "From your perspective, when did we start dating?"

"I think it was the cuddle date for me. And you, Sam? When do you believe that we began to date?"

"For me, it was Austin when we consummated the relationship at Randi's bachelorette party. Are you dating other guys?"

"I'm not going to answer that question. Aren't you dating other girls?"

"Well, we really didn't talk about exclusivity."

"No, we didn't. Sam, I see you 4 to 6 days a month. I figured you were dating other women. I like you and enjoy spending time with you, but I'm keeping all my options open."

I picked up my latte and blew the heat off of it. "So you are dating other guys?"

Amy sat back in her seat like a kid being scolded. "Yes, I go out on dates with other people, but you are my number 1."

My curiosity was getting the best of me. "How many others are there?"

"Not many, and I'm here spending New Year's Eve with you, right? Can we not talk about this anymore? It is ruining a perfectly fine evening."

We sat for a while in silence. It became a little unnerving for Amy. She began to show her insecurity as she fidgeted. "Sam, are you dating other women, and if so, how many?"

I sat in silence. She continued, confused. "Were you planning on marrying me?" I looked up at Amy. I didn't answer her questions because I wasn't quite sure how I felt about her, but I did know that Hope was correct. Her exact words were streaming in my head as if she was whispering it in my ear at that very moment. "Amy is active, and there are many." We returned to the hotel and proceeded to do what we always did. As we continued with our usual act, I no longer felt present. I felt like I was just going through the motions. The specialness of the relationship had disappeared. I was searching for the "one," not just any companion. Knowing is as much of a curse as not knowing.

The firm was quiet. It was February 2008, and the office was noticeably smaller and slower. The high energy of the past 5 years was gone. The office had the air of a ghost town. Everyone was concerned that things could get worse. Bill Hiroshi had retired from SocMedia and started an angel investment company. An angel investor is a wealthy individual who provides capital for start-up businesses in exchange for equity. He visited the office because he was considering an investment in CropFuel, a renewable energy company. Bill was always a little over the top when it came to investing. "These guys claim to have rights from Kansas State for some new hybrid sorghum. These CropFuel guys are engineers that believe the future of energy is in building a biomass facility or an ethanol plant."

"Bill, can you educate me a little about the industry?"

"Biomass can be used as a source of energy. It most often refers to plants or plant-based materials that are not used for food or feed."

I put my pen down and stated, "So energy through plants. What makes this idea any different than other energy plants?"

"This hybrid sorghum is drought-tolerant with 3 harvests and yields 3-times that of traditional sorghum."

"I don't know much about crops, but that just sounds too good to be true, Bill. Let me check some other data." I pulled up some data sheets on the computer.

"The ethanol market share grew in the US from 1 percent in 2000 to 3 percent in 2006."

"That is a good sign, Bill. Oil prices were fluctuating in the high 70s in 2005, dipping to the high 40s in 2006 and are now on the rise again. Commodities are tricky. I wouldn't invest in the building of a biomass facility or ethanol plant. The budget on those is in the hundreds of millions, plus 3-4 years of construction time, permits, and potential delays. The play here might be to invest in a company with all the rights to the hybrid sorghum. The goal is to become a value-added seed company."

"I knew I made the right move by contacting you first, before making any investments. Can you meet me for dinner tonight?"

Glancing at my calendar, I responded, "Sure."

We reserved a private room at Sakana. Bill began by saying, "Are you always going to keep talking the talk, or would you ever consider walking the walk?"

I chuckled. "Well, that was an interesting way of putting things. For the right idea, I could be persuaded to walk the walk."

"Time is of the essence. I was wondering if you would visit KSU and learn more about the crop, meet with the CropFuel folks and gauge if they are real. If so, devise a business plan to monetize this opportunity."

"Bill, that would take about 2 months, full-time." I never liked to beat around the bush when it came to my time, and as the old adage goes, time is money.

"Sam, I will pay you $100,000 for your time."

"I don't want any conflict-of-interest issues, Bill. I have 2 months of vacation reserved. Why don't I use this time to conduct due diligence on this project? I'll provide you with a report. You can pay the firm $150,000 for my time."

"If it is a green light, how do you want to work?"

"Bill, I'm not greedy. I think 25 percent equity would be fair, considering the risk and the potential future dilution. I don't need a large salary. I could survive on $60,000 annually for the first 2 years."

Bill was pleased. We shook on it. As I headed back to the office, my adrenalin began to escalate about our next venture. I called an emergency meeting of my team and announced my decision to take 2 months off. "Mark is in charge while I'm away. I will still be available by email and phone but will be in areas with limited reception so it might take me a day or 2 to respond. Mark, please prepare an email to send to all the clients and copy me. I'm going to learn more about this renewable-energy sector starting next week."

Kansas Baby, Kansas Baby, here I come rolled through my head as I researched short-term housing near KSU. After securing a place to stay, I packed my car with 2 months' worth of clothing and headed for Manhattan, Kansas. I broke out the GPS and calculated my drive. "Hmm, looks like it will take me about 2 days. Jules, please schedule a meeting with Prof Vincent Friedman and Curt Lassiter of CropFuel."

After an uneventful 2 days on the road, I arrived at KSU and was greeted by Dr. Lassiter. Curt led me down to the boardroom and began a presentation detailing the investment opportunity in CropFuel, its business model, and the amount needed for the initial investment. I was surprised by the dollar amount. A proposal to raise only $5 million for the initial financing seemed a bit low, especially considering they required funding to build either a biomass facility or an ethanol plant. I inquired about the hybrid sorghum and was told that they had not executed any exclusive arrangement with KSU. They were only considering purchasing the seed from KSU and growing the crop to generate feedstock for their facilities. That was good news for Bill.

I spent the next 30 days following Dr. Vincent Friedman, a peculiar man. He talked to himself a lot. I assumed that this was his method of working through his thoughts. His mannerisms were familiar to me. I was taking advantage of the time I was spending with him. My goal was to learn all about him and as much as I could about the hybrid sorghum. We visited the green room, and I was amazed to see crops measuring 20 feet in height. It was a spectacular sight. I took pictures and lots of notes. According to Dr. Friedman, the crop would continue growing after each harvest until the first frost. He pointed at the tallest of the crops. "These crops have the potential of reaching 20 feet twice a year and possibly 3-times in tropical climates or hot weather areas like Florida, Hawaii, and Arizona. Through classic breeding techniques, not by genetic modification, I have produced a new seedless sorghum that has both male and female characteristics."

As I listened to the professor, I began to realize the potential for the plant, but how was I going to create a business model from all of the information that would make sense? On SocMedia, I located an old classmate from Kubasaki High School who lived nearby in Larned, Kansas. I sent him a quick message on SocMedia. *"Hey, Butch Haney, Sam Rivtoc. I'm trying to learn more about farming. Do you have time over the weekend to talk to me? I have questions about land costs, water costs, planting, harvesting, and all other probable expenses. Where is Larned, and how far away is it from KSU? Can you recommend a hotel?"*

It took all of 3 seconds for him to respond. *"Yes, I have time. I'll bring my hired hand, Sean Klein. Only 2 Restaurants in town. Pizza or burgers?"* I chose pizza. Butch hit me back with *"Only 1 hotel in town. You can't miss it! It's about a 3-hour drive from KSU."* I sent him a quick okay, gave him my digits, and headed to my temporary lodging to pick up some essentials to take with me.

After college, Butch moved back to Kansas and took over his father's land and kept reinvesting in more land. He had more than 1,000 acres of farmland. Butch knew the ins-and-outs of farming. He was my go-to guy for the information I was seeking. Driving in, I passed the sign "Welcome to Larned, population 4,000." I arrived at noon and checked into the local gas station. I asked for directions and inquired if they knew a Butch Haney.

∞

The front desk attendant said, "You aren't from around here, are you?" I was curious if it was what I was wearing—a Robert Graham shirt and flip flops—or if it was my Asian characteristics. He leaned forward over the desk and said, "I wouldn't go looking for him. That guy is crazy. Rumor has it he unloaded a magazine with his AK over someone trespassing on his land."

I had no idea what he was talking about, so I asked, "Like a machine gun?"

"An AK-47, a rapid-fire machine gun that holds 30 rounds in a magazine. He's done that on multiple occasions. Folks around here don't mess with that crazy Butch."

"Can you point me in the direction of the pizza joint?"

"Sure can. Turn left onto that road over there. Go until you see the stop sign. The burger joint will be on the right. Turn left, and the pizza joint will be on your right 2 doors down."

I thanked the attendant and headed to the pizza joint. Butch and Sean were waiting for me by their Ford pickups. Sean glanced over at Butch in a suspicious way; I'm assuming that he had never seen an Asian in person before. We headed inside for pizza, where Butch and I reminisced about the old high school days.

Sean chimed in. "Where did you learn how to speak English so well?" Not wanting to offend him, I quickly responded, "I'm a military brat, met Butch on Okinawa, and lived in Atlanta as a lawyer."

"You look kinda funny in that get up out here in the country." Apparently, I had 2 strikes against me because Sean was raised not to trust any "city folks" or "lawyers." The conversation over lunch was very basic. I didn't know quite how to take Sean and kept the jokes to a minimum.

∞

Casually, I brought up the AK-47 story to Butch, and he smiled. "Guilty as charged. Folks around here know not to mess with me. I don't bring a knife to a gunfight. I bring my AK." Good Ol' Butch. He definitely knew how to stand his ground. I gave out a little chuckle.

I asked, "Hey, Butch, you married yet?"

Sean let out a holler and laughed uncontrollably.

"Hush, Sean! No, I don't have the time. I have all these animals to deal with on the farm. A thousand goats and 300 head of cattle. No time to deal with women and romance."

Sean grabbed a glass of water. "Butch has the time. He just prefers to talk to the animals."

"Baaahhhd, Butch, you know buggery is illegal in Kansas." Butch and Sean both belted out a laugh. Butch reached across and grabbed a slice of pizza and said, "You're sick, Sam."

After lunch, Butch invited me to visit his farmland. I got out of my car, took a few steps and landed flat on my ass. Everyone got a kick out of my fall. I even laughed myself. I was wearing flip flops. Damn flip flops. My thinking was that I could blend in by looking casual. But as an Asian, driving an S-500, dressed in a loud Robert Graham shirt and flip flops, I stuck out like a sore thumb. They were driving pickup trucks and wore boots and t-shirts. Note to self: I need to pick up my country game. Sean put his hand out, and Butch pulled out a $20 bill and gave it to him. "Sean bet me $20 you would fall flat on your ass within 20 minutes of being here."

Sean gave the bill a good stretch and put it in his pocket and said, "Thanks for making my day, Sam." I was glad I could be the butt of everyone's joke. There was a time when Butch had been the butt of many of my jokes in high school. Turnabout is fair play, I guess.

Butch introduced me to the various farming methods he performed on the thousand acres he owned. Dry farming, pivot and flood irrigation. Two hundred acres were being irrigated on pivots, a method of irrigation where equipment rotates around a pivot and crops are watered with sprinklers. Four hundred acres were dedicated to dry farming and irrigated by the rain. He had another 400 acres for raising 300 head of Black Angus and 1,000 boar goats. Sean brought up fertilizer and mentioned NPK.

"What is NPK?"

He kicked some of the dirt off of his boots and explained, "It has something to with nitrogen." For a second, I thought he was talking about a brand. Slowly, I realized he was talking chemistry. Nitrogen, phosphorus, and potassium. Our conversation moved to grain crops. They start explaining the differences between grain sorghum and grain corn versus forage crops without grain, which including sorghum, grain, rice straws and hay. We then talked about dry matter, the part of the feed that remains if all its water is removed. I was a little overwhelmed by all the information. Butch explained, "for example, if you were to yield 20 tons and have 60 percent dry matter, then people would only pay for the 12 tons."

I then asked him about harvesting. Sean explained grazing, round baling, square baling and silage. I was glad I drove the 3 hours to meet Butch and Sean. All this information was Greek, and I knew I needed to spend more time with them to become familiar with all the nuances. I had probably missed some relevant information already. I was learning something entirely new, and that was exciting, but I needed to provide Bill with a coherent summary of all the risks and rewards. I prepared charts and summarized the findings. I projected it would take another 2 weeks with them to confirm and reconfirm all the data.

∞

I began to shadow Butch and Sean. My first 2 days, I did not dress properly. Sean hollered, "Butch, does your city slicker lawyer friend here know that there are heavy metals, chemicals and rattlers out here? He's still wearing those flip flops. He's not too bright, is he?"

"Sam, there is a store in town where you can get some boots to protect your feet. It's next to the burger joint, a couple doors down."

"Thanks. When I get back to town, I will make it a point to check it out."

They explained the differences between dairy (milk-producing cows) and cattle (beef-producing cows). Butch leaned on the side of the post. "Cattle can eat up to 20 pounds of dry matter each day. The important factors in the feed are total dietary nutrients, energy, and protein. For cattle, the important metric was net energy gain, whereas, for dairy, it was net energy lactation." Butch had 300 head of cattle and needed about 1,000,000 tons of feed per year to maintain their growth. Boar goats were different. Butch had 1,000. The nutritional analysis was similar to cattle but on a much smaller quantity per animal basis. I was in information overload. I kept repeating my questions to Butch and Sean.

Finally, after the 5th reconfirmation, Sean looked at Butch and said, "I thought lawyers were smart. He keeps asking us the same questions over and over again."

Butch said, "Sam is just thorough. He has always been that way." At that point, I explained to them about Dr. Friedman's hybrid sorghum product and all its benefits.

"Sam, it seems too good to be true. I've never seen a 20-foot crop that you harvest twice a year." I showed them pictures of the crop, and they both looked at me in awe. "I wouldn't mind planting some of that in our fields to test it out. Do you know what the nutritional value on that might be?"

"I don't have a clue. You guys are the first folks to explain animal feed and nutritional values to me. I'm sure it has a lot of sugar, which converts to energy. It was bred as a possible ethanol feedstock." I left Sean and Butch pondered the idea of planting the hybrid stock.

I returned to KSU with more questions for Dr. Friedman. I spent the next 3 weeks discovering how much NPK was used to achieve the 20-foot crop on a per-acre basis. He calculated, "That would translate to 300 units of nitrogen, 100 units of phosphorus, and a hundred units of potassium, along with some products only permitted to be used at the University."

I inquired about how much water was used. Dr. Friedman was vague, which is unusual for an agricultural scientist but par for him, and said only, "I watered it regularly."

"Are you familiar with the planting protocols since the seed is 10-20 percent the size of forage sorghum and corn seed? How deep should one plant? Should you drill it in or air plant?" My 2 weeks with Sean and Butch were invaluable, and the professor seemed to enjoy the line of questions. I asked him if I could purchase four 50-pound bags of the seed for R&D purposes. He agreed to sell it to me for $400. I drove back to Larned in late March with the 200 pounds of seed and discussed a test proposal with Butch. I wanted to plant 2 pounds of seed per acre on a plot of 50 acres of pivot irrigated land to determine maximum yield. I had another 2 pounds of seed I wanted to test on 50 acres of dry farming land. We agreed to plant 50 acres on a pivot. Butch would supply the land; we would supply the seed, and we'd split the costs for fertilizer, water, and labor, 1/3 to me and 2/3 to Butch. Harvesting cost would be divided in the same manner. We estimated that the growing costs, including land and seed, for the 50 acres would not exceed $40,000. We agreed to silage the pivoted crop. With 2 harvests at a 12-ton per acre dry matter basis, the cost should not exceed $10,000. Butch agreed to purchase the finished product at a 25 percent discount on the market price at the time of harvest. Theoretically, we would nearly double our money. On the dry farm, I suggested an experiment of 25 acres of forage sorghum and 25 acres of forage corn, in 2 fields. Butch asked if I wanted to do the same deal as before. I declined but offered to provide the seed for free. He agreed, and we made a plan to plant the seed the first week of April.

I prepared a summary for Bill, explaining the issues. I divided it into 3 major categories: Planting Costs – planting, seed, fertilizer, and water; Maintenance Costs – weed abatement, watering, and fertilizer; Harvesting Costs – silage, bale. "Here is the difference between winning and losing. It's all about minimizing costs, maximizing yield and the crossing of your fingers that the market price for feed at the time of harvest is high." I also warned Bill, "Don't rely heavily on Dr. Friedman's results. They're ivory tower, best-case scenario results. He didn't account for weather, insects or the use of excessive fertilizer and water." Technically, the excess would be commercially unreasonable. The professor did not take into consideration the dry-matter analysis either. "Instead of 40 tons per acre, we should model the results based on 12 tons per acre on a dry-matter basis. I have provided a farmer in Larned, Kansas, with seed. We will test on 50 acres of irrigated land and two 25-acre parcels of dry farm land. Our costs will not exceed $15,000. The potential profit is $30,000."

Bill was a data-driven decision maker. "I am not concerned about profit at this time."

"This is the cheapest way to figure out if you should proceed with the investment. Instead of a $2 million mistake, this would be a $15,000 pilot."

Bill replied. "Yes, let's move forward. This is great news. I can't believe you were able to learn so much in 2 months. What about CropFuel?"

"They have no rights to the hybrid sorghum. We could do a feedstock deal with them in the future and include them on the advisory board. We should also allocate a percentage for KSU if we succeed in a securing a license." Bill agreed, and we moved forward with the process.

Amy had visited me once during the 2 months that I was in Larned. Sean commented, "Butch, I might have to take a job out there in the city. The fishing ain't as nice here as it is there."

I asked Amy to sit with Butch and Sean while I searched for a place to stay. "You see that? Sam ain't bright at all. He's leaving Amy to hang out with us."

Amy and I were used to iconic 5-star hotels. The only hotel in Larned was a 2-star hotel. I wasn't prepared for the blue-collar community, which was a culture shock for both of us. All in all, I didn't mind, since I was there to immerse myself in farming culture. Amy was a city girl, though, and there was no reason for her to be here except just to be with me. She complained about the food, the odor, the lack of activities and the room. She hated all the flies and bugs. We had our first fight traveling; perhaps the honeymoon was finally over.

The night before the planting I asked, "What time should we start... 8:00 am?"

"Butch, I don't think Sam's gonna make it as a farmer." Then he looked at me and continued, "We don't work no banker hours. Most of us start at 6:00 a.m. and work until 6:00 p.m. And that's outside, not in the AC all day." I wasn't afraid of hard work. I worked 12-hour days and longer. But my days were in the office and involved brain power. Sean was right. This work was outside. Primarily physical power. I was at a disadvantage but hardly out of the game. On the day of the planting, I noticed a group of more than 20 farmers observing the planting. News had spread that Butch and Sean were planting a next-generation super crop that could reach 20 feet. We were the big news of that small town.

Sean was methodical in planting the 50 acres of hybrid sorghum. He might have been slow by my standards, but he was not stupid. He "profiled the field" on the pivot land by applying water 1 day before planting so there would be water underground to help with germination, applied 50 pounds of nitrogen, and meticulously followed the 4 pounds per acre and ½ an inch planting protocol. He deviated on the planting protocol on the dry farm's 5 pounds per acre and 2 inches on one 25-acre dry farm similar to corn and at 3 pounds per acre and 1 inch on the other 25-acre dry farm. The seed germinated in 3 days. I was excited as I drove back to Atlanta.

"Jules, I'm back. Please invoice Bill Hiroshi a flat fee for $150,000 and describe it as research and meetings on the feasibility of the CropFuel project."

Jules smiled and retorted with sarcasm, "I'm glad you actually took time off to work. By the way, the management committee is coming by in 15 minutes to meet with you."

Three of the management committee partners, including the chairman, visited my office. They were concerned that I was being recruited by a competitor to leave Billings, Day and Knight. To ensure that I was happy, they offered me a position on the 7-person management committee starting in June. The chairman pulled me to the side and whispered, "I'm thinking of retiring in 2 years, and you have a great shot at becoming the next chair." On any other day during my entire time at Billings, Day and Knight, I would have been jumping for joy at the news of joining the management committee, but not today. My guard had dropped while I was away. Something had changed. Something had germinated in my soul.

Chapter 23

Tying Up Loose Ends

Ping! Ping! Ping! I left the meeting on cloud 9 but wanted to talk to Sean and Butch about the progress of the hybrid sorghum. It had been 5 days since the crops were planted and 5 days since germination. Each week the boys would contact me and let me know the progress.

Butch reported a week later that the crop was at 2 feet. Two weeks later... 4 feet. In May, it had reached 6 feet.

"Have you ever guys seen anything like this before?" I asked.

Sean seemed shocked and responded, "No! It's starting to look like a jungle out here. I hope there aren't any gators lurking."

"SWEEEEEET! I need to share the great news with Bill."

We cut the crop at 5 feet to determine the nutritional value. It was comparable to corn forage on energy but in the form of sugar versus starch. Much easier for the cows to digest. It also had significant amounts of protein, which forage corn and sorghum lacked. The quantitative numbers were great, and the bonus was the qualitative numbers. Traditional forage corn and sorghum had energy maxed at 20 percent, with a TDN of 55. In other words, 12 percent was actually digested by the cow. The hybrid sorghum had energy at 18 percent and protein at 10 percent at a TDN of 70 percent. In other words, 13 percent of actually digested energy along with 7 percent protein, which the other crop lacked. Nutritionists would approve of our solution to traditional forage because it eliminated the need to mix any additional crops with protein, thus reducing potential error, waste, and inefficiencies. These were amazing results! I called Bill to share the good news with him.

"I'm ready, Bill. Whenever you are ready to move in the renewable farming direction," I said confidently.

We agreed to form NewAgri, investing $100,000 each for 50 percent of the company. Bill would invest an additional $2 million at a $6 million pre-money valuation after we secured the hybrid sorghum exclusive license from KSU. If everything went as planned, Bill would own 75 percent, and I would end up with 25 percent. I was ready to announce it to the world but needed to negotiate the technology transfer from KSU.

We contacted the KSU Transfer team and proposed a term sheet. We explained the business plan to KSU and highlighted many of the risks.

"We want a 20-year exclusive license. We are willing to offer escalating minimum guarantees of $100,000 the first year, $500,000 the 2nd year, $1 million in year 3, plateauing at $2 million for 20 years, provided, however, that you receive 10 cents for every pound of seed sold annually along with options to purchase 5 percent of NewAgri at a $8 million price per share valuation."

They countered with an annual technical support agreement for $150,000. All parties agreed to the term sheet, and we asked KSU Transfer to prepare the definitive documents for signing over the weekend.

I returned to the office the following Monday with the hybrid sorghum contract in hand for NewAgri.

"Jules, do you want to grab coffee?" She got her coat, and we headed out the door.

I am not usually one to shy away from a tough talk, but this was different.

"Jules, you have been an anchor for me for the past 6 years."

"Sam, is your health okay?"

Jules had a worried expression on her face until I answered, "Yes, I'm fine, better than fine."

"Sam, I know you are going to move into management. My salary is too high, isn't it? I don't need a raise. I love working with you. I can live on $80,000 a year. You can cut my salary from $110,000 to $80,000."

"Jules, you are perfect. I couldn't ask for a better person to work with. If I could pay you more, I would. I've decided not to accept the management committee job. Things are going to get worse, and I don't want people to view me as KOD."

"KOD?" she asked.

"The Kiss of Death. I'm Mr. GSD, and even I can't turn this tide. I'm leaving the firm."

"Which firm are you going to? I'll go with you."

"I'm leaving the practice of law. I'm getting into renewable energy farming." Jules was stunned and rightfully so. This was a complete 180.

"What? You don't have a clue about farming. Are you having a mid-life crisis? You are really good at law, and the clients adore you. I think this would be a horrible mistake."

I laughed. "Jules, it's time for me to walk the walk."

"Does anyone else know?"

"No," I paused. "You are the first. I'm going to let Mark know next and the team and then the firm."

Jules let out a deep sigh and gave me a hug. "I hope you know what you are doing."

I walked over to Mark's office. He was deeply engrossed with an M&A transaction, so I knocked lightly so as not to alarm him. He looked up, smiled, and invited me in.

"Mark, remember what I said to you in San Francisco when we were working out the details on the Absorb financings over a year ago?"

"Yes. You said I would be on partnership track in 2 years."

I inhaled deeply and exhaled. "Mark, you know that the market is spiraling downward. What is your book at this year?"

"Yes, I'm aware. I was at a $2 million book of business at the time we first spoke, but last year, I didn't hit $1 million, and I would be lucky if my book is $500,000 this year." He sounded almost embarrassed.

"Well, my book has fallen too. Last year, we were saved by the Wireless Tower year-end Hail Mary. I'm not projecting any miracles this year. I'm looking at something closer to $5 million."

"Sam, I appreciate this conversation. Thanks for giving me a heads-up. I guess I won't be up for partnership at the end of the year. I'll just keep plugging away and hope the market is kind to me next year."

"Well, that's not what I'm saying, Mark. Although I do hope that next year will be kinder to us all." I paused, not for dramatic effect but because every time I told someone about my plans, it made them more real. "I am leaving the firm," I continued. "I've only told 1 other person about my decision."

Mark looked stunned. "Which firm are you jumping to?" Even Mark believed that I was jumping ship to another firm. He must have thought that I was crazy to give up the management committee job.

"I'm not going to another firm, Mark. I'm leaving the practice of law. I'm going to announce to the group next and then to the partnership. I'm going to tell them to make you partner immediately because I'm transferring my entire book of business to you. I kept my end of the bargain. Now you need to make sure that you take care of the remaining folks on this team. Deal?"

Mark was flabbergasted, saddened and overjoyed at the same time. I gave him a minute to let it all sink in and then said, "Let's go tell the rest of the team now."

I think everybody feeks that they are indispensable. After my notice, my messages dropped from thousands a day to hundreds in the first week. By the 3rd week, I was fortunate if I received 10 messages a day. I had accrued enough airline miles and hotel points to travel for 2 weeks. I decided on DC to spend my last few weeks with Randi and Ron before embarking on my next adventure. I hadn't spoken to Amy in over a month. I called her.

She was her usual bubbly self and mentioned, "Hey, Sam, I'm in DC this weekend and staying at the Plaza near the airport." I didn't let her know that I was going to be in DC, too. I thought a surprise would be nice for both of us. It would be just the pick-me-up I needed.

After I had checked into the Willard, I grabbed a bottle of wine and headed to the Plaza. "Excuse me, Amy Hunter's room, please."

"Room 404, Sir." I would never have checked into a room with so many unlucky 4s.

I knocked on the door, and a middle-aged Asian man answered. "Is this Amy Hunter's room?" I asked, looking at the numbers again.

"Yes," he replied. "She's just stepped out for a walk."
"Who are you?"

"Jack Tanaka. I'm a friend of Amy's." He sized me up and continued, "And you are?"

"I'm Sam Rictov."

"Oh!" He nodded. "*You* are Sam Rictov."

Caught off guard, I asked, "how do you know me?"

"Amy talks about you all the time. You are her number 1. You're lucky you get to see her 2-times a month. I'm like number 3. She spends time with me every other month."

"How long have you and Amy been dating, Jack?"

"About a year now."

"Does she go down on you too?" I asked, almost sickened that she might.

He laughed. "No, she doesn't like to do that. I guess she only does that for her number 1."

A little stunned that anyone would accept being anything but number 1, I mockingly replied, "Well, I'm not going to be her number 1 anymore."

"Really! You're ending it?" he asked, and then it dawned on him, "I get to see Amy more often now?"

I was dumbfounded that this man would so willingly put himself in this position, even if she was hot. I felt sorry for the guy. I'm a numbers guy, and the numbers, in this case, were not good. I was still reeling from shock and disgust when Amy stepped out of the elevator and screamed, "Sam what are you doing here?" I nearly dropped the bottle of champagne.

"I called you, and you said that you were in DC. Well, I was in DC, too, so I decided to surprise you," I said indignantly and shook my head. "Boy, am I surprised!"

Amy burst into tears. "This wasn't supposed to happen."

"Jack, go back in the room. I need some time to talk with Amy." Jack looked at Amy and acquiesced.

"Sam, I didn't expect you to be here," Amy sobbed.

She was gorgeous even when she cried. I'm not comfortable with awkward emotions, and I don't like to see any woman cry, especially if I am the reason for her tears. I wavered for a second. She seemed to care so much...No, I thought. I need to end this now. I should have done it a while ago. Convenient fun had evolved into something deeper for me, and now I was clear that it was time to cut bait.

"Although we never agreed to be exclusive, Amy, I've been exclusive with you. You are a play-the-field type, and that's your prerogative. I'm more of a 1-woman-guy."

"I really like you, Sam, and I would stop seeing all these other guys if you wanted to marry me."

I laughed out loud, not to be mean but at the naiveté of her words.

"You and I both know that you aren't ready to be with just 1 guy. You're more into an open relationship and carefree lifestyle now, and I'm just not, nor have I ever been. Plus, I'm gearing up to go farm renewable energy, and we know how much you like the country lifestyle. You are better off dating guys like Jack." She looked bored at the thought of Jack, so I continued, "I have a friend, Craig. You met him at Randi's wedding. He's a lot richer than I am. Worships attractive girls like you and only knows the city life. I should introduce him to you. Maybe he can gradually become your number 4." I smiled at the zinger. Even when hurt, I can create a sharp and perfectly timed retort.

"Not funny, Sam." Still, she cracked a smile. "Are you staying at the Willard?"

"Yes," I reluctantly replied.

She looked at the bottle of bubbly and then playfully into my eyes. "Can I stop by for a final goodbye hookup?"

"I don't think that that is a good idea, Amy. But…" I paused, thinking about how I might extricate myself from this hot mess with little to no complications. "I'll forward your number to Craig. Let me warn you about him. For Craig, it is all about the physical hotness. Let me break it down for you. I love cats but am totally allergic to them, so I avoid dating women who own them. The best way to keep me away from a girl is to tell me she has a cat."

Amy, looking less emotional now, seemed surprised by this rather important fact about myself.

I continued, "Craig is also allergic to cats. He, however, will 'take 1 for the team' if she's at least an 8 on the hotness meter." I laughed.

"I remember Craig chasing after a girl with 2 cats. After every visit, he would have severely swollen, red eyes, severe sneezing, nasal congestion, and hives. I would ask Craig if she was worth it. His answer was almost always the same, 'Sam, she's smokin' hot. If I can hook up with her, it is worth being out of commission for a few days.' Amy, according to Craig, you are smoking hot, so you shouldn't have any problems on his front. He's 100 percent Asian and wealthy, the type you are attracted to. Do you mind if I give him your number?" Amy looked at me in disbelief and nodded. With that, I hugged Amy and made my exit.

As I walked down the streets of DC, I felt a sense of freedom and excitement course through my body. The weather in DC in May was invigorating, and I began to think about my next adventure. The streetlights and neon signs gradually lit up the dusk sky and made the gray cityscape seem vibrant. I seemed to be seeing things more clearly and with renewed enthusiasm. I needed to tie up a few loose ends. I laughed and with a firm sense of direction, I called Craig.

"Hi, Craig, it's Sam. Wanted to let you know that I'm going to be an entrepreneur partnering with Bill on a renewable energy project," I said, trying to play it cool.

"I heard," Craig said. "Congrats but be careful; the market really sucks at the moment."

I knew this, but now was not the time to balk. "I might need you to come in on the later rounds with additional capital."

"Shit, Sam! Bill's got more money than I do, mainly because I like fast cars and fast women. Still, I'll think it over."

"Hey, speaking of women, do you remember my date for Randi's wedding?"

"How could I forget?" I could almost hear him drool. "She was the bomb diggity, and I still dream about her."

I laughed. "Craig, simmer down. We broke up today."

"Can I call her?"

"What? The body isn't even cold, Craig," I exclaimed.

"Oh, sorry," Craig said with contrition.

I laughed, and Craig joined in.

I balanced the phone between my ear and shoulder as I fumbled for change for the metro. DC metro stations have very distinct interiors, and I almost lost my train of thought, pun intended and enjoyed.

"Actually, I'll give you full disclosure so that you don't sue me later for an omission of a material fact. Amy has yellow fever and only dates Asian guys."

"She's hot, Sam." I agreed and shook my head. Craig was completely comfortable with his unapologetic shallowness.

"Well, I'm half Asian, and you're full Asian, so I'm sure she'll eventually like you more. Warning, Amy plays the field and dates many guys. We broke up because she has 3 to 4 other guys on rotation."

"Oh, that's nasty." He paused for what I'm sure was a visual and continued, "I like that, Sam!"

"You will be 1 of many guys if you pursue her," I warned again.

"Don't worry, Sam. I'm going to pursue her. The chase is on."

"If you are okay with all of that, I'll give you her number." Then I remembered how excited Jack was to be moving up in priority with Amy and I quickly added, "Please wait until next week to contact her because she's with Jack, formerly known as number 3, and I feel sorry for him."

As I got off the Metro at Farragut West, my status was no longer ambiguous. I was single without any strings attached, ready to conquer the renewable energy vertical.

I started thinking about Caroline again. It had been a while since we last spoke although she was never far from my thoughts. I texted her to let her know that I was in town. *Hey, pretty lady! Dinner at 8:00 pm? I want to discuss my exciting new adventures with you.*

I am a creature of habit, and when she agreed, I told her to meet me at Sake, a nice sushi place in the city. I was delighted when she said that she could join me. As usual, I arrived early. To my happy surprise, she did too. She looked amazing, and as I told her so, she blushed, smiled that radiant smile of hers, looked down and touched her hair. The hostess asked us to follow her to our seats. I put my right hand on the small of Caroline's back; she smiled, and I breathed in the comfort of being near her again.

Once seated, we ordered our drinks and dinner. We made small talk until the drinks arrived and then I shared that I had officially retired from the practice of law and was heading off to be a renewable-energy farmer.

"Oh, Sam," she giggled, "be serious!"

I began to describe the new hybrid sorghum and its potential. She was so cute, as she stared intently while listening to my every word. I could lose myself in those eyes forever.

I broke out of my fantasy when she asked if I was seeing anyone. "I had been dating someone, but things didn't work out. Once I took on this new venture, we decided it was best to end the relationship." I quickly changed the subject and asked about her situation.

"My husband moved out right before the Christmas holidays last year. He was spending it with his new girlfriend, who, by the way, is 26 years old."

I gave Caroline my sincere condolences while feeling almost giddy with the thought that she might be available now. Or was she? My mind detoured into practical matters, and I asked, "Have you secured counsel?"

"Yes, Sam. I took care of that the day he moved out."

The melancholy in her voice told me she was still very hurt by it all. I decided to tread gently. I placed my hand on hers to show support and asked, "What are your plans?"

"Virginia has some odd rules. They have 2 types of divorces. Divorce from bed and board where the couple is legally separated but are not permitted to remarry. The 2nd kind of divorce is from the bonds of matrimony. One can file after living separately and apart for a year when there are children involved or adultery. I'm not sure what I'm going to do. My youngest is in 9th grade now, and I don't want this situation to impact him negatively. I'm probably going to wait until he graduates from high school before filing for the divorce. I don't want to have to sell the house and move. That would be too traumatic for my son."

"Do you plan on dating?" I asked, not sure that I wanted to know the answer.

"No," she said, "I don't want to complicate the divorce proceedings."

"If he came back to you, would you take him back?" Again, why did I keep asking questions that I wasn't sure I wanted to know the answer to? I mentally shook my head. I knew why. Caroline was my Mona Lisa, and I just wanted her to be happy.

"No, Sam. I'm way beyond loving him at this point. It is about the best interest of my kids."

"How do your kids feel?"

"They are so mad at him. Honestly, I don't think they will ever speak to him again. They say that they won't. Realistically, I know that they will." She looked at me and changed the subject. "Where are you moving to?"

"Manhattan, Kansas."

"Where is that?" I could almost see her pulling out a mental map.

"Near Kansas City," I replied and quickly added, "It is where KSU is located."

Caroline nodded and said, "Promise me you will stay in touch."

"I will Caroline; I promise."

"Don't forget about my postcards."

I placed her hand on my knee, and she giggled. We were so engaged in our conversation that we barely noticed the near emptiness of the restaurant. We reminisced about Okinawa, our school friends and our dates, especially the 2nd date. We had been dancing all night, Kona Garden, and I walked her to the door. It was our first passionate kiss. I was dazed by it all and stumbled over a bush. We laughed about it, but I was truly head over heels for her, and she knew it.

Leaving the restaurant, we held hands. It was an escalation of intimacy from Joe's wedding, infused with a sense of familiarity may be even more meaningful than it was 19 years ago. As I walked her to her car, she said, "Don't even think about kissing me, Sam."

I smiled, "I wasn't thinking about it, Caroline. Friends don't kiss friends. But," I continued playfully, "If you wanted to kiss me, I would let you."

At that moment, she leaned in and pressed her lips against mine. It seems corny, but I was transported in time. I was a kid again. My heart began to beat faster. My breathing labored. I closed my eyes so as to savor every moment with Caroline. I didn't want to scare her off, but I didn't want this to end, so I wrapped my arms around her. She pulled me in closer. Tighter. Our lips played together, touching and pulling away for just enough time to eagerly come back for more.

I could feel her passion. She was hungry. When was the last time that she had been made to feel loved and desired? I didn't care, not really. I wanted her all to myself. I pushed the thoughts from my head and focused on the warmth and curves of her body, the eagerness of her mouth and the smell of her perfume. She was soft and yet hard in all the right places. I parted my lips ever so slightly, and she seemed to anticipate and reciprocate the move. Our tongues began to touch, almost in a tease. Caressing, sucking, even a little playful biting. I was near heaven. Our bodies began to sway as our tongues danced to the rhythm of our hearts. They were beating as one again. It was energizing— enchanting—and I lost myself in it. If

Caroline had asked me to stay in DC and forget about farming, I would have said yes in a heartbeat. And just as if she could hear my thoughts, Caroline stopped and pulled away. She said, "I'm sorry, but I needed this tonight." She left without another word.

I wasn't sorry. That kiss was a complicated dance of varying intensity, a work of art. It sent tremors down my body. My hands were still shaking, my knees were wobbly, and I had the biggest smile on my face. I was born again. It had been 19 years sequentially converting to the letter "S." What a "surprise!" Could there be a "second" chance with "sweet" Caroline?

After what could only be classified as a successful trip, I returned to Atlanta with a runner's high and secured a rental unit to move all of my office and household items into. Then I contacted the same realtor that I had purchased my Craftsman through and listed it to rent. I packed my car with only "farming necessary" items: 1 suit, 1 dress shirt, 1 tie, 1 pair of dress shoes. The rest were tennis shoes, jeans, t-shirts, sweatshirts, the Mont Blanc pen and, of course, the Ba-Ba-Ri coat. I packed all my valuables: rings, watches, sports memorabilia, photo albums, and coin collection into the storage unit. I had received a cowboy hat and boots as going-away gifts from the firm and friends. Placing the hat on my head, but leaving the boots, I was off to Kansas.

By June, the crop that we had planted in Larned was 15 feet tall. Sean had some concerns that his chopper would get stuck and recommended that we swath the crop before it got any taller. The first harvest on the pivoted land had yielded 8 dry tons. Butch figured $150 a ton was fair. After the calculation, we had netted $20,000 on our portion, a profit of $5,000 on this experimental field, and we still had a 2nd harvest to look forward to. Our crop was outperforming the other forage crops, yielding 6 tons per acre. Yes, 2

∞

tons less than the irrigated field but still 3 tons better than the competitive forage product. This was great news for our test plot. Bill was excited and said that we should plant more seed this year. He was a numbers guy, too, and did a straight-line math analysis. "If we plant 1,000 acres, we can make this much more money," he said as he pointed to the figures. His goal was monetary, but he also knew that if we were going to be successful in the renewable energy space, we needed to be farming on at least 5,000 acres.

Bill and I started to discuss different business models. The prospects of money can often blind people to the simplest risks. Mother winter would be here in October, and we were blissfully unaware of what that might entail. Still, the local farmers who had observed Butch's field were impressed and wanted to plant some of the feed in their fields. Since Bill was the majority owner, and 95 percent of the capital was his, I deferred to him reluctantly.

We agreed to farm 1,000 acres: 500 acres that we would pay for 100 percent and 500 acres that the other farmers would provide. We would keep 2/3 of profits while 1/3 of the product or profits would go to the other farmers. There were corn and sorghum in their fields, and we couldn't begin planting until the first week of August at the earliest. We spent $400,000 on the 500 acres that we were 100 percent responsible for and $325,000 on the other 500 acres. On October 10th, everyone was concerned about the winter frost, so we decided to harvest the crops. On Butch's field, the 2nd harvest yielded an additional 8 dry tons. The feed price dropped from $150 during the summer to $120 per dry ton. Excluding Butch's portion, we spent $17,000 on his field, and the hybrid sorghum value was $36,000, giving us a profit of $19,000. The 1000 acres only yielded 4 dry tons due to the late planting and early winter. On the 500 acres that we 100 percent farmed, we spent $430,000 and the hybrid sorghum value was $240,000. We lost $137,500. On the partnered 500 acres, we spent $330,000, and the hybrid sorghum value was $240,000. Since we had agreed to profit-split the 3rd, our portion was $160,000, and we lost $170,000. Our test farming for 2007 resulted in a loss of over $450,000 due to an error to plant late in the season. We also paid the KSU license, rented office space, bought insurance, paid salaries and other expenses, resulting in a combined loss of $900,000. Butch's field was the silver lining to the thunderstorm of losses. We revised our model: assuming we planted the entire 1,000 acres in April, we projected a profit of over $1.7 million based on a yield of 12 more tons per acre. We encouraged each other there was a valid business model here. We lost money for farming so late, but we were excited and working on gearing up for next March.

During the first year, I followed Sean and Butch's suggestions, but I wanted to collect some data. So I placed markers throughout the field, testing soil and crop performance. Sean would always chime in with, "This isn't rocket science. Why are you paying an additional $100 per month for testing?"

Chapter 24

Things You Don't Know You Don't Know

Ping! My email messages were coming in at a snail's pace. For some reason, I was being trolled by timeshares. The idea of a timeshare would have been nice, but the markets were taking a turn for the worse. By the end of 2008, the capital markets were on the verge of collapse. Lehman Brothers had levered or borrowed significant monies taking risks in the housing-related assets. Although highly profitable during a boom market, a downturn of 5 percent would eliminate the entire book value. It resulted in the largest bankruptcy in US history. That bad news was followed in December with the collapse of and the arrest of Bernard Madoff. The Madoff investment scandal defrauded thousands of investors of billions of dollars. I was sad to hear the news and realized the impact that it would have on my friends, past clients and the folks at Billings, Day and Knight. I was also relieved that I was not going to have to deal with that mess. We had lost close to $1 million, but there was light at the end of the tunnel. By November, Bill and I were convinced that we needed to farm on a minimum of 5,000 acres. The cost to farm was $5 million. If we planted correctly, with the expected yields, we should expect a profit of $4 million. We had $1.5 million in our account and were short about $4 million to execute this plan. Bill looked at me and asked, "Do you believe in this project?"

"Of course I do," I replied.

"Let's go big or go home," Bill said confidently. "I'll put up $3 million more if you can you come up with $1 million."

I shouldn't have answered so quickly. Bill had made $200 million in SocMedia. His total $5 million only represented 2 percent of his total net worth. I had $1 million in liquid assets and a home valued at $1 million. If I put in $1 million more that would be 50 percent of my total net worth. I was on the front line. I wanted to walk the walk, and I was comfortable with the business plan. So, right or wrong, I went big.

In the middle of December, I received a message from the storage unit where I had stored my mementos. There had been an explosion, and a fire had broken out, destroying many units, including mine. I quickly called back and asked the lady about my particular property and if it was a total loss. She sounded tired from what I can only assume was a result of calling all of their customers and answering their questions about the explosion and their personal property in the storage units. She responded politely, saying, "You have 5 days to come down and inspect the unit and collect the items that you want to keep. Afterward, we will clean up and trash everything else."

I immediately drove back to Atlanta to assess the damage and see if anything was salvageable. It was a total loss. Everything had burned to ashes. My Robert Graham shirts, the suits, all the clothes, sports memorabilia, stamp collection, coin collection, diplomas, yearbooks, transcripts, letters, all my pictures, furniture – and the list went on and on. I didn't want to believe the news. This was a nightmare. I was stone-faced and unemotional. Randi, Jean, Jules, and Caroline cried for me, but for me, it was all surreal. I took pictures and recorded the loss, but my mind dutifully protected me from the truth. This had been my life, and now it was gone.

As I sifted through the ashes and smoke-damaged items, I found a red box. Inside was a Cartier watch that I had purchased in 2000 to celebrate my academic achievements. Later, I had replaced that with a Rolex Submariner. The Rolex had an entirely different meaning. It reflected the years of excess. This Cartier watch, however, signified all the achievements from hard work and determination. As I continued rummaging through the debris, a light bulb came on. This watch would be a symbol incorporating all of the past worldly possessions that I once had that were now lost in the fire. Lost in a material sense but not forgotten. It would become my physical reminder to view the silver lining in everything because the glass, at whatever level, is that percentage full. Depending on the angle and the dimension, my watch contained various numbers, reflections, and recordings from the past. Every time I looked at it, I was reminded to be mindful of the present and hopeful for the future. With the watch, I came to terms with the loss. Awareness gained, my mind suddenly returned to the comments Hope had made at the beginning of the year. Fire. Ashes and a phoenix rising.

Between the insurance check for my property and the selling of stock and mutual funds, I was able to secure my $1 million portion for our farming venture. KSU only had enough seed in storage for us to farm on 2,000 acres. We needed to commence seed production in the Dominican Republic by late December if we wanted any chance to farm on 5,000 acres by April 2009.

Bill and I flew to Santiago to meet with the locals. Dr. Friedman introduced us to LatinSeed, a seed production company and our only heart-line in the Dominican. Time was of the essence. Although we could have negotiated a slightly better deal, it was important to commence seed production. We needed to ship male and female plants to LatinSeed and secure land and equipment. We agree to the $3 per pound, a cleaned and treated deal. We were farming on the border of the Dominican Republic and Haiti. The hotel was 1-star and lacked hot water. Bill and I did not know what we were getting ourselves into until we were knee-deep. LatinSeed paid their Haitian farmers $8/day and Dominican farmers $10/day.

The pay surprised both of us, so we agreed to budget an additional $9,000: $900 for each of the 6 employees, to be paid in monthly installments, and the remainder for lunch every day during the 3-month period. Productivity during the first 2 days was sluggish, but once they realized that we were providing healthy meals daily, productivity increased. At the end of the month, I called all 6 of the employees and handed each of them $300. They didn't know how to react. That was the most money they had ever made in a day. I told them to keep up the good work, and we would reward them with $300 each at the month's end if everyone worked together as a team. Throughout the week, groups of farmers would stop by to visit. While visiting, they would inquire if we needed more help with our crops. On the 15th day, I noticed a woman on the farm. One of the workers introduced her to Bill and me as his wife. He had gotten married recently. I congratulated him and handed him $50. At 7:00 p.m. as the sun was beginning to set, a group of 25 Haitian farmers wielding machetes approached our field. The Dominican farmers in our group had shotguns. All I heard was yelling in Spanish, Creole, and French. Bill and I were afraid somebody might get shot, or there would be a fight involving machetes. I grabbed one of the Dominican farmers and asked, "What is going on?"

He explained, pointing to the other side of the field, "That girl was promised to that man over there, but a broker rerouted her to the man who just got married."

I had no idea about farming, but I was a master negotiator. Naturally, I walked into the mix. I started with "Unless everyone puts away their machetes, I will never hire anyone here on any of our projects." Since we paid the most and treated everyone with respect, everyone put away their weapons. I learned that our friend

194

paid a broker $50 as a bride wealth payment to secure a wife from Haiti. I asked him, "Do you like your new wife?"

He replied, "Yes. I've been saving for years. It gets lonely at night. I like her much more than my hand, and she has mad oral skills." Everyone laughed at his comment. I could relate. Oral skills were most definitely worth fighting for. Then I turned to the 24 people on the other side of the fence.

"How many of you guys are single?" Ten hands went up. "Remind me never to shake your hands again." We all laughed. I figured group peer pressure would work. I offered everyone $10, which was more than a day's pay, to consider this matter closed. Naturally, the other 24 people were on our side. I also asked our farmer to give me back the $50 I gave him as a wedding present. I handed that to the aggrieved individual along with another $10. What had started out as a potentially deadly situation was resolved smoothly by me taking control of the situation with calm, reason, and some cash to line the pockets of those offended. It was good to know that my negotiation skills hadn't rusted. Everyone was happy, and we had peace in the fields.

Chapter 25

Better To Be Lucky Than Good

Ping! I received a text message from the Dominican Republic indicating that they had produced 60,000 pounds of seeds. That was enough for 15,000 acres. Our cost was $240,000 including freight charges. Our strategy was to farm in Arizona, Kansas and New Mexico. These were locations with lots of dairy and cattle. The plan was for 3,000 acres in Kansas, 1,000 acres in Arizona and 1,000 acres in New Mexico with 50 percent of the fields irrigated and the remaining 50 percent dry farming. By April, we were on schedule and had planted on time, spending only $4 million. We had about $260,000 to cover salaries, office, and any emergencies.

With that settled, I came to realize that I had to part with my S-500 as it was not conducive to or effective for farming. The dust, the crops, and the mud were all wreaking havoc on the engine, and the rough dirt and gravel roads tore up the paint. I loved that car. It was a part of who I am. Well, who I was. So I drove her down to the local dealership and traded her in for a new F-150 Lariat LE. It had all the comforts that I had become accustomed to as well as a rugged exterior that could take whatever it came across. Kind of like me. I had now transitioned from lawyer to farmer. A stylish farmer but still a farmer.

Our irrigated lands were on track in performance, but our dry farms were suffering. We had not accounted for the worst drought in American history. Although all the other dry farming crops were dying due to stress, our crop was drought tolerant. It didn't die, but it wasn't going to grow tall either. We decided to harvest our irrigated fields in the 3 states by July. Each harvest averaged approximately 6 tons. In turn, we generated $1.8 million in revenues. Harvesting costs were double due to the rising fuel costs. Initial investment in those fields was $2 million, and we made back $1.4 million. Harvest from the dry farm fields could not be achieved. We made an equal $2 million investment and became nervous. By October the results were in: another 6 tons on the irrigated and a total of 2 tons on the dry farms. Farm costs reached $4 million, and harvesting costs came in at $1.3 million. Total cost was $5.3 million. Revenues were $3.6 million from irrigated and $600,000 from the dry farm. Total revenues, $4.2 million. Altogether, a loss of $1.1 million from farming and an additional $400,000 in administrative expenses. We had lost another $1.5 million and had $2.5 million to spend the following year. My investment to date was $1.1 million and my share $625,000, or a loss of $475,000. I was deferring a salary until we made money, so this setback had a double negative effect on me.

I visited Butch and Sean to get feedback on the farming lessons learned. We decide to party at the Veterans of Foreign Wars (VFW) Post #7271. It was your typical VFW bar, complete with smoke-yellowed walls, covered in memorabilia about wars from long ago to items fresh from the front. Most of the patrons sitting at the bar were in some way still fighting those wars; others were trying to forget. I mentally chuckled when I remember a line from the movie *The Breakfast Club* when John, played by Judd Nelson, starts to criticize Brian's choice of clubs with, "So it's sorta social. Demented and sad but social. Right?"

Butch started in with another round of "Let's Bash Sam" as our drinks arrive.

"What the hell was the drought all about?" He took a long drink of a national beer and continued, "Sam, I've never seen one like that in all my 15 years of farming. Have you, Sean?"

"Hell, no! It has got to be Sam, the city slicker lawyer gone farmer. That there's proof that Mother Nature doesn't like lawyers." Butch and Sean had a good laugh and continued to play around with the idea that Mother Nature had placed a drought in the area to spite me.

A few beers in, though, Sean shook his head and said, "I have to admit, those damn cows are picky eaters, and they sift through all the other feed to eat your shit."

"Can I swing by tomorrow and see for myself what you are talking about?"
Sean didn't want to talk about work anymore. He was all about getting drunk and chasing women. He asked, "Where's that smokin hot Amy, Sam?"

I grimaced at the thought of Amy, but answered simply, "We broke up because she was seeing multiple guys."

"Can I get her number? She's smoking hot!"

"I would give it to you, but she only dates Asian guys."

"Sam, if I look into the sun, I can look a little Asian."

I laughed. "I think she is a little too crazy for your blood."

"Sam, all girls are a little cray cray," He said, moving his pointer finger in a small circle near his temples. "I'm dating this really hot girl, but she texts and calls me like 15 times a day."

"Sean, I don't do needy unless there is a real emergency," I said as I took a sip of my beer and leaned back in the chair. "My rules of engagement are reasonable and mellow 360 days a year with 5 days of drama allowed. Be careful not to escalate, or the drama will be justified, Sean."

"Sam, I can handle all the drama so long as there are rewards. The more drama she provides, the more chunks I'm going to knock off."

Sean consistently used the term "knocking off a chunk" when referring to sex. "Sean, so what is the going exchange rate for cray cray and sex?"

"So, 3 days of cray cray converts to 1 night of sex, but the variables could change. Like that girl you brought, Amy. She could cray cray all year long, and I would be smiling." He paused with a big grin creating deep, sun-leathered lines. Then he stopped, tilted his head and continued, "But this girl I'm dating right now… 3 days of cray cray seems like a fair deal."

"Sean, you are so risk-averse when it comes to farming, I don't get this. That kind of cray cray risk clearly outweighs any benefits for me. It would be too painful to be in such a dramatic relationship. Are you sure that you aren't related to my friend Craig? You 2 have more in common than you realize!"

The next day, I showed up bright and early. I noticed a lot of birds flying overhead. Sean and Butch put out straw to feed the cows and they nibbled at it. Then they pulled the hybrid sorghum out and the cows didn't just nibble, they began to eat in earnest. The guys then mixed our sorghum with other sorghum and straw. Amazingly, the cows sifted through the different types of food and ate our sorghum first. They then proceeded to eat the other sorghum, but only after waiting to see if we would add more of the hybrid. "Butch, that was pretty educational. Hey, did you always have lots of birds on your land?"

Sean said, "Don't mention the birds. It is a sore spot for Butch. He thinks they are the reason he will lose money this year. Damn birds eat all the crops and animal feed. Have you ever shot at any birds, Sam?"

"Me? Never. I don't own a gun, much less know how to shoot one."

"Come by around 5:00 p.m. and let's drink some beers and go bird hunting."

"Butch, the early bird, gets the worm, and the late one gets shot! Sure, I'll try anything once."

Five o'clock rolled around, and Sean handed me a shotgun and gave me a quick tutorial. I had heard stories about shotguns and felt sorry for the birds, thinking that they had no chance. Butch and Sean fired and hit a bird apiece. I fired and hit the air. I tried again and again. Same result: air. By the 5th round, Butch and Sean were laughing hysterically.

Sean commented, "Can't teach common sense. Sam couldn't hit an elephant with that shotgun."

Butch finally said, "I'm better off letting the birds steal my feed than have Sam try to stop them because I'd be wasting money on the bullets. Sam can't hit the target out on the farm."

The guys had a nice laugh at my expense. I didn't mind, though. This world was a lot simpler than the one I was used to. It was interesting how I had transformed from Mr. GSD to Mr. KOD.

Sean would continually point out the fact that Mr. KOD was collecting data again. "Hey, Butch, there goes Sam again looking professorial. He could be drinking more beer and chasing women if he stopped doing research."

Finally, by year 3, I had enough data to support my findings. "So Butch and Sean, I noticed that your soil salinity pH went from 8+ to 6 in the course of 2 years."

"Sam, please speak English to me. We know what low, high and balanced mean, but what do the numbers mean?"

"I am a numbers guy. Your soil pH is balanced. I think you are going to have a bumper crop this year. Also, based on the data, we don't need to use as much NPK to achieve similar results. You'll save thousands."

Sean looked at Butch. "Well, damn, I told you that Sam knew what he was doing. That professorial shit really works." Sean and I had developed a friendship over the years. I learned how to turkey and beaver hunt. I was never able to actually catch or kill an animal, but I had become "one of the guys." They forgot about the flip flops and RG- wearing city lawyer. I became known as the professorial farmer. I also got to know most of the folks in town.

Before working here, when people asked me if I had traveled a lot in the US, I said yes. My perspective was skewed. My view of America was seen through the lens of a city boy. Living and working here was a true eye opener. This was the heartland of America where folks left their keys in the car ignition or cup holder, and doors were almost always unlocked. This was a good wholesome town, where people said good morning and good evening even to strangers, and a handshake was more binding than the 4 corners of a contract. We took pictures throughout the 3 years as evidence that I was a real-life farmer. The early ones were quite different from the later ones. The later ones depicted that smile. A lifetime of friendships had indeed been forged.

The farm life had eaten up a lot of my time. I had become a horrible brother and friend, only touching base with Jean, Jules, Randi, and Caroline on an annual basis, forgetting birthdays and holidays. I was obsessed with making this venture successful. I *needed* this venture to be successful. Bill and I regrouped. We studied the data, and the numbers didn't lie. Dry farming was the reason for our loss. We needed to shift our focus to irrigation farming exclusively. We had 40,000 pounds of seed in storage and decided to double down in 2010 with only irrigated fields. If we had

∞

solely focused on the irrigated fields, we would have made at least $2 million. I agreed with the revised plan and sold my house, netting only $600,000 because of the housing market pullback, and invested it all in this project. Bill added his prorated portion of $1.8 million. Bill had tripled down, and I was all in.

I traveled throughout Kansas, Arizona and New Mexico to secure only irrigated fields. Prices had increased for irrigated land due to the recent drought. Accordingly, our cost would increase by $200 per acre. That was a price Bill and I were willing to pay to mitigate against the event of a drought. We had barely enough to farm on 5,000 acres. Our cost was $5 million, and we planted in April. We followed all the planting protocols, and things were on course. Finally, we had worked out the kinks and begun to turn the corner. By June, our crops were 15 feet tall, and we were getting ready to harvest. When I asked about feed prices, I was anticipating them to be in the $100-$120 range. I was told by all 3 markets that, due to high feed prices in the past 2 years, there had been overplanting in Brazil and Ukraine this year, resulting in a glut and subsequent drop in price to $70/ton. We had budgeted $3 million on the low end, but the reality was $2 million. I became concerned because our growing cost was $5 million and our harvest cost was close to $1 million each time. With 12 tons per acre at the current price of $70/ton, we would gross $4 million, resulting in a $3 million loss for the year.

That was the most likely scenario, but things could get worse, and they did. The harvesters in July had accidentally damaged some of the crops on 2,000 acres, so our regrowth would likely be less than the projected 6 tons. At the end of October, we averaged a total of 10 tons/acre on the fields and sold the feed at $70/ton. Revenues were $3.5 million, and costs were $7 million. We lost $3.5 million in 2010. At the end of the day, we had $1.6 million in our accounts. Bill waved the white flag, and we split up in November. I had $400,000. Butch was right; I couldn't hit a target in farming.

It was mid-November. The stress of the past 3 years, travel, and a loss of over $1.5 million caused me to wake up with paralysis of the face. I had never experienced such a thing. I could barely talk. Alarmed, I called the emergency room, and they told me that I had either suffered a stroke or had Bell's palsy. I knew what a stroke was, and that wasn't good, but I had no idea what Bell's palsy was. It sounded bad, so I looked it up on the internet. Bell's palsy is defined as a one-sided facial nerve paralysis. The cause is unknown. I was prescribed antibiotics along with steroids. The doctor suggested that I purchase a transcutaneous electrical nerve stimulation ("TENS") device to stimulate my facial nerves through electric current. I told Bill of my physical condition, and he suggested that I contact Craig.

"Craig had Bell's palsy years ago and was treated in China by a healing monk," he said with concern.

My life had been upside-down for a while. I needed a little peace of mind right now, so I texted Craig and told him about my situation. Craig responded, *I need to contact my friends in China. I will get back to you soon.*

I looked in the mirror. Wow, there really is a basement under the floor. Who would have imagined? Healthwise, I was out of shape. I didn't care. I had insurance and no real medical issues other than being slightly overweight. Now, I had this Bell's palsy thing. I couldn't talk or eat properly. My smile was off, and it wasn't clear if this condition would be permanent. About 4 years ago, I was on top of the world. The only worries I had were whether my practice group would hit $10 million in revenues. If I was wrong, it didn't matter; Billings, Day and Knight got paid, and I got paid. I stayed at the finest hotels and ate at the fanciest restaurants. I didn't think it was excessive and didn't appreciate the luxury. Funny how everything changes. Well, not funny. Sad, really.

For the past 3 years, I hadn't made any money. I spent a lot of money and lost a lot of money. I drove everywhere and didn't fly because it was too expensive. I even became frugal about hotels. I was no longer staying at 5-star hotels and would often wonder if the 2-star hotel was too expensive. Or I stayed home. Meals were another fall from grace. I became a good cook out of necessity. I used to complain about having only a $200-per-person dinner budget. Now I was excited to dine at a $40-per-person restaurant. The 3 years had grounded me. I felt bad and looked worse. I felt that I couldn't face Jean, Randi, and Jules, much less Caroline. I was feeling sorry for myself but who could blame me? Had life killed a dream I had once lived? Who would love me? I was physically impaired, financially unsound, and emotionally lost. I was a wreck, and I knew it.

Craig called and said, "I can get you in to see the monk, but you need to stay for 90 days." He listened for my response and seemed unsure if I was still there or if the call had dropped.

"Sam, you still there?" I gave a half-assed sigh and thought, How am I going to pay for all that? Craig continued, "This Healer is 1 of 2 monk healers. He is very difficult to access. The cost will be $100,000. That will cover room, board, transportation and translator. Do you want to do that?"

"A, uh, $100,000?!" How was I going to swing that now? I exhaled. I've got to regroup, I told myself. This is about my health and getting back into life again. I breathed in deeply and exhaled slowly.

"Yes," I said, not as emphatic as I could have been, but I was beginning to think that my luck was about to change.

"I can pay for it, Sam, just write me a check when you return." He paused and then quickly added, "or whenever you can."

I often joked about Craig and his propensity for all things naughty, but he truly was a good guy. He made you wonder about his choices. And he often said that he'd rather be lucky than good. I laughed at the thought of that. Wouldn't we all?

I refocused and heard him going over some more details about the temple. "Oh, and by the way," he warned, "you get 1 bag and no cell phones. Make sure you follow the orders. That monk still scares me to this day."

Chapter 26

Time Heals All

I printed pictures of Mom, Jean, Randi and Caroline, packed lightly, and included a deck of cards for entertainment since there would be no TV, radio or civilization. I was going from city to farming to meditation. Before I left, I mailed my watch to Caroline with a note.

> *I am entrusting you with the only meaningful possession I own. I'm okay, but I have some health issues to attend to. Will be gone for 90 days or longer. I want to see you in person, but time is of the essence. Please keep this watch safe and think of me every time you look at it, as I will be thinking of you. I am sorry that I am not present in person to support you, but know that I am mindfully thinking of you from afar. Look forward to spending time with you when I return. Your friend, Sam.*

With that, I was off to China. The flight was long but uneventful and to prove just how much I had changed, I didn't flirt with any of the flight attendants. I landed in Beijing and was greeted by Mr. Yang. As I walked outside the terminal and into city life again, I was accosted by the smog. It burned my eyes and nostrils, and I tried taking shallow breaths. I noticed the countless people, many with hospital masks, hurrying into buildings that were almost as gray as the sky. As we walked further into the city, I noticed a small flower that had pushed its way through a crack in the pavement between the curb and the road. It didn't sadden me. In fact, I mentally rejoiced at the balls it took for the flower to take on the city. *Life will find a way*. It wasn't the flower's gumption. It wasn't fighting. It was surviving with the hand that it was dealt.

Was this who I was now? Take away the smog and this city would resemble any major US city. The world hadn't changed or sped up; I had slowed down.

We caught a train to Hubei, and from there we rode a bus for 5 hours. There was no small talk or any conversation, for that matter, during that whole time. It suited me, and I was glad that Mr. Yang was a man of few words. We checked into a humble hotel, and Mr. Yang said, "Rest." That was it. If that was a harbinger of things to come, well, I might be in for a bigger shock than I had planned.

The next day required us to hike up Mount Wudang for 10 hours. Then we rested in a temple. The Wudang Mountains are a range of mountains in the northwestern part of Hubei. They were stunning, home to a famous complex of Taoist temples and monasteries renowned for the practice of Tai Chi and Taoism.

The next morning we hiked another 10 hours and finally arrived at our destination. Simple structures provided basic shelter and paled in comparison to the nature surrounding us. I closed my eyes and breathed deeply. Upon opening them, the landscape seemed... brighter and more vivid. There were many monks at the temple, but only 8 of them were in constant contact with me. There were also many patients, both elderly and young, with varying issues. Mr. Yang attracted my attention. He had walked on and was a good 30 meters away. I caught up, careful not to trip on the uneven road. He showed me to my room, turned, and walked away. No words. I guessed none were needed. I placed my belongings in the room and tried to settle in. It was winter and freezing in the mountains. I didn't notice the cold while we were hiking, but it was noticeable now.

My very first meeting with the Healer was outside on the walkway. The walkway was simple but artfully crafted over a waterway that was now foggy due to the evening change in weather.

The Healer told me to undress and proceeded to push me into the water. The water was ice cold, and I was sore everywhere.

"Where does it hurt?" he asked scornfully.

"Everywhere," I replied with more whininess than I had counted on.

"For someone as young as you, you are in bad health. Money isn't everything." I watched as he jumped into the stream and did exercises for 10 minutes without shivering.

"My circulation very good," he explained.

He was being humble. His circulation was actually amazing. His theory was babies have great circulation, so they seldom bruise. "When you have poor circulation due to old blood you tend to bruise more." With that, he got out and walked away. I quickly got out too, but I wondered what I was supposed to do next. Just then one of the monks came to take me to my room. When I arrived, what looked like a dinner was waiting.

The next morning the Healer informed me of his expectations. After the first week: "A hundred squats, a hundred pushups, 6-mile hikes, 2 hours of meditation, 100 shoulder exercises and 2 hours with pillows under your back." I couldn't even do 20 of any of the above, so I needed to start getting into shape.

He took me by the arm and said, "Please lay on the floor so I can work on your circulation." His strength was indescribable. He palpitated each pressure point with precision. After an hour of what seemed to be 10 hours of torture, he selected a cup, spread a lotion made from plant extracts onto my back, and started to rub my back with the cup. The friction from the cup caused suction, and the cup just hung there, filled with smoke. His assistant explained, "Cupping is an ancient form of therapy in which suction is induced on the skin. Suction is created by using heat, with the belief that it will mobilize the blood flow to promote healing."

I nodded as I bit my tongue. That was the most pain I had experienced. Ever. And gobs and gobs of dark, jelly-looking blood poured out of my body and into the cup. The Healer also administered acupuncture, inserting 108 needles in my face. I looked like Pinhead from *Hellraiser*. Clearly, I was less threatening. I laughed silently and then it occurred to me that 108 was a significant number. I remembered… Hope springs eternal. Hope had mentioned the significance of 108 the last time we spoke. I am not sure this was what she meant, but I continued to endure the feeling of being a live pincushion. The next day, I was extremely sore and tired. I noticed the bruises all over my body. The exercising, meditation, hiking, blood removal, and acupuncture continued for weeks.

By the 3rd week, China was in the peak of the winter season, but I was no longer cold. I was still struggling with the 100 units of exercises but was gradually getting there. I could sense the nerves in my face. I spent my free time playing with my deck of cards. I would wake up every morning to check my notepad. I could see new words. "Get it done" and "Car." I was happy but confused. I would catch myself staring at the picture of Mom and Dad with their Mona Lisa smiles. Jean and her kids and their Mona Lisa smiles, and my picture with Caroline and our Mona Lisa smiles. During my hours of meditation, I would focus on the things that were important to me growing up. I became aware of how things had started to blur. I had fed the status quo and the material lifestyle for an extended period of time, and they had begun to eat away at the most important values of meaningful relationships, family, and friends. I was chasing a dream, and that dream didn't care about me. Work should be a means to an end, not the end itself.

By the 2nd month, my body was healed, but I still had to work on my mind and soul. I decided to stay an extra month for long-term clarity and a complete cleansing. Craig was right. This place was difficult, but all the players in the orchestra came together in concert to bring me back to health and back to life: Tai Chi, the exercises and the treatments for my body, the walks stimulating my endorphins, the meditations for the calming of my mind and spirit.

Sometimes the student becomes the teacher. I even found joy in teaching my new friends a Western game. The monks and the Healer were curious about my deck of cards. We played for bowls of rice. Naturally, they only knew how to tell the truth; bluffing was foreign to them. So I won often, but I always returned their bowls of rice for fear of reprisals during the healing one-on-ones.

As I went on my walks, I met with the common folk and farmers in the nearby areas. Everyone knew of the Healer.

One story was about an elderly farmer who was struggling to make ends meet, and was being harassed by a gang of youths. The Healer went down to the farm and waited for the gang to return. He confronted them and said, "Do not ask for things from those that have nothing. Go elsewhere or suffer the consequences." The leader of the gang foolishly attacked the old Healer and was killed instantly. Five members stayed while one ran back to get reinforcements. He returned shortly with 20 others, along with the gang leader. The leader recognized the Healer. The gang leader was an orphan; the Healer had taken him in as a child and given him a 2nd chance at life. The Healer said, "Why do you try to take from those that have nothing? I gave you a 2nd chance when you had nothing. Would you have taken from yourself when you were begging for food?" The gang leader went to his knees and asked the Healer for forgiveness. The Healer said, "Don't ask me for forgiveness. You have burdened this family; you need to help them this year. If there is excess, I'm sure they will pay you." The story goes that 5 members were assigned to assist with the farming during the year.

It reminded me of a story I heard growing up in Japan about an assistant shogun who roamed the country as a peasant to fight corruption and would help the little folks in his travels. Maybe I could help. Since I knew a little about farming, I also knew that soil erosion was becoming a big concern for the average farmer due to the pH imbalance in the soil. I was part Asian, but a complete foreigner in China in more ways than one. I was an American and a former lawyer, a city person to them.

I found it surprising that after a few weeks, there was a true, deep connection between the Chinese monks and myself. The human spirit and love transcended our different paths. The Healer told me on my final day that he only healed people who promised to do something good for society with their 2nd chance. He also said that the monks only kept 25 percent of the $100,000. The rest went to help the orphanages and surrounding farmers. Then he handed me his prayer beads, closing my hand around them, so I knew they were a gift. I realized how special they were to him; I had never seen him without them. He told me that his master had made the string by hand and left it for him upon his passing. He said, "There are 108 beads to remind you of 108 different vices you should avoid." I thanked the Healer and handed him my deck of cards in exchange for the prayer beads.

I walked the 10 hours to the staging ground in complete joy. Then another 10 hours, then a bus back to Beijing and a plane to DC.

As I boarded the plane, I assessed my current status: my face was had fully recovered, I had lost all of my excess weight, and maybe more importantly, I was spiritually content. It was March and time to return to America. I had found myself again.

Chapter 27

Rising From the Ashes

Ping! I checked my messages: hundreds of unopened emails. I had been away for what seemed an eternity. Upon my return, I only had $100,000 remaining in my account. I didn't want to go back to to Atlanta because I knew too many folks there. The likelihood of running into someone from my former life was extremely high. I decided to move to Vienna, Virginia. I guess a part of me wanted to know that I would be close to my friends Randi, Joe, and Caroline. I had gone from being a workaholic lawyer to a workaholic farmer to near hermit status, isolated from civilization. Intermittently, I would receive text messages from Jean, Randi, and Caroline wondering how I was doing. Surprisingly, even Amy sent me messages. What should I do? All these guys are hitting on me? Or the random Do you think I look sexy in this dress? I miss pitching to you! I didn't reply to Amy nor did I want to. I did want to respond to Jean, Randi, and Caroline, but I was too embarrassed. What could I say? They might get all freaked out too. Silence is golden. Or is it no news is good news?

I had not prepared a resume in over 10 years. I drafted one but needed to dumb it down somewhat because I knew I would be overqualified for the corporate paralegal position that I was applying for. It was a small firm located off the orange line. They offered me the job at $70,000 a year. I shared an office with Cheri, an ambitious 20 - year-old. Her plans were to work her way through college and attend law school afterwards. She reminded me of myself when I was 20. There were 2 senior partners, a junior partner, 5 associates, 3 paralegals, and 4 legal assistants. I was in my own simplified world.

Newly baptized, I woke up at 5:00 a.m., walked for an hour and a half, did tai chi for 30 minutes, showered, dressed and then went off to work at SmallFirm from 8:00 a.m. to 6:00 p.m. After my daily ritual, I would head home for exercises, meditation, and sleep. Gradually, my days at SmallFirm became challenging. I was inundated with a lot of busy work. I was asked to review and revise all the documents and mentor new attorneys. In my previous life, I had stopped mentoring attorneys by my 4th year of practice. I rationalized that it was an inefficient use of my time. At SmallFirm, I was working with 3rd year and 6th year attorneys who needed some help. In my former capacity as a partner, they would have been ecstatic to be mentored by me. I was certain my comments would be received differently as a paralegal. I felt like the assistant shogun who had concealed his identity to help the underdog. By the 4th month, I had made numerous comments, common knowledge, and materiality comments.

After all I had been through, I had determined that my health was a priority. My choice of work facilitated that commitment. In comparison to Billings, Day and Knight, SmallFirm did not require any heavy lifting on my part, but old habits die hard. I was reviewing a set of documents when I noticed a big mistake. The structure of the transaction was a reverse triangular merger. They desired a tax-free reorganization. The non-stock consideration was greater than 20 percent of the total, which would blow the tax-free reorganization. I made sure to copy the partner on the transaction for fear that the associates would miss this important aspect of the deal. Three hours later, all 3 partners and both associates came knocking on our door. Cheri looked at me nervously and exclaimed, "Oh my!" She was always nervous around any of the partners.

The senior partner approached me and said, "Those were very impressive comments, Sam. Have you thought about joining the firm as an attorney? I remember your resume stated that you attended Duke. You would have to pass the Virginia Bar, of course. In the meantime, we would like to promote you to corporate expert and pay you $100,000, effective immediately."

Everyone congratulated me. I thanked them but said that due to recent health concerns, I preferred to maintain a balanced life. "I appreciate the offer, but I would like to stay in my current capacity until I fully recover."

After the partners and associates had left, Cheri was incredulous. "Uh, hello, Sam!… what were you thinking? That was your golden ticket to be somebody. People don't get a golden ticket every day, and what do you do? You decline. I've never met anyone like you before. Are you sure there is any intelligence in that brain of yours?"

I laughed. "Cheri, you don't understand. I have traveled a long road, and I am looking for a quiet life with the least amount of stress possible."

After that day, Cheri started to open up more about herself. She was the eldest of 2, and distrusted men because her father was never around. Her goal was to make something of herself. She was going to take care of her mother and brother. Cheri would constantly tell me that I would be perpetually single if I didn't socialize more.

"Guys need to continue to improve their social status by progressively moving up the corporate ladder," she scolded. Little did she know that I was there 5 years ago. "I should set you up with my mom. You guys would make a good couple," she said with amusement.

I smiled. "That is very sweet of you, Cheri, but I'm focusing on my health and don't have much time for anything else. Besides your mom would never date a paralegal, and her daughter would never approve."

There were several attempts to get me to join in the reindeer games and various social events, but I always graciously declined. That didn't stop Cheri from inviting me.

"The office is going out for happy hour this Thursday. Want to join us?"

"Thanks but no thanks," I replied with a smile.

"If you aren't doing anything for Thanksgiving, you can come over to our house. My mom is an awesome cook."

"Thanks, Cheri, but that's more than 30 days from now. I've probably got plans."

By mid-October, all the associates were coming by the office asking me to review their documents and discuss negotiating strategies for their deals. Cheri was a real estate paralegal. She worked on real estate investment trusts or REITS. REITs are companies that own and operate income-producing properties such as commercial buildings, apartments, warehouses, hospitals, shopping centers and hotels. It was 3:00 p.m., and she was noticeably annoyed, confused and lost. I could hear her mumbling, "Why is this deal still here? I've been researching for months and don't really understand the subject matter or substance of the documents."

I interjected, "Hey, Cheri, maybe I can help?"

"Sam, you know everything. All the attorneys say it. They can't believe you don't want to be a partner here because they say you know more than anyone." She handed me the sheet. "It is a term sheet with code names written on it. In a nutshell, 3 different

∞

investors plan to invest $20 million total, in phases, based on milestones, into an existing company. The company is a phytoremediation company that uses living plants to clean up contaminants in soil. We will retain 60 percent and the investors 40 percent if the first test is successful. It involves land remediation testing of cesium, technetium and heavy metals."

"Cheri, you won't believe me, but I was a farmer for 3 years, and I know a little bit about what they are talking about. But they use code names and are very cryptic regarding investors and company. What is the target date for the deal?"

Cheri flipped through the pages. "After Thanksgiving."

"Great; we have time. Let me work on it after Halloween, and I can give you a more definitive answer." It was October, which in my sequential conversion was an "I." Time for Mr. GSD to roll up his sleeves to be "Impactful" and "Involved."

∞

Chapter 28

Strengthening the Soul

I turned off all my forms of communication, minus my email, the week of Halloween. I didn't want to be bothered. I was looking for my place of solitude. I planned to visit the monuments and memorials. I wanted to thank those who served, personally, for the sacrifices they made for our country. As I walked along the path, I remembered growing up on Okinawa. I reminisced about Mom and the Ba-Ba-Ri coat; Jean and her kids playing rock, paper, scissors; Joe's wedding; Randi's wedding; my time at Billings, Day and Knight; my encounter with Hope; my Wudang friends; my mentee Cheri; and of course, Caroline. I was reflecting on the past and searching for direction for the future. I laughed. I remembered Hope telling me to find my patience. I guess I had finally found it.

Upon leaving China, I had made a promise to my Healer that I would do something good for society with my 2nd opportunity. I was at a loss. I kept searching but found no answers. Hope had predicted the last 3 years very accurately. It might be good to schedule an appointment with Hope before the New Year. I thought, Maybe it would be best if I started by taking baby steps and find some small good deeds I can work towards. I was mulling my options.

I remember hearing once that there are no mistakes in life. Maybe I was destined to help Cheri. No adult male had been reliable for Cheri. She was angry at her father and had vowed never to be dependent on a man to succeed in this world. Why not surprise her with a complete and definitive agreement when she returned on Monday? I researched phytoremediation, cesium, technetium, and other heavy metals. I dove in. "Hmmm... cesium is a soft, silvery-gold metal with atomic number 55. It has a half-life of 30 years and would take about 150 years to become safe." I researched more to explain the half-life. I find some articles to put it into perspective for me:

> *...the 1986 Chernobyl accident site should be clear of cesium around 2116. The cesium is generally found in the top two to three inches of the soil.*
>
> *Technetium is a light element and is produced synthetically, with a half-life of hundred and eleven thousand years. It follows water and could be fifteen to twenty feet under the surface soil. Heavy metals, such as cadmium, mercury, and lead, are highly toxic. Most are found four to eight feet below the surface soil.*

I realized, This is some interesting stuff. I devised a testing protocol to be attached to the draft definitive agreement, extrapolating from my past farming experience as to when to commence the planting, and marking up the documents to include the key elements of agriculture.

I stopped, knowing that this test would be incomplete. I played both sides of the equation. "What are you going to do with the crops once they absorbed the hazardous elements?" I drafted an option of burning them in closed-chamber biomass facilities. These facilities would need to have sensors to detect the elements so that they wouldn't be reemitted into the air. The organic matter would burn, generating electricity and reducing to ash or 5 percent of its original state. My proposal would be to encapsulate the ash and bury it in a coal mine for the duration of the half-life. I realized what the term sheet was requesting, but I feared that $20 million would be too little for the project. It reminded me of the CropFuel issues. I researched soil erosion and discovered that China was losing approximately 1 percent of arable land a year. Crops were unable to grow in high pH environments, due to salinity. Much like I was shown when I was in Hubei. I prepared a 2nd protocol with a 3-year plan to balance pH in lands for better utilization. I was in need of more information, and it was a holiday weekend. I worked 12 hours each day, and I still managed to meditate, walk and exercise.

Monday arrived, and Cheri returned stressed and disappointed. It was typical for lawyers and legal assistants to be stressed out. The legal field is pretty demanding, but from Cheri's face, I could tell her emotions were boiling over; she just couldn't take it anymore. "My dad is such a jerk, and I am a fool for thinking he could be anything more than what he is! He was supposed to meet me for coffee and dessert on Sunday." She grabbed a cup, poured herself some coffee and plopped down next to me. "He was a no show. I should have known better," Cheri sighed and shook her head. A pained grimace took the place of her usually brilliant smile. "He has been AWOL since July, and I thought maybe, just maybe, we could discuss what had happened to him." Tears began to well up in her eyes.

I felt compelled to reach out and comfort her. "Everything is going to work out."

"Why aren't guys more like you, Sam? I mean not just my dad, but men in general?"

"Looks are deceiving, Cheri. I'm equally a jerk. That's why nobody wants to date me."

Cheri gave me a slow punch in the arm. "Haha."

To lighten the conversation, I changed the subject. "Cheri, Trick or Treat? I did a little work over the weekend on the term sheet that you were having trouble with."

Cheri looked at all the exhibits. "Sam, when did you have time to enjoy Halloween?"

"Don't worry, Cheri. The information was a little tricky to decipher, but the treat was well worth it." She smiled. "Now that is what I wanted to see. I also put some time into the definitive agreement and exhibits, but they need another week."

Cheri looked unsure. "That might be tough, Sam. The senior associate is a little antsy."

"Well, we just need to meet with the senior associate and explain the issues to him."

We met with the senior associate to request more time. He looked puzzled but decided to run with what we had found. He wasn't going to wait on anything additional. There was a meeting scheduled with the client for mid-November. Apparently, the client was waiting for a business partner to return but hadn't heard from him in over 6 months. Regardless, they planned to move on the deal by the end of the month.

By November 8, Cheri and I figured out the costs and scenarios for the phytoremediation of soils to balance the pH, remove the cesium, technetium, and heavy metals. We also identified the legal issues, including nuances that would not be in a standard cookie-cutter agreement. The partners were impressed but required multiple days to be debriefed. I told them, "This is Cheri's project; too many people attending the meeting will give the impression that we are overbilling the client." None of us knew who the client was except the senior relationship partner. They were using code names throughout the term sheet and definitive agreement. It was confusing not to be able to put a face to the deal.

Cheri invited me to dinner as a thank you for helping her out and wouldn't accept no for an answer. "You like sushi?"

I perked up. "That is my favorite dish, and I haven't eaten any in over 3 years."

"Please, let me treat you for all the work you have done," she said with a smile.

Over dinner, Cheri and I discussed her life in greater depth. Seeing how she was baring her soul to me, I slowly began to share a little bit about my past. "Once upon a time, I was a pretty good lawyer and decided to get into the business of farming. We made some bad decisions. Along the way, I got really sick, and I've been on the road to recovery ever since."

"What? Did you have cancer or something?"

"Not that bad. Let us just say that I was the cause of my sickness. I am no longer that person and have been newly baptized." I excused myself to the restroom and grabbed the waitress along the way. I handed her my credit card. "I am going to the restroom. Can you please cash us out? I will come back here and sign in a few minutes."

I returned to the table. Cheri saw the waitress and asked for the bill. The waitress told her, "The bill has already been taken care of."

Cheri looked at me. "But Sam, I was supposed to treat you."

"Cheri, your company is payment enough." She gave me a hug and thanked me for restoring her faith in the male gender. It felt good knowing that she could trust me. I believed that that trust could transfer to others in her life, other good men she might meet. I was changing the world, 1 person at a time.

∞

Two days before the meeting, I presented Cheri with a gift. It was a Louie V business card case. "This is your first business meeting, right? You can't go into a client meeting without business cards."

Cheri stared at the card case. "Sam, you are too much!"

"Let's just say I am your guardian angel and am here to guide you through this event." Intently, she listened as I went through the formalities of how to introduce and accept business cards. After I had finished, Cheri's eyes looked a little glazed. "Don't worry; everything will be alright. Go break a leg, Cheri."

The firm was abuzz. There was a large group of people visiting to wrap up the phytoremediation transaction. The buzz continued. Reports that it was a large firm with 3 lawyers, the client and 3 groups of potential investors were circulating the office. Over 12 people sat in the conference room. Looking on as a spectator, I thought.... Man... I really do miss those high-powered meetings. I was both nervous and excited for Cheri. The meeting started at 10:00. A couple of hours passed – and nothing. I wasn't sure if I should leave for lunch. By 1:15, I was famished and had to leave and get something to eat. I ate quickly and rushed back. It was 1:45 and still no movement. I began to look for things to occupy my time.

At 5:15, Cheri appeared in front of my desk. "The senior partner wants you to come to the conference room because everyone has questions about the protocols. We aren't able to explain the protocol in a way that makes everyone comfortable."

"Give me about 5 minutes." I paused and meditated for those 5 minutes and then headed to the conference room. I walked in and saw Mary, Mandy and Debs from Absorb; Suzy from Wireless Tower; Craig from SocMedia; Mark and 2 associates from Billings, Day and Knight; and Bill from the farming venture.

Jaws were agape, and everyone screamed, "Sam Rictov!"

The questions were flying at me.

"Sam, did you know we were meeting today?"

"No."

"Are you a partner here?"

"No."

"Are you advising them?"

"Uhhh, no."

"What have you been doing since March? Everyone has been worried sick."

"I was recovering from some health issues."

"What do you know about this deal?"

"It is very cryptic due to code names."

"We all think Bill is a good guy and great with numbers, but we don't trust his business skills."

"Are you going to be the CEO of this venture?"

"No. Seriously, I've been recovering from some health issues and working here in the meantime."

"Did you draft the protocols?"

"I worked with Cheri on them."

"Should we put $20-$30 million into this deal?"

"Depends on what the deal is. If you are doing phytoremediation and are responsible for the biomass facility, no. You'll need over $400 million. If you are staging this to prove the effectiveness of this means of solving farming problems throughout the world, yes. Possibly. The hybrid sorghum will grow tall, about 15 to 20 feet, so its root systems will go that far too. It can handle the cesium, heavy metals, and technetium, and performs well in sand loam soil under pH levels in excess of 9. It will be a good crop to balance pH in places like China and New Mexico."

Suzy looked at the group as if she was communicating with them telepathically, turned to me and said, "Well, we aren't going to invest unless you run this company, Sam. We'll put in $30 million as a group and own 40 percent of the company. You will get 15 percent, Bill 25 percent, and we'll reserve 20 percent for new employees. We will also pay you $200,000."

I responded, "Thanks for the confidence and the offer, but I need time to think about it. Can we reconvene here on November 28th at 2:00 pm?" I left the conference room and headed to my office. My cover had been blown. In my old life, I would have strategically manipulated the situation and accepted the offer, but I was no longer a 1-dimensional numbers guy. I had evolved into a multidimensional numbers guy. I drafted my resignation letter to the senior partners and asked it to be effective immediately.

Cheri came into the office and closed the door. "Wow, I didn't expect that. You were a partner at Billings, Day and Knight! Everyone at that meeting totally respects you, Sam. I'm so confused. I mean, I'm not confused about why they respect but, well, you know."

"I'm sorry for not telling you everything, Cheri. It is a long story." I expanded on my previous successes, failures, the fire, and my health issues. Everything had come full circle. My eyes began to well up as I felt comfortable enough to let my guard down. This was the first time I could remember that I had opened up to anyone about my life. She hugged and comforted me. "Cheri, I will miss our conversations and mentoring you. Please don't give up on guys. We are not all bad."

Cheri winked and smiled. "Thank you for the Louie V business card case. When Suzy and I exchanged business cards, we both noticed how similar they were. She mentioned that her favorite lawyer in the whole world had given it to her as a gift. Sam, I hope you find what you are looking for. If anyone deserves it, you do. I'll see you on the 28th."

"Cheri, I'm sure our paths will cross again soon."

The 3 partners met, and I was sure it was about me. I walked in and handed them my resignation. They asked, "Would you reconsider and join the firm as a partner?"

I smiled and said, "Thanks, but my legal days are over." I knew I had all the leverage in the world. They wanted to do the deal, and there was a significant probability that I would be the CEO of this new $75-million venture. They didn't want to offend their future boss.

What a turn of events! The ride home was a blur as I did a mental recap. There was 1 person who had been right about more than a few things, and it was time for me to pay her a visit. I went home and packed for a drive to New Orleans. In the past, Hope had shown that she had the gift of predicting events. I had heard her, but I hadn't wanted to listen. This time, I was going to be mindful.

I drove all day to get to New Orleans. Without checking into a hotel, I exercised, meditated, and went straight to Hope of Life. Hope came out of the corner with her big coffee cup. I paid for a 3-hour session, and she pointed to the chair.

"What, no tea?"

"Sam, would you care for something to drink? You seem centered, so I did not offer any this time." Fair enough, I thought.

"Thanks. No, I don't need a drink."

"Why are you here?"

"Hope, you know why I'm here. I just pray that I hear you this time. I want to ask about my future job."

"What is the question?"

"I have an opportunity regarding land remediation via phytoremediation. I'm concerned because I was a farmer for 3 years and failed miserably. What is the likelihood of success?"

She looked around and returned her gaze back to me. "Define success."

"I'm interested in monetary, societal and personal success."

Hope put her cup on the table and straightened the tablecloth. "In regard to money, you will not make a significant amount for 3 years, but I see a silver lining by the 5th year."

"Will we be beneficial to society?"

"Phytoremediation... will you be using crops to clean up land for better use?"

"Yes."

"That would be beneficial to mother earth, the animals, and humans. Personal... you made a promise to the man who returned you to health and provided you with this 2nd chance to do something good."

I spent the next couple of hours discussing my setbacks and the trip to China and how my health was impacted.

"Speaking of health, how is my health?"

"Health is physical, mental and spiritual. Physically, you are in the best shape of your life. Mentally, you are still sharp and analytical. Spiritually, you are meditating often." She smiled. "You are starting to read the Bible and are curious about Christianity. You are starting to become compassionate about other people. Your path has been realigned with your destiny."

I turned to the important people in my life.

"Jules?"

"She is not healthy. You should visit her before April."

"It's that bad?"

"Visit her," she said. Okay.

"Randi?"

"She is expecting." I paused a moment to digest this. I felt a wave of warmth and excitement.

"Debs?"

"She is dating someone seriously."

"Mark?"

"He is nervous about the practice group. He needs some encouragement."

"Jean?"

"Focused on kids and worried about you."

"Caroline?"

"Her ship has sailed. She is divorced and waiting. She keeps staring at a watch. Waiting, infinity, watching. Sam, you don't have to win every battle."

"Finally…"

"Yes, Sam, what is your question?"

"Ice cream?"

"Sam, everything is good in moderation, bad in excess. Always remember, if you want something badly enough, you can always move the mountain to get it. The power has always been within you, Sam. You just have to choose to make it so."

I acknowledged, "Fair enough."

Chapter 29

You Don't Have to Win all the Battles, Just Win the War

Eager to start acting on some of the advice given to me by Hope, I decide to drive back the next day. I stopped in Atlanta and called up Billings, Day and Knight.

"Mark, can you and I meet for lunch at Korean BBQ?"

"Sure, Sam."

I arrived my usual 10 minutes early and was pleasantly surprised to see Mark walking up the sidewalk as I approached. He walked up, smiled, and gave me a firm handshake. I supposed that I hadn't really taken the time to look at Mark or the others when we reunited at SmallFirm. My time with the monks had taught me to be mindful, but the meeting that day had thrown me for a loop. I made it a point to be mindful as he approached. Mark's suit was sharp but not overly stylish. He seemed to have acquired a few more lines on his face, and his hair had more salt than pepper. It was nice to see that I was not the only one who had changed.

It was evident that there was something bothering him. After the hostess sat us at our table and took our order, I wanted to ease Mark's worry.

"Mark, I want you to know, confidentially of course, that I'm leaning toward taking the offer. I would like you guys to keep the representation but plan to throw some business to SmallFirm in DC."

"Thanks, I appreciate the vote of confidence and candor. I've wanted to call you but it never seemed the right time, or I didn't know what to say or how to say it. Things have been rough."

"I know," I offered reassuringly, "for us all. I was in a bad place and couldn't help myself, Mark, much less anyone else. I'm looking forward to reconnecting and working with you and your team. I do have a favor to ask of you, though."

Mark perked up. "Anything. What can I do for you?"

"Please keep an eye on Jules. I don't think her health is good."

"I've been noticing that, Sam."

"Can you check to see what her vacation days look like?"

"Probably pretty good, Sam. She's been wanting to go on a cruise and has been saving them up."

"I'd like to make that happen for her. Let me know what it will cost. I would like to pay for half of it."

"That sounds great. And she's been working pretty hard, so I'd like to cover the other half."

"Do you mind if I offer it to her later today?"

"That works for me."

There was a lot left on my plate. American-sized portions had led to some of my issues in the past, and I didn't want to go back to where I had been. As I listened to Mark, I recalled Hope's words, "Everything is good in moderation and bad in excess."

Mark and I wrapped up lunch with a mutual, "See you on the 28th." He headed off to his next appointment, and I walked to Billings, Day and Knight to see about Jules.

I picked up a hydrangea flower arrangement on my way to see Jules. Mom loved the purple hydrangea plants, and whenever I saw them, it made me smile.

I walked over to Jules' office, flowers in hand, and poked my head in.

"Hey, Jules, remember me? Sam."

∞

Jules looked up from her pile of paperwork. Her smile was the length of the Rio Grande as she jumped up to give me a hug. "It has been so long. I've missed you more than words can express."

"Me too." I handed her the hydrangeas. "These are for you." She took the plant and placed it on the desk as I continued, "Do you have time for coffee?"

Jules eyes sparkled, "Of course I do!"

I shared my experiences over the last 3 years of chaos and explained why I had not been in touch. She told me about what was going on in her life, but she didn't mention any health issues. So I asked, "Do you have a week of vacation time?"

"Yes, Sam. You know me, always planning for a vacation but never taking one. Why?"

"Do you want to go on a cruise with me at the end of November? You may have to go on a 6-day tour."

"Why YES, Of COURSE!!! I've been dying to do that."

"Then it is set! After the 28th, we will go. By the way, it's on Mark and me. We have so much to catch up on." She looked at me skeptically, and I smiled. "It's important to me that I spend some quality time with you in the next 3 months." I'm not sure how Jules felt about our conversation and the impromptu trip with me, but I felt good about it.

As I drove to DC, I called Jean and Debs to catch up and explained my recent absence. I purchased a baby car seat, some generic baby clothing, and headed to Randi and Ron's house. Randi opened the door to greet me. "Sam?" She turned around inside the door and yelled "Ron, it's Sam! Come inside and sit." Randi looked at me frantically. "It's been forever since we talked, BFF. I've been calling everyone to see where you were. How have you been?" She frowned and punched me in the shoulder, "Where have you been?"

∞

But before I could speak, she pushed me into the sitting room, smiled a wildly contagious smile, and demanded that I sit down on the sofa. "I have so much to tell you. Great news…."

I smiled as I looked at her twinkling eyes and glowing skin. Before she could continue, I said, "Congrats on the upcoming child!"

Randi tilted her head to the side and looked at me curiously, "What? How did you know?" Randi looked across at her husband. "Ron, have you been talking to Sam without me?"

I laughed, "A little birdie told me. Sorry for being absent for the past few years."

Just as with so many of my old friendships, the lack of communication was forgiven, and we spent the next couple of hours catching up on my missing years.

To give myself a break, I refocused the conversation back on to the happy couple. "I am so happy that you all are procreating."

Randi gathered some papers and put them on the side table. "If he's a boy, we are calling him Sam. If she's a girl, we'll call her Sammi."

"Your kid is going to need a lawyer to lay claim to more space from you, Randi. Maybe, along the lines of a prenup, a pre-natal?"

"Haha. Very funny!"

Before I left Randi's, I checked my messages and emails. My heart skipped a beat as I noticed one from Caroline.

> *Sam, I have a bone to pick with you, mister. It has been over 3 years since we last talked. Thanksgiving is around the corner, and no matter where you are or what you are doing, I want to be the first to wish you a Happy Thanksgiving. The watch was the sweetest thing. I think you of you every time I*

look at it. I have lots of news to share with you, and I am excited to see you again. Hopefully soon.

I became a little lightheaded. I must have held my breath too long when I read the message. I quickly emailed her back.

Dear Caroline, Your prayers have been heard. I am in the DC area and wonder if you have time to meet tomorrow for a long dinner. Lots to catch up on! Meet me at 6:00 p.m. at the Pentagon City mall. You know where.

I rushed home and gathered the items that I had collected over the years for Caroline, but was unable to give her due to timing. I never got around to writing comments on the postcards much less putting them in the album. But I did have the jewelry box. I asked a jeweler to fix it to my specifications. I knew he must have thought I was a loon. I asked if he could set it so that it would play a piano version of *Beautiful in My Eyes*. He said he could, took the box, and I left the shop.

I was nervous and couldn't wait for the next day to arrive. It had been 22 years or sequentially a "V" since Caroline and I had dated. I wanted to see her soon but needed to work on a business plan, revising test protocols and growth strategies. It was too much to think about, so I did some meditating and went to sleep. It wasn't very restful sleep.

The next morning, I awoke feeling unsteady. I hadn't felt like this in a long time. It was as if I were going on my very first date. I supposed, in a way, I was. Hope had said that Caroline's ship had sailed. Things had changed for her, too.

∞

I made an appointment to get my hair cut at 9:00 a.m. and drop off my one Brioni suit and dress shirt to be pressed. I hadn't worn that suit in nearly 4 years. It was loose from the 25 pounds I had lost, so I asked the woman at the cleaners, "Is it possible to take the pants in? Can you get it finished by today at noon? I'll pay for the rush job, but it must be done by today." I needed to go shopping for a smaller size belt just in case. I was debating on flowers. Would roses come off too strong? Hydrangeas were always perfect for any occasion. I got the hydrangeas. I ran to the jeweler, picked up the box, and put all the magnets from San Francisco, New Orleans, Atlanta, Nashville, DC, Kansas City, Phoenix, Santa Fe, Wichita, Odessa, Manhattan, Lawrence, Larned, Beijing and Hubei into it. I thought, I also need to wrap the jewelry box. It was 10:45 and I was a nervous wreck. To calm my nerves, I decided to get a massage. I emerged from a deep-tissue massage somewhat more relaxed. At noon I rushed back to the dry cleaners and picked up the suit and shirt, drove back to the house and got ready.

I arrived at SmallFirm 30 minutes early and asked for Cheri. "Cheri, do you have time for coffee?"

"Yes. Wow, you surprised everyone at the firm. We all did more research on you and talked to people at Billings, Day and Knight. A $10 million book! You are a rock star attorney."

I laughed and asked if she wanted an autograph. "Actually, Cheri, I was a pretty good lawyer, but it consumed my life, and I needed a change. What did you do for Thanksgiving?"

"I spent time with my family. Mom is single, and I think the 2 of you would make a good couple. Do you want me to set you guys up?"

"Cheri that is sweet of you. The story of my life – a day late and a dollar short. Actually, I reconnected with someone very important to me, and we are going to start dating. I'm all in, but I'm sure you'll be able to find someone wonderful for your mom." I looked at her as I stood up, "You have so much potential, Cheri. I want you to be at the meeting today at 1:00."

She was in awe and thanked me. Not knowing what to say after that, Cheri asked, "Hey, Sam, tell me about your farming experience."

"Bill and I got our asses handed to us. We were number and book smart, but sometimes it's better to be lucky than good. By the by, how many more years do you have in school?"

"I have 2 more years."

"What does it cost these days?"

"About $25,000 a year," she said with an I'm-barely-getting-by look. Slightly embarrassed, she regrouped, "Well, we better head back. If I forget to tell you, thanks for your friendship and mentoring, Sam." She had a charming smile. Sincere and demure.

"Oh, Cheri, you can't get rid of me that quickly. I'm sure our paths will cross more often after this deal."

Charlie, Suzy, Mark, Mary and Mandy, Debs and Bill entered the conference room followed by the SmallFirm team.

"I want to begin the meeting with a power point describing the opportunities, hybrid sorghum solution, the proposed stages of growth, the proof of concept testing to be completed in New Mexico, and how the funds from the $30 million would be deployed." I then made recommendations on the strategy. "Our goals in year 1 will be to achieve germination and plant growth to at least 4 feet. That will balance the pH and provide organic matter to the soil and help with growth in the following 2 years. So we shouldn't deploy many resources in terms of fertilization and irrigation. Depending on the results, we will either follow year 1 protocol or increase resources. Certainly, we should increase by year 3. Our goal with the test in New Mexico is to determine if the plant will uptake the cesium. Since cesium and technetium are on the same periodic table line, we can assume that if we're successful with cesium, then the process will work for technetium. There is already published data on sorghum's ability to absorb heavy metals. Based on the data from the past 3 years of farming, we know that the root system will extend to 15 feet and is capable of uplifting all the elements. Bill and I have lost 3 battles in the past, but I am confident that with appropriate resources and learning from past lessons, we have a great chance to win the war."

Everyone agreed. Then Suzy asked pointedly, "Will you run the company? We all talked about it and want you to be the CEO. Although we mentioned at the last meeting a $200,000 annual salary with 15 percent equity, we are comfortable increasing the salary to $225,000."

I smiled and thanked everyone for the opportunity. "With every venture, there is risk. The risks you know you know, the risks that you know that you don't know, and the risks that you don't know that you don't know. In the course of this venture, our business model will change. It will be a living business model, requiring agreement from the folks in this room. I've thought about it carefully and here are my conditions. I will not accept $225,000. I will agree to $120,000 annually and a $30,000 scholarship awarded to Cheri for 2 years. Also on the equity, I would like the 15 percent to be allocated as follows: 3 percent to the Wudang monk fund, 4 percent to my sister Jean, and the remaining 8 percent to me. If you can agree to those terms, we have a deal." I smiled and looked at the group. Everyone was happy; Cheri was stunned. Mission accomplished. "Mark, can you draft the documents with hard page breaks? I have an engagement. As a former lawyer, I would never advise my client to do what I'm doing, but I'll sign 5 sets of all the documents. Please keep my signatures in escrow with Cheri to be exchanged."

I pull out the Montblanc pen that Suzy had given to me several years prior. "Suzy, remember the pen that you got me? Well, here's to breaking it in. Can we take a picture of the whole group? I would like to keep it for historical purposes." Mom would have been smiling proudly. After the picture, I said my goodbyes, grabbed my Ba-Ba-Ri coat and headed home to get ready for my date and the flight.

As I stepped onto the pavement, a message from Caroline popped up. *"Unable to meet at 6 p.m., please call me when you get a chance."*

I looked at the message and said to myself, "I should never schedule anything with Caroline at 6:00 p.m. Nothing good happens at that hour." I flipped through my phone and called Caroline. "Hi, Caroline, is everything okay?"

"Hi, Sam, I am soooo sorry. I completely forgot about a family dinner I need to attend tonight. Please forgive me!"

"I totally understand. Can we do it tomorrow at 8:32 am?"

"That would be much better. I am so sorry! You did say 8:32 a.m., correct?"

"Yes. No worries, just glad everything is okay. See you tomorrow," and I hung up.

After Caroline had hung up, I decided to grab a scoop of ice cream, partly to reward myself and partly to quell my disappointment. It did the job. I headed home and gathered my thoughts for the next day.

Morning came quickly, but the minutes until 8:32 a.m. dragged. By 7:30, I was a nervous wreck again. I gathered up the hydrangea plant, postcards, jewelry box with magnets, and dashed off to Pentagon City. I arrived 15 minutes early and headed towards the lobby of the Ritz.

Caroline sent me a text that read, *"Let's meet in the lobby where last we met."*

Our eyes met, and we melted into each other. I felt at home there. No words, just the excitement of seeing each other again. Eight minutes passed, and I loosened my hold on her to ask, "Are you hungry, Caroline?"

"Not right now but I do need a drink." I could sense she was nervous and I was nervous, too. We made our way to a quiet booth to talk.

I motioned for a server. "What would you like?"

"Bloody Mary, please."

"That sounds good. I'll have 1 too."

The waitress took our order and whisked away. I looked at Caroline and smiled, eager to catch up. "Caroline, tell me everything that has happened to you since we last spoke."

Touching my arm, she replied, "No, I want to hear from you first."

"Before I begin, here is a hydrangea. Mom used to love these. They were her favorite, and I wanted to share them with you."

Caroline's eyes softened. "Thank you, Sam. I know how much you miss her. I'm sorry that I couldn't be there for you. She was an amazing woman, and I know that she is proud of the man you have become." Then she chuckled and continued, "Well, except for not contacting your friends and keeping us worrying about you."

I described the painful lessons that I had learned farming for 3 years and my recent health issues. We laughed about my sometimes painful recovery period in China. As I continued to talk, Caroline placed her hand on my leg. I noticed that she was wearing the infinity necklace and the Cartier watch. I felt confident that the gifts that I had collected would be well received. I handed her the jewelry box and said, "I've been collecting these for you."

She opened it, and it began to play a familiar tune. "Didn't we dance to that at your friend's wedding?"

"Yes. That was the song."

She peeked inside and began to smile. "Magnets... I LOVE magnets!"

"Yes, I know. They're from all the places that I've visited." She smiled. That smile brightened up our booth and my soul. "Your turn, Caroline."

"Well, I told you that we were separated last time we spoke, right?"

"Yes."

"Well my youngest graduated and the oldest has been in college for 3 years now. Once the youngest graduated, I filed for divorce. We finalized the papers this past November." She paused to inhale. I knew it was still a bitter pill for her to swallow and admit. She noticed that I noticed and quickly hid the pain behind that stunning smile as she continued, "Hopefully soon, the house will sell."

"Then what?"

"I don't know. I'd like to stay near to my kids in Virginia, but who knows? Atlanta?"

She winked. "What about you? Where are you these days?"

"I'm planning on doing something exciting with land remediation." Her hand squeezed my leg, and I placed my hand on top of hers. "Caroline, I'm thinking of living in Northern Virginia. You must stay here. Don't go anywhere else. Promise me."

She smiled and said, "I have something for you, too." She opened her purse and handed me a dollar bill. "I'm returning this dollar that you gave me in the elevator."

"Caroline, that was the consideration for us to be friends."

"Yes, I know. I'm afraid that since you are a lawyer that you will sue me for breach of something or another because I don't want to be just friends anymore, Sam. I want to date you. I want to move slowly, so we aren't going to be date dating. Just dating."

"Caroline, you and your definitions. I need to clarify the differences between dating and date dating."

"Sam, dating is going out, having fun, holding hands, kissing...and date dating is, you know, much more physical."

I reached for my wallet and grabbed a $20 bill and handed it to Caroline. "Consider that a binding agreement with this consideration."

"Oh, Sam! You are such a lawyer."

I grabbed Caroline and leaned in. I had been longing to kiss her and didn't want to waste any more time. We behaved like high school students again.

By 9:00 a.m., we were both hungry. Caroline suggested we have brunch at the Ritz. We headed towards the restaurant, hand in hand, oblivious to our surroundings. At brunch, she wanted me to retell my China stories, including the Texas Hold 'em. After that, I described the plants we would be working with and their unique ability to clean up many of the toxic fields in the world: Chernobyl,

Fukushima, New Mexico lands contaminated by past military tests, and the Hubei Chinese farming lands.

"Sam, I really want my kids to meet you."

"Caroline, I only want to meet your kids when we are dating dating. I don't want to develop a relationship with them unless we are seriously dating. It's better that way, for all of us."

Caroline agreed, and she began to describe her kids in general terms. I knew very little about them. "My oldest is clever, but she is very ambitious and stubborn. My youngest is the opposite, carefree and more into athletics."

Over brunch, I felt compelled to ask something that was gnawing at me. I probably wouldn't have asked, but knowing Caroline as I did, I didn't think that she would be offended. "Caroline, I'm asking for clarification because the last person I dated, we never talked about it, but it subsequently caused some issues. By dating, are we talking about exclusively dating?"

"Sam, I haven't dated in 20-plus years. Do you want to date other people? What are your expectations, Sam?"

"I have none, but I think you are my 888."

"What is an 888?" she asked.

"Long story," and I grin. "Oh, Caroline, I only want to date you, and I don't intend to date anyone else."

She smiled and said meltingly, "Me too." I couldn't keep my hands off her and could not resist the urge to kiss her constantly. When the check came, I asked Caroline if she could take 3 weeks off to travel.

She paused and with a coy little smile said, "The proper southern strategy would be to respond in 3 days."

I smiled and said, "We can sign a non-disclosure agreement to preserve your reputation."

"Yes. I have 3 weeks. Why?"

"I would like you to meet some of the special people in my life. I am planning a cruise for my dear friend and former assistant, Jules. Her health is not well, and she's been wanting to go on a cruise for the longest time."

I handed her the postcard from San Francisco. "You have always wanted to visit Golden Gate and Napa. So let's go. I'd also like you to meet my family."

"Sam, that would be wonderful!" And with a head tilt and looking for assurance, she added, "Separate rooms, though, right?"

"Of course, we are only dating, not date dating."

"Sam, I always thought things came easy for you. I didn't realize how much time and energy you put into a project."

Eye opener. I thought I've been working on dating you for the past several years. Nothing good comes easy. You have to earn it the old-fashioned way. I felt content in her presence. We embraced and kissed until it was time to pack. I forgot to mention that our flight departed at 6:00 p.m., but that we should get there by 4:00 p.m. since neither of us were A-List on SWA or TSA PreCheck. "Wow, Sam, 4 hours notice is not a lot of time." Was that a sign? I gave an apologetic grimace but was happy that Caroline and I were going to make new memories together.

Chapter 30

Vacillating

Ping! Ping! Ping! Over the intercom came a lovely voice. "Boarding all business class, boarding all business class now."

I was excited to go on vacation with Caroline. I checked in early with a seat assignment of B-66. I was anxious, and I needed my ice cream to calm my nerves. As the flight was boarding, there was no sign of Caroline. I texted her, *"Are you at the airport yet? The plane is boarding. I'll save you a seat."*

At 7:45 p.m., the plane doors shut, and I receive the KOD text message. *"Hi, Sam, I'm sorry, but I can't go on this trip with you. Call me when you land in Florida. Travel safely! Take care."* I was devastated, but I had been warned that it takes time to be available after a divorce. My mind somewhat accepted it, but my heart felt otherwise.

On that flight, a part of me died. My dream of the perfect vacation of doing anything and everything with Caroline had just shattered. I encouraged myself: I've waited 20 years; what's another 6 to 18 months? As I landed in Miami, I had a strong desire to call Caroline but thought it best to text her instead. *"Just landed in Miami. I'm happy with whatever you decide so long as you are happy. Words cannot express how much you will be missed. Call me if you want to talk."*

The phone rang; it was Caroline. I scrambled to answer it. "Hi, Caroline?"

"Sam, I'm sorry for not telling you beforehand. I thought it would be best that you travel without me. Your friend needs you, and I would get in the way of that. I have so much going on with the divorce and all. The decision weighed heavily on me, and I felt that this was the right thing to do. Please forgive me for not saying something sooner."

"Caroline, it is fine. I will miss your smiling face."

Caroline ended the call with, "Sam, good luck, and I hope your friend makes it!"

I stared at the phone with a stone in my heart but knew her act of kindness was more important than the sadness I felt... And thought, "V" was for "vacillating" not "vacationing."

As I looked up, Jules came around the corner. "Hi, Jules!"

Jules was taken aback. "Sam, you look so sad. I've never seen you look so sad before. I thought you were bringing a friend?"

"Jules, I am a little disheartened. She decided at the last minute to cancel on me."

Shocked, Jules responded, "Wow! Well, that's never happened to you before, Sam!"

"To make a long story short, Caroline just went through a divorce, and her emotions are all over the place, but that is not why she canceled. She was doing the most unselfish thing anyone could do, and I shouldn't slight her for that."

"Oh, yeah, I understand," Jules said, nodding. "How long has she been divorced?"

"About 5 months. "

"How long was she married and are there any kids involved?"

"About 15 years with 2 kids."

"Are they in school?"

"The oldest is in college, and the youngest just graduated high school."

"Oh my gosh, Sam. As you know, I've been divorced and so have many of my friends. Be there to support her, give her plenty of space, and know that Caroline won't be ready for any relationship for at least 6 months, possibly 2 years. It takes time for a person to process a divorce fully. It's a mixture of emotions: anger, regret and the best interest of the kids. Caroline is not going to want to hate her ex because of the kids. It will take time for her to figure things out."

"Thanks for the heads-up, Jules. I've waited 20-plus years so what is another 2 years in the scheme of things, right?" As I said that, I wasn't quite sure that I believed it, and I think Jules saw a tell in me that gave my feelings away.

"Make sure you are there for her for a soft landing but try not to suffocate her. I know how Big Bang, Carpe Diem-esque you can be. The best way for me to explain to you is in deal terms so you can easily relate. As you would say, Sam, let me break it down for you. How long does it take for a family-owned company CEO to retire and sell his company?"

"2-3 years."

"Exactly!"

Of course, I knew this. Still, I think it was therapeutic for Jules to mentor me just as much as it was ideal for me to have someone to commiserate with.

"Jules, I'm at a fork in the road. Do I continue when she is confused and unready, or do I just let her go for a while? Someone once said this when I was in 'dating mode' and not 'relationship mode.' 'If you love someone, let her go. If she returns, she was always yours. If she doesn't, she never was.'"

"Sam, you are a farmer. I think relationships are like crops and require attentiveness: constant watering and sunlight along with periodic fertilizing to stimulate growth. When there is a break in the connection, the relationship, not unlike a crop, remains status quo, dies, or evolves in a different direction."

"Jules, it is tough to put aside my personal feelings and desires so that I can be there for her as a friend."

"Sam, it is tough wanting to find oneself again without the pressures of getting involved or sending the wrong message."

I guessed Jules was right. In the end, it was best to let the heavens fall and let her go. Perhaps that was the essence of true love...

"So how are you doing, Jules, healthwise?"

"I'm so glad that you made this vacation happen for me. It has been a lifelong dream to go on a cruise. I just never made time."

Evasive. Redirect. "Jules, how is your health?"

She looked out at the ocean. "The biopsy indicated that I have stage 2 ovarian cancer. I went through chemo. After this cruise, I will need to go back for re-evaluation. Best case scenario, surgery to remove my ovaries and, or radiation." She looked down briefly but then seemed to gather her strength. After a few nanoseconds of silence, her eyes reconnected with mine. She smiled and said, "Thank you for making this happen."

"I'm sorry for being so selfish, Jules. You have my undivided attention. Is there anything I can do to help?"

"Well, you know I have a daughter. She is in college," she paused. "Sam, I can't think of anyone that I could turn to if anything should happen to me."

Wow! I was taken aback momentarily. Jules exhaled and gathered the courage to continue what must have been so difficult to admit, let alone say. "Can you please watch over her in case I'm not around?"

I felt my throat tighten and as my eyes began to tear up, I forgot to breathe. I needed to be strong for her. Cancer sucks!

I took a good look at Jules and noticed that she was really quite striking, although a bit frail and pale. She was wearing a wig again. When I had met her at the office, before I had learned of the seriousness of the threat to her health, I assumed it was one of her new fashion statements. She never mentioned that she was sick, much less battling cancer. Jules was a strong woman, and I knew she would fight this with all she had. I resolved to be there for her daughter in any way I could. What would I be to her? A distant helicopter parent? I'd be stealth-like and helpful… The Secret Asian Man, perhaps? I mentally chuckled, stepped up to my new role and refocused on my friend.

"Of course, Jules. You can count on me to be there. But I want to focus on you and have faith that you'll still be around. I need to invite you to my wedding in 5 years."

"Sam, you crack me up. Only you would have a 5-year plan to marry someone that you aren't even dating." We laughed, and then she sighed. "Thanks for your friendship and support."

On the cruise, I thought a lot about emotional attraction and how a very abstract quality, so difficult to explain, might be the superglue to any relationship. My focus was on Jules, but my thoughts gravitated toward Caroline. I thought that of all the people in the world, and she was the most extraordinary woman to enter my life after my mother and Jean. The older we got, the more beautiful Caroline became in my eyes. I pulled out my cell phone to review the pictures of us together from Joe's wedding and her birthday celebration. I noticed my Mona Lisa smiling. That smile gave me joy. I came to terms with Caroline's decision about the cruise and was happy because it gave me perspective about where she was emotionally.

At the bar, a late 20s, early 30s attractive woman approached me. "Hi, I'm Linda, I love your shirt."

I hated it when my shirt did that. I forgot that my shirt was a chick magnet. It was like walking a dog. May I pet the shirt? Ummmmm…Or would it prefer a treat? Down, shirt… down, boy…

"Seriously, thanks, but I'm sure there are other guys here willing, able and ready."

"Yes, your shirt caught the attention of my eyes. Your personality piques my interest. Your non-threatening demeanor makes me comfortable. Your hard-to-get attitude is a challenge. Now, roll over, be a good boy and bark like a dog. You're like, what, 28 or 30? Can I buy you a drink?"

I laughed and responded, "Umm, no, and I would only accept your offer if you weren't hitting on me."

"Well, that's a first. I thought that it was 'What happens on a cruise, stays on a cruise.'"

"No offense, you are attractive, but my heart has run away from me to be with someone else."

"In all seriousness, there are 3 aspects to this person your heart left you for."

"Which are?"

"The person you think she is, the person she really is, and the person she becomes."

"Let me turn the tables. You think I'm a single, quasi-intelligent, hip guy looking to hook up. But I'm really a quasi-intelligent, hip guy who is totally in like with someone. I want to become the man who is in a serious relationship with that person."

"Are you telling me that I have no chance at all?"

"I'm sure you get hit on all the time since you are attractive, but no hard feelings."

At that moment, I knew that a meaningless encounter would not heal my emptiness. I had transformed. I finally realized what F. Scott Fitzgerald had meant when he said: *And in the end, we were all just humans drunk on the idea that love, only love, could heal our brokenness.*

It was 1:00 am, time for me to turn into a pumpkin. I heard a knock on the door. "Room service!"

"I'm sorry, but I didn't order any room service." I opened the door and there was Linda, asking if she could come in for a nightcap. "What time is it?"

"Why? It's 1:08 a.m."

"Interesting… The Cubbies first office was located at 108 W. Madison Street, and they haven't been to the World Series in a long, long time. Besides, a really wise man once told me that there are 108 vices, and nothing good can happen at this hour."

"What do you mean?"

I counted 4 vices that might occur if she entered my room… so I would be a good boy and decline. "Listen to me Linda, I'm totally flattered, Linda, but not interested!"

She replied, "You aren't gonna turn this down, right?" As she posed and waved her hand from the top of her breasts to below her thigh, she smiled provocatively. "She'll never know."

"Linda, listen to me, I will know… As Bogart said, *maybe not today… maybe not tomorrow, but for the rest of my life, I will regret it…*' So I'm gonna pass. But I think the guy 2 doors down might be hungry. Good night!"

That evening, I slept dreaming of only 1 person… Yes, visions of Caroline and only Caroline. I woke up the next morning and looked at my notepad. It read, "Get it done" and "Caroline's the 1." Was I that blind? Even my subconscious knew the obvious!

When we docked at Miami, I helped Jules to a cab and then I had the sudden urge to telephone-consult with Hope.

"Hi, Hope, it's your favorite client!"

"Sam, why are you calling me?"

"First, how'd you know it was me? I mean I know that you're psychic, but…"

"Sam, I have caller ID. What is it that you need to know?"

"I have questions about the one."

"What do you want to know about Caroline?"

"So she IS the one?"

"Sam, listen to me or listen to your subconscious. She's the one for you!"

"How do you know she's the one for me?"

"Sam, have you been drinking? I'm a numerologist, so I deal in numbers all the time. I'd never met anyone who views relationships solely in numbers until I met you. But I need to clear something up for you. There are no 5-year plans for love. You have this theory. Yes, the physical and intellectual are quantifiable in numbers, regarding IQ and beauty in relative scale. But emotional attraction is not quantifiable… It is the feeling of wanting to kiss someone… not the act of kissing. A relationship lasting a lifetime… not defined by time and space. The feeling of sharing your life with her. Not being with her. The feeling lasting beyond the act in time and space. Emotional attractiveness is not quantifiable… It is infinite, Sam. I know you have OCD, so save your money. I have a message for you from your mom."

"What is it?"

"She's yelling at you again. She wants to know why you haven't introduced her to Caroline yet. Oh, and stop asking me the same question in 3 or 4 different ways. Go get some ice cream. Everything is going to work out."

"Thank you, Hope, and send me the bill!" *Damn she's good,* I marveled as I hung up the phone.

Shortly afterward, I received an email from Amy. Oh great, I thought sarcastically and sighed. Another test. First Linda. Now Amy.

> *Hello, Sam,*
>
> *I find myself in DC at the Willard and feel it is a sign that I should reach out to you for many reasons. I have so many things to say....When we met, I had been dating promiscuously. I never considered a serious relationship with anyone. Being with you scared me to death. It was the first time in my life that I felt secure. I will never forget the romantic gestures. I enjoyed the stories and the crazy things you did. You showed me a different way to look at life. Over the last 2 years, I have worked hard to change my life and begin again with Craig. The person I am today is not the one you said goodbye to 2 years ago. I have fond memories of us and treasure the pictures we took together. Thank you for being part of my life, and I am sorry for not being forthright. I have learned and hope that I will not make the same mistake with Craig.*
>
> *Always,*
>
> *Amy*

Wow, this wasn't another test. Amy had moved on. I was glad that she was happy now but a little sad too. It honestly surprised me. Maybe the sadness was just a transference from missing Caroline. Caroline, I sighed. Not yet my Caroline. The emotional attractiveness was more than evident to me now. As I left one terminal for another, I wondered if it was the same for her. Were things as clear as they were becoming to me?

Oddly, when it rains it often pours. The storm's power separates what is important from what is illusory – a deal junkie realizing that the true cure to that fix was Caroline. I was so glad that I could spend the quality time with Jules. It helped us both, but neither of us healed. As I headed to the airport for San Francisco, I was excited to see Jean, but I still carried a feeling of emptiness.

Chapter 31
The Smell of Cheap Alcohol and Perfume

Ping! I checked my messages while I boarded my flight from Miami to San Francisco. A single message came up... *Sweet!* I thought. I finally have my life back. I laughed at the absurdity but quickly looked to see if Caroline had sent me anything. I let out a deep sigh after I saw nothing from her. It was Jean wishing me safe travels.

I sat down in the emergency exit row next to the window (the one with the extra leg room). I stretched my legs and stared at my smartphone, which showcased a picture of Caroline smiling. It was bittersweet. Whenever I thought of my Mona Lisa or gazed at her picture, I smiled and took a moment to recover from the pleasant trance. I had leaned in to kiss her picture when I felt someone petting my arm like I was cashmere.

"Well, here's the all talk no action, Robert Graham sportin' Sam who fumbled the ball last night!"

"Linda from the cruise? What are you doing on this flight?"

"No, Linda from room service! I'm here to give you a 2nd chance to score."

Yes, it was really her, and she was sitting next to me. *Ugh!* "Listen to me, Linda; you smell like cigarettes, alcohol, and cheap perfume! I'm sorry, but my wipers don't work on your model!"

"Yes, I'm still drunk. Wipers?! I don't get what you're talk'n about, but just to let you know, I live in the Bay Area and am returning home. Why are you going to ESSS EFFFF? Business or pleeeeeeasure?" I wasn't sure if it was her drunken state, but pleasure ended up sounding like play-sure. *Ick!*

∞

I wasn't about to explain the boob joke or the head movement. I quickly replied in one long breath, "Long story about the wipers – I'm visiting my sister – please don't hit on me."

"What's wrong, Sam? Every guy likes it when a girl hits on him. I'm open, throw me the ball so I can score!"

I kept wondering what perfume she was wearing. It was making me nauseous. "My name is Sam Rivtoc. I'm not the kinda guy that likes to be chased. Hate it, actually. I'm totally in like and am pursuing the one… the one that got away… not the one 'you'… You are nice, but I'm not interested. I'm tired and need to sleep." I turned away and worked on getting to sleep. Linda rustled around and mumbled something under her breath.

Sweet Southern Caroline. Ever since Caroline, my love life has not been the same. We met in high school, but due to distance and circumstances, it ended. With the white noise of the airplane droning on, I drifted back to 7th grade, Kadena Air Base, Okinawa, Japan. I was with Jim, Jack, and John, my 3 cool Little League baseball buddies. We had all just been rejected by the girl next door.

"Well, guys, looks like we all struck out. She throws one wicked curve ball and sadly, a perfect game tonight. She wins, we lose! Let's go to 31 flavors outside Gate 2 and wallow in our losses." It was 10:30 p.m., the night was young, and we had the excuse of a slumber party that allowed us to be out. John suggested, "Let's go to the KozaVu strip club." We had never gone to that club before, or any club for that matter, except for John. Due to his overly manly appearance, he got into a couple of clubs. But we were cool, and none us wanted to admit that we weren't experienced. To work up the nerve, we went to the nearby Mama-san store and bought some Akadama punch. It was a mild rose wine with a 3 percent alcohol content. We egged each other on and eventually got a little buzz going. Amazing the amount of peer pressure we went through at the age of 12. After we had consumed our liquid courage, we headed to KozaVu.

John knew how to get there and led us through this tiny roadway he called "Whisper Alley." At every turn, we were propositioned by the "ladies of the night." I was nervous, scared, and wanted to leave, but I didn't want the other guys to think that I was chicken. We approached a road marked BC Street and ran smack into KozaVu. Outside, there was a short-statured man was wearing a tropical shirt with a wife-beater underneath. He continuously yelled, "Irasshai.... Irasshai masen" while fanning himself with a gray fedora. We snuck past him as a couple of GIs distracted him and entered the doorway. Upstairs, you could hear the sound of loud rock and roll music. The decor was circa 1960, old and torn. The joint reeked of cigarettes, alcohol and cheap perfume intertwined with the distinct smell of old body odor. The strip club was pretty empty, with the exception of three 40-something gaijin (non-Japanese foreigners) sitting in a booth by themselves. We sat down, and 4 scantily-clad women approached us. I only had $8 in my pocket. Back then, that was enough to buy 2 drinks. I didn't want to be rude nor a prude, but I really didn't want to be there. I was noticeably uncomfortable as one lady put her hand on my legs. It was hard to tell her age, as she was seemingly a full-blooded Okinawan woman. Her hair was wound up tight on the top of her head, which made her look even more Asian. When she put her hand on my leg that night, I felt a part of my innocence drift away. We all manned up and ordered the "purple haze." It was horrible. It tasted like black jelly beans and had a hellacious kick. Suddenly all the women walked onto the stage and started to yell "Show time... Show time!" The music started, and one lady began to take off her clothes. She spotted us, approached, and yelled out, "Come, baby-san!" I was totally embarrassed, and the 4 of us ran around to avoid being caught. I made a beeline for the exit, and the other 3 followed suit. "Holy shit! That was close," I exclaimed. With all the excitement, the purple haze began to make its way back up, but I managed to keep it down. We sat on a curb a safe distance away from the club and laughed about the purple haze, nudity, and the chase, but all I really wanted to do was throw up. I was broke, more than slightly intoxicated, and terrorized by the memory of the little stripper lady chasing me.

∞

Chapter 32
Okinawa

Ping! I heard the fasten seatbelt sign come on. I opened one eye and looked around. Linda was fast asleep with mouth agape. I thought, Probably a good thing she's still tanked from the night before. I wondered what had brought about that trip down memory lane. It must've been a combination of Linda's smell and her behavior. It reminded me that the KozaVu incident was when I had acquired my powerful aversion towards women who chase me. I looked away and slid even further back into my childhood.

The classroom bell rang. It was late April. The last day of class, and I was no longer an elementary school kid. I'm going to be in middle school next year, I thought. I was so excited about the upcoming summer of fun and playing ball with my boys. My number was 3. I batted 3rd, played 3rd base and pitched occasionally. Mom always told me that the number 3 meant good fortune. I had a mean split-finger fastball; my voice had changed, and middle school girls were hot! Life was about to be amazing! I should've known something was strange when I got home that night. I looked around, the house was a mess, everyone was moody, and they were packing everything up in boxes. I asked if we were moving neighborhoods.

Jean looked at me in horror. "We are moving to Okinawa. Dad just accepted a new civil engineering job. I can't believe they are moving now just when I'm starting high school!"

"Where is that? Is it here in Korea?"

Screaming, "Oh my God, I have an idiot as a brother! Didn't you learn in your history class about the battle of Okinawa? It is in Japan."

All I could come up with in response was, "I don't speak Japanese."

The thought of having no friends, being an outsider and unable to communicate in Japanese raised serious concerns in my adolescent brain. It must have shown on my face.

Mom stopped packing, gave Jean a "Mom" look and came over and comforted me. "Don't worry. You will make new friends. We are moving to Kadena Air Base on Okinawa. It's like a little, transported piece of America. They're Americans, and they all speak English. You will be fine. I bought you some ice cream. Do you want any?"

"Yes, Mom, is it Rocky Road?" She nodded her head, and I immediately relaxed. When it came to stress, ice cream was my drug of choice.

As she handed me the bowl, she whispered, "I am worried that you are behind in school. We should continue to pay Jean $5 an hour to tutor you."

Jean heard those words, focused on the economics and instantly began thinking of ways to spend her newfound source of income. No longer was she bothered by the move. It took a couple of days, but we eventually got everything packed. I said goodbye to my buddies, we all stated that we'd write but knew we probably wouldn't, and the Rivtoc Family was off to a new adventure.

Chapter 33

Boys of Summer

Ping! "Please fasten your seat belts, we are experiencing some turbulence in the area."

I asked for some water and dozed back off into middle school.

We landed at Naha International Airport. There was a distinct smell of salt water in the air, and we hadn't even made it out of the terminal. We retrieved our luggage and headed outside. As the doors opened, I gasped. I felt like I had hit a brick wall of water. The humidity felt like 150 percent. My head whirled as if I were about to pass out. I looked at Jean and noticed her hair had frizzed up. Mom and Dad didn't seem fazed by it at all. I thought, This place SUCKS!

We exited the front of the airport where we were greeted by a driver from the Civil Engineering Department. It took 37 minutes to get from Naha Airport to Kadena Air Force Base. I was overwhelmed. All of this was very new to me. A new country, a new climate that was hot, thick, and salty; a new home, next to the base entrance; and the sound of roaring F15s taking off into the horizon. Yes, okay, some of it was cool, but it was a bittersweet feeling. I was excited about my new beginning, but I was overwhelmed with sadness. For the first time, I felt a sense of loss – my Korean friends.

To make me feel comfortable, Dad signed me up for Little League baseball. For guys at that age, friendship was based on one factor and one factor alone – the coolness factor. The brands of your glove, shoes, and bat mattered, but if you could play ball, hit dingers or throw hard, you automatically were elevated to the cool group. On Okinawa, the three Js – John, Jim, and Jack – were it when it came to Little League ball. Apparently, as Dad was chatting up the coach, I needed to be tested by the three Js to see where I fit. They hurled fastballs at me, which I hit out of the park.

"Did he get lucky?" One J would say.

The other J would follow with, "Let's do it again."

All about the numbers, I hit 5 dingers that day. Then I struck out the three Js. I was now cool with a capital "C." I proved myself that day and became one of the notorious 4, Sam and the three Js. Being on top of the cool food chain had its benefits. Guys wanted to be your friend, and girls would give you the eye. Not the stink eye, but what I called the "hey you" eye. The 4 of us were joined at the hip. We went bowling together, to the movies, and into the little boonies all over the base. The Keystone Theater was our favorite place to go and watch the latest movies.

We also shared the same likes and dislikes, even about Ann Marie Jones. We talked about her all the time and decided that on Valentine's Day we would settle it once and for all.

Ann Marie was as cute as a button. Sweeter than sweet tea and the first girl I ever liked. We weren't the only ones sweet on her, so we decided that we needed to move fast. The 4 of us came up with a code of conduct and a plan for good faith and fair play to see whom Ann Marie would ultimately choose. Our plan came together at a slumber party at Jim's house. We dubbed our method the CKCC. The Cool Kid's Code of Conduct. We met at the skating rink Friday night and invited all the girls. We played rock, paper, and scissors to determine who would go first. Each had 45 minutes; if she didn't respond favorably, then it was the next guy up. I lost and was dead last on the "Ask Ann Marie Out Skating Rink Game Show." Jim went first and failed. I was happy that he failed but sad at the same time because I could see the pain and embarrassment on his face. Jack's turn was next. He saw how it went with Jim, and I could tell he was hesitant. Still, he dug in, and he struck out as well. Oddly, my feelings for Jim and Jack started to outweigh those for Ann Marie. They both looked sad, and that was totally uncool. John went next, and he, too, returned dejected.

It was my turn. I wasn't nervous at all. Perhaps it was because I had grown up with a sister who was smarter than me and always knew how to put me in my place.

I approached Ann Marie, and she said unhappily, "Not you, too, Sam?"

I responded, "I'm glad I'm last. The original plan was to ask you out, but now that you've rejected all my best friends, I don't want to ask you out anymore."

Startled, she replied, "Why not?"

"I'm in a conundrum of sorts." I used my $8 Jean word on her.

"What's a conundrum?"

"It's when you are in a dilemma. If I ask you out, and you answered 'no,' then I'd be sad that you rejected me. But I would be happy along with the boys because we all got rejected tonight. You and I would never go out again because you would only get one chance with me. So I'm not asking you out at all, but if I did, you know you would say yes. Then I would feel real bad for my best friends. So I'm better off telling them that you rejected me too without asking you out at all. That will make everyone happy. Besides, you wouldn't know how to date a smart, emotional guy."

Ann Marie laughed and let her guard down. "Sam, I like smart guys. You are obviously not smart because I would go out with you if you asked me out. I didn't know you had such a tender side."

"Well, I'm not going to ask you out officially tonight. Unofficially, remember you turned me down. That is the story. OK?

∞

But I'll come by your house tomorrow and ask you out because I'm really smart. I could teach you a thing or 2."

"Like what?"

"Like conundrum and diplomacy."

Ann Marie and I laughed the whole time. It felt great knowing that I had just created a win/win situation for everyone.

That evening, we celebrated the Ann Marie rejection by going to KozaVu. I began to feel nauseous and woke up.

Ping! "Please fasten your seatbelts. We are experiencing some turbulence" came over the P.A. system. I double-checked my seatbelt and fell back to sleep, reminiscing about the aftermath of my bittersweet Ann Marie and KozaVu experience.

The next morning, I was still slightly buzzed from the purple haze and akadama wine and that *smell*. It wasn't a nightmare; KozaVu had actually happened. The three Js were off to the batting cages and asked if I was interested. I told them, "I'm broke from last night. I think I will take another hack at Ann Marie."

All 3 looked shocked. Jim said, "Remember how fast I ran from that stripper last night? I hated the feeling of being rejected last night by Ann Marie. Sam, you are one brave man to face that rejection storm again. Good luck because I wouldn't do it!"

I responded, "I'm not laying an egg. I need more 'at bats' to hit that wicked curve. Maybe she'll be off her game and walk me. Either way, I'm getting on base one way or another."

We all laughed, but I knew they thought I was insane. I rushed home and showered 3-times to rid myself of the smell of deceit, but I couldn't remove the dirty feeling that came with it. Washed and looking good, I waited 58 minutes for the bus to take me to Ann Marie's house. To up my game, I decided to write Ann Marie a poem. I wasn't much of a poet, but I figured she might be impressed with my ability to put words together with some meaning attached. When I arrived, I adjusted my shirt and rang the doorbell, praying that she would be the one to answer. I was in luck.

Ann Marie said, "Well, it's about time you showed up. I still don't think you are that bright, Sam."

"I came as fast as I could, but the bus just took a while to get me here. I've been thinking about you all day, and I wrote a poem for you."

Ann Marie let me in and asked, "What poem?"

"Ann Marie, roses are red and violets are blue. Yesterday, my heart bled knowing I had to wait a day to be with you." I know, it wasn't by any means savvy, but I figured I would throw it out there and see if she would bite.

"Sam, that's corny. Did you really write that?"

"Yes," I replied sheepishly, "on the bus ride over."

"I want to go out with you, but you need to talk to my dad. My parents have to say yes before I can say yes. That's the rule."

Ooooooo. Almost got away with it. "Today? Like as in now?"

"Yes, now!"

It was the bottom of the 9th, the window of opportunity to go out with the most beautiful girl in the whole wide world was on the line, and the umpire wanted to inspect the bat. It was hit or miss. Ann Marie left the room and returned with her father.

"Young man, Ann Marie tells me you have an important question to ask me?"

"Uhh, yes, Sir. My name is Sam Rivtoc, and I have a very important question to ask of you, but before I ask you, I want you to know more about me so that you have all the facts to make an informed decision. This is all new to me, and I have no experience in matters of the heart, but I do have my mom and older sister, and they mean the world to me. I love them dearly even though they make my life difficult at times. I adore and respect them. I have similar feelings towards Ann Marie. I don't make any money yet, but I will in the future. I'm smarter than the average bear. Last time, my report card was six A's and one B. Mom wasn't too pleased with the B. Of all the guys in school who like Ann Marie, I am confident that I am the smartest. So now that you know a little more about me, I was wondering if you would allow me to ask your daughter to be my girlfriend? This is a *yes* or *maybe* question, Sir, because I'm not sure if I could handle a *no* today. I hope you say *yes*, but if you say *maybe* I will honor your wishes but I think it would be a grave mistake." I said it in one fell swoop.

"Sam, you should have stopped at 'girlfriend.' My answer would have been yes. But since you continued, why would *maybe* be a grave mistake?"

"Well, Sir, I am very nervous and can we just pretend that I stopped at girlfriend?"

"No, Sam, we are all curious now."

"Okay, Sir. Imagine if your wife's parents had said *maybe* to you. It would have been a grave mistake because maybe you wouldn't have gotten married and had the most beautiful person I've met in my entire 13 years on this earth."

Suddenly, Ann Marie and her mom were advocating for my cause.

"Dad, I like Sam. Please, Dad, please say *yes*."

"Honey Dear, he's only 13 and very sweet."

This was my first major negotiation with a total stranger. It was not like asking for ice cream from Mom. The stakes were high. Dating Ann Marie was the most important thing in the world for me… at that time. I learned the valuable lesson that in every negotiation, it is important to convince the influencers because there is something about *power in numbers*. Ann Marie was my 1st girlfriend.

Near the end of 7th grade, I had assimilated to Kadena Middle School. I had been dating Ann Marie for 7 months. I had acquired a standing in the cool crowd based on my baseball skills and the girl I was dating.

Whereas Dad put me into Little League to help me assimilate better, Mom was concerned that I might get bullied at the new school, so she enrolled me in judo. I was in the advanced class, which started with middle school students, went through high school and included adults. Monday, Wednesday, Friday and Saturday. Two hours a day, 4 days a week, approximately 50 of us attended classes. Every day we did 200 regular pushups, judo pushups, situps, and burpees to start. Then we practiced our techniques for 30 minutes and then it was hand-to-hand combat for an hour. We gave it 100 percent because we all feared and respected Fukushima Sensei. He was stern, fair, and a master instructor. I had been the recipient of so many knuckle sandwiches that my head hurt. By the end of the 2nd year, I was a brown belt and champion of my age group on Okinawa.

I recalled a tournament where they combined the 14-15 age groups. It was the final match for the gold or silver medal. I was at a disadvantage for 2 reasons. I had injured my ankle slightly in the previous match, and my opponent outweighed me by about 100 pounds. I was losing by one yuko to Ishikawa-san. There was about a minute left in the match. I looked up and saw Mom glaring at me. I was hurt, and he was bigger, but I was more afraid of Mom's wrath if I wussed out. I summoned all my courage and energy and then boom, a wazari to win the match. This was huge! Since he was 6 years old, Ishikawa had never lost a match. I got my win and saved my proverbial behind in more than one way.

We were taught only to use martial arts for self-defense. Fukushima Sensei was very explicit. There had to be balance. The 2 years of judo had molded my mind and body. I was in excellent shape physically and mentally. I had learned to push my body beyond the threshold of physical and mental exhaustion and pain. Although I had kicked and screamed in the beginning due to the daily "torture," Mom was right. My self-confidence was high. I knew I could defend against any bullies. I had a network of "older brothers" to turn to for guidance and support. I also made many local Okinawan friends during competition. My standing earned me honcho judoka. I had Mom to thank for that.

My dad was a civil engineer. We lived close to Gate 1, and in my neighborhood, everybody's parents were either translators or editors. It felt like the UN of neighbors: Russian, Chinese, Taiwanese, Korean, Japanese, Vietnamese and Thai. The neighborhood kids generally got along. We had only one bully. He was in high school but constantly harassed middle school guys. The bully had been harassing my 8th-grade friend for 2 weeks. I was fed up. It wasn't any of my business, but I just couldn't stand the injustice any longer. My compassion had finally outweighed the fear I had for him. He was a junior who wouldn't pick on someone his own size. So one day when he was laying the hammer on my friend, I yelled out, "Leave him alone!"

He came up to me and said, "What are you gonna do about it?"

"I'm going to defend my friend from your tormenting, even if it means I end up getting my butt kicked. I'm tired of watching you bully and torture him." We got into a scuffle. He was much older and stronger, and I ended up with a shiner. Yes, I lost, but I was the neighborhood hero.

I got home, and Mom saw my disheveled look and swollen eye. She was concerned at first; she got angrier as I told her what had happened.

"He's a junior, and he's picking on us. I just got tired of it, Mom. I'm sorry for fighting and disrespecting martial arts' main rule."

Mom had tears in her eyes. She was compassionate and pissed at the same time. She sat me down and said, "I want to go over to their house and have a word with his parents, but first I need you to learn how to fly. Did I ever tell you about the birds on the islands in Korea? On one island, there was so much food. The birds on that island couldn't fly at all. They didn't need to. But on another island, there was no food. The birds on that island—the same species —could fly high and wide in search of food. I want to help, but I think it would be best if you handle this yourself."

"Thanks, Mom!" I hugged her and left. I had this cool reputation to uphold and didn't want people to think that I was a mama's boy.

"Okay, now you go get ready to go to judo class."

I went to judo class, and everyone noticed my shiner. Fukushima Sensei called me over and asked what happened. I explained to him about the neighborhood bully.

"I finally got tired of him picking on the neighborhood kids and, in this case, a friend, so I tried to defend him and got beat up."

Fukushima Sensei said, "Today you know what the word 'Konorebi' means. There is sunlight that filters through the leaves of trees, Sam. You'll see the sunlight tomorrow."

Sensei then called over 4 of my "older brothers" in high school for a meeting. I wasn't invited to that meeting. They approached me afterward and asked for the bullly's name.

The next day, I was the talk of Kadena middle school. The kids in my neighborhood exaggerated the story at school. After that, nobody dared mess with me again. When I got home from school, the bully was waiting for me at the bus stop with my 4 older judo brothers. As I got off the bus, my older brothers pointed to him. They had made him an offer he couldn't refuse. He got on his knees, bowed low, and apologized to me and all the kids in the neighborhood. He promised never to bully us again. The interesting lesson I learned that day was that it is always better to surround yourself with powerful people. Also, sometimes one must lose a battle to win the war. I killed 2 birds with one stone. By getting beat up, I finally resolved the neighborhood bully issue that had lingered for 2 years. With my brothers in arms, no one would ever mess with me again. Judo had served a twofold purpose for me, and I could see the sunlight filtering through the experience of getting beat up.

Classes were relatively easy for me. My report cards were mostly A's with the occasional B. Why did it matter what my grades were? I couldn't have cared less about my grades. All I cared about was spending every possible waking moment with Ann Marie. She was my first girlfriend, my first kiss, and soon to be my first heartbreak as her father had just received orders. Her family was transferring to Texas in 2 weeks.

Ann Marie, "Do you think we will ever see each other again?"

"Of course we will. I will write to you every day. I don't think that I will date anyone else again, ever. What about you?"

"I want to run away with you, Sam. I can't imagine my life without you."

"Don't worry, Ann Marie, I'll talk to my parents about moving to Texas next year so we can be together in high school. We might have to just suck it up for a year, but time will fly, and we will be together again."

When I entered the house after 9 p.m., Mom and her straight-A grade-enforcer, Jean, were waiting for me.

"Where is your report card?"

"I got five A's a two B's, Mom."

Jean immediately said, "See, Mom, I told you that he was failing middle school. I'm really concerned that he might end up being a *nobody*, Mom!" Emphasis on nobody.

"Yes, I agree with you, Jean. Come outside with me!" Mom grabbed a medium size stick. She hit me 3 times, paused and then hit me 7 more times. Why 3 and 7? In Korea, 3 meant good fortune and 7 meant luck. I didn't feel fortunate or lucky. The physical punishment paled compared to what would come next.

Mom said, "You are grounded for 2 weeks for the two B's, and from now on your sister is going to tutor you 15 hours a week so that you won't fail in school anymore."

Jean smiled and said, "Mom, it's a lot of work. When he was in 4th grade, it took me nearly 2 years to get him to understand what 'x' was. I need to make more money this time. At least $6 an hour because Sam taxes my brain." No amount of pleading on my part would do. Arguing was futile. Mom agreed to Jean's terms because she went shopping with Jean all the time. They were both shop-a-holics: clothes, shoes, make-up, accessories, perfume, crystal figurines, plates, knickknacks. You name it, they bought it! She needed her enabler and was happy to pay for it.

Man, my body was bruised from the 3 and 7 lashes. I felt like a failure and loser intellectually for receiving the two B's. Most importantly, I was an emotional wreck, unable to leave the house to see Ann Marie before she left for Texas. I threw a tantrum, breaking Mom's favorite watch by throwing it against the wall in anger. It was a low moment in my life. I was a kid and Mom forgave me, but I still hold regret to this day.

I always remembered Ann Marie and the wonderful times we spent together. She was my innocent, first-base girlfriend. After she moved, we never contacted one another again. I learned some valuable lessons from that evening. First, Mom had a one B tolerance. I needed to keep the B margin of error to that; anything else would result in severe punishment. Second, a guy shouldn't get too romantically and emotionally attached to a girl at such a young age. As a dependent, one had zero control over one's destiny. Romance at this age would only lead to heartbreak. My new rules of engagement were to just date, but not get too serious. If I began to cross a certain threshold or became unsure, I would break it off.

My 2-year sentence had begun right after Ann Marie left. Why 2 years? Because I had broken Mom's favorite watch, and Jean would graduate high school by then. I would be as free as a bird. I just needed to endure the tutor torture marathon. I knew that I was in for a long 2 years.

In English, we expanded my vocabulary to include $800 words like amalgamation, illusory, pragmatic, benevolent and tenacious.

Jean would always say, "Mom, it's hard teaching an imbecile. Hopefully, Sam will be a *somebody* one day, but for now, he's bordering on being a *nobody*."

We also covered novels like *Les Misérables*, Richard Bach's
Jonathan Livingston Seagull, and *Antigone*. By the time we covered
Cyrano de Bergerac, I was hooked. All this time, I thought girls
liked boys solely based on physical attributes or athletic ability,
strength or beauty. I finally discovered the intellectual and emotional
components to attraction. The learning curve was steep, but I was
hungry to learn more. These tutoring sessions were endurable
because I always had my favorite scoops of Dulce and coffee to
medicate my pain and suffering. Would I ever experience a kiss like
the one described in *Cyrano* as "too intimate for the ears?" Ann
Marie and I did kiss, but I didn't get those *Cyrano* feelings.

We covered lots of academic ground in a year. When it was
time to graduate from Kadena Middle School, the intensive tutoring
had prepared me for a junior academic program at Kubasaki High
School. Freshman year would be a walk in the park. My body was
developing and the years of pushups and judo training finally paid
off. I had earned my black belt in judo when I turned 15 years old,
and I was ready for high school athletics, especially varsity
wrestling.

Kubasaki was the main high school on Okinawa. Eventually,
they built another school, Kadena High School, to accommodate the
influx of new families on the base. Half the cool friends from
Kadena Middle School went to Kubasaki, and the other half went to
Kadena for high school. When I reached high school age, I attended
Kubasaki. I wasn't interested in girls after Ann Marie. My soul was
lost without her. Well, that was until I walked onto the Kubasaki
campus. There were lots of girls at the school. After that, my interest
in the opposite sex was rekindled. There were Ann, Becky, Cindy,
Dana, Elizabeth, Francis, Grace, Kathy, Kathleen, Lisa, Liz Mary,
Nancy, Ronnie, Sheila and the list just kept growing. It was like I

271

was in Baskin-Robbins heaven for the first time, with 31 amazing flavors to choose from. I was narrowing it down to Sara or Susan. John had made the transfer to Kubasaki too, and he and I were always rubbernecking it when the girls walked by.

John was always pretty frank when he spoke. "So Sam, I think Susan is way out of your league. She has juniors and seniors hitting on her all the time. As freshmen, we are at the very bottom of the dating pool. Sara is only a year older, so you might have a chance, but not with Susan."

"John, I can't decide between Sara and Susan. Susan is hot, mature, and sweet. Sara is really smart and cute. I like them both and can't decide. It would be like asking me if I would pick a scoop of Rocky Road over a scoop of Pralines."

"Well?"

"I'd order a double with a scoop each." I laughed and continued, "Patience John! I'm planning my next move soon. You will be the first to know. How about you? Who do you have your eyes set on?"

"After that crushing rejection from Ann Marie several years ago, I'm still a little gun-shy. That affected my self-esteem when it comes to asking girls out. Sam, have you been back to KozaVu?"

"Good Lord, no! I still have nightmares about that older woman chasing us around. Every time I smell that smell, I freak out. Have you been back?"

"Yes," he said with a devilish smile, "I've gone back at least 5 more times."

"You know that is just an illusory world where lonely guys pay to play? I'm never gonna be like those 3 guys. You are young... funny and cool, John. Chase a real high school girl."

Chapter 34

Fight Only to Defend

Ping! The 3:00 p.m. bell went off. School let out. It was November, and I was leaning on asking Sara out. Stop the presses; the rumor mill circulated that I was cruisin' for Sara. That didn't make Frank too happy. Frank was an upperclassman who had the hots for Sara. He claimed to know karate and had spread another rumor that he would crush me for crushing on Sara. Frank informed my buddies San, Bin, and John that I would be doomed after school the next day.

I sighed, "I am really not into this machismo thing that is going on." Side note: machismo was one of those $800 words that Jean was so adamant I learn.

The next day, I waited until lunch and met him in the cafeteria.

"I don't know you, Frank, but don't you think it's silly that we need to fight over a girl? It seems a bit barbaric. Shouldn't Sara have the right to choose who she likes?"

Frank seemingly didn't hear a single word I said. "I know karate, and I'm gonna kick your butt. Sara's going to realize what a wuss you are. Freshman, you're messing with the wrong guy. Do you want some?"

"Yup, I want some at 3:30. Off campus, Frank, so no one can bail you out. You and I have a date with destiny. If I win, you back off Sara. Period!"

"What if I win? Who are you anyway?"

"I'm Sam. I have a duty to warn you that I am a black belt in judo, and I am an All-Okinawa champion. You don't have a chance!"

I noticed that Frank was nervous. His modus operandi was to instill fear through intimidation. He had probably never fought his equal in his entire life. He preyed on younger, smaller guys with low self-esteem. I had trained for 3 years in the art of hand-to-hand combat with older, skilled judokas. I sensed that Frank was no martial artist. Anyway, no true martial artist would ever use his art as a sword. I always remembered what Fukushima Sensei taught me, "Only use judo as a shield. Your duty is to warn them." I had warned Frank, and the 3:30 fight was approaching. I was calm, but I could see he was nervous and anxious as we passed each other between our last few classes. At 3 o'clock, the bell let us out. A bunch of us headed down the road and out of the gate to a local park.

Ping! The fight was on. He threw a punch, which I blocked. I proceeded to throw him with an ippon seoi-nage, or Japanese wizard. To onlookers, it would've looked like an over-the-shoulder throw. Immediately, I put him in Osaekomi, or holding technique, and continued with my patented arm bar. At that point, I had total control over the situation.

My message to Frank was simple, "That was less than 30 seconds. I have you in an arm bar and could easily choke you out. I will let you up. You have 2 choices. Concede and agree to our noon deal, or you can think that I got lucky and re-engage. If you do, I will break your arm next. You have been warned!" Just like that, Frank was neutralized.

The next day, John came running up to me to let me know, "Sara wants to talk to you at lunch time."

"Do you know what she wants to talk about, John?" as if I didn't know.

"No, but it seems important. It might have something to do with your fight with Frank yesterday. She wanted me to let you know."

At lunch, I walked over to Sara and asked, "You wanted to talk to me?"

Boy, was she adorable. "Yes, Sam, I've been noticing you and think you might be interested in me too, especially after yesterday. I normally like older guys, but you seem so much older than you are. I wonder if you would be interested in going to Homecoming with me?"

And just like that, Sara triggered all my fears from that night at KozaVu. I liked Sara and had planned on asking her out but not this way. No, no, no! A thousand times no. I couldn't get the visuals of KozaVu out of my head... and that smell. I became sick to my stomach and quickly said, "Sorry, Sara, but I can't go to Homecoming with you. I'm not interested in you that way." I made a quick exit, stage right, and headed straight for the restroom in an attempt to purge that feeling from my bowels. In a split second, Sara had gone from giving me a toothache to giving me abdominal spasms.

John followed me and said, "What happened, Sam? What did she want?"

"Sara asked me to Homecoming, and I said no."

John shook his head, "What? I'm confused. You fought Frank yesterday because of her. Don't you like her? Weren't you about to ask her out?"

"I like to pursue. I hate being pursued. It takes me back to that awful KozaVu night." *The smell of cigarettes, alcohol, and cheap perfume.* I was getting sick to my stomach. I blamed John for my fear of being asked out and that recurring smell. "It's nasty! Damn you! Yeah, I liked Sara, but she is no longer the person I want to ask out." KozaVu had doomed me for the rest of my life.

I had just said no to Sara, the person that I had hoped to date. None of this made any sense to anyone, including me. Sara was never going to like me again in this lifetime.

I got home that evening, and Jean asked, "What happened today?"

"Nothing different from any other day. Why?"

"Everyone is talking about a freshman fighting some guy for Sara. Sara asking a freshman to Homecoming and that freshman turning her down. This freshman is a total imbecile. He must be my little brother. Sara's really nice, cute, popular and a good person. I'm so confused. Don't you like her? Why did you say no?" She tapped her nails on the table, sighed and continued, "I'm not sure if I can teach you common sense."

"Long story. The smell of her perfume and timing was bad. I probably won't go to Homecoming now."

"Why? Oddly smart people think my little brother is cute. It's gross. Even my friend Susan wanted to know who you are going to ask to homecoming!"

"Susan! Do you think she would go with me if I asked her?"

"Yes, but getting into a fight won't work this time. You better ask her out soon, like tomorrow, because lots of guys are interested."

Jean could make fun of me, but if anyone outside the family joined in her bashing, she would turn into momma bear and come immediately to my defense. I needed to come up with a clever angle to ask Susan to homecoming, but I also felt bad for Sara. I needed to pull the trigger tomorrow.

I told John to let the homeroom teacher know that I had an important errand to run and that I'd be about 5-10 minutes late for homeroom. I proceeded to the administration office and told the secretary that I needed to make an important public announcement. She turned on the mic, and the rest is history.

"Good morning, fellow Dragons, this is your savvy freshman, Sam Rivtoc, with an important Homecoming announcement. To Susan, the girl everyone wants to ask out. I take thee at thy word. Go with me to Homecoming, and I will be newly baptized! I'm sorry, guys, but Susan's spoken for." As I finished, the principal was standing by my side, so I handed him the mic.

I knew I was going to get detention, and there would be a lot of upset upper-classmen, but if my little antic worked, it was well worth it. I walked into homeroom and received a standing ovation from my classmates.

Throughout the day, strangers came up to me and said that that was one ballsy move. I had earned the respect of even the guys that liked her. During lunchtime, I spotted my new conquest and approached her.

"Well, I didn't expect that from a freshman, Sam. A line from *Romeo and Juliet,* right?"

"You've always got to be on your toes around me. I figured I'd put my best foot forward. Plus, I need a great translator to help me navigate off base."

"I don't think anyone's going to ask me out now after those theatrics. It was sweet, but way over the top. You don't need a translator; you have an army of local judo fans."

"Great!" I said with an internal wellspring of enthusiasm. I cooled it down enough to ask, "What color is your dress?"

"Blue. I guess I'm going to Homecoming with you, Sam."

I had just created major chaos in the high school Homecoming order. I pulled out my notebook and pen and created a checklist for homecoming. Corsage, check. Pick up Susan. I don't have a car, much less a driver's license. That might be a huge *date* obstacle. Dinner reservations at Sam's by the Sea, check.

I had a major transportation problem, but I had a solution. It was time to call in my chips. Two months prior, I was at a popular beach hangout called Maeda point. Butch Haney and 6 other upperclassmen were there with me. A group of locals were talking to some of our girls and the guys, namely Butch, got jealous. They had about 30 people, and we had 5, excluding the girls. Those were horrible odds for a beef. The problem was, they called in the cavalry. Suddenly, there were 30 cars blocking the entrance and about 100 more locals approaching us. I braced for a massacre. No matter how strong or well-trained we were, there was no way 5 of us would be able to manage to fend off 130 guys. As they got closer, I recognized many of them from the judo tournaments, including Ishikawa-san. I bowed and asked Susan to help me out because she was fluent in Japanese.

"Susan, please let them know that it is an honor to see him tonight. There is some confusion because those 2 guys thought some of these guys were hitting on their girlfriends. Unfortunately, due to language barriers, it escalated. But we do apologize for the misunderstanding." Susan translated.

Ishikawa responded, "We were told a bunch of gaijin were causing problems at the beach."

"I understand your concern. But there are only 8 of us and 3 are women. I don't think they needed to call all of you. But I'm glad they did because we didn't get a chance to get to know one another outside of the judo tournaments."

We heard a lot of mumbling and the name Sam. "Susan, what are they saying?"

Susan responded, "They are all talking about you, Sam. They know you as the only guy that could ever beat Ishikawa and are glad that they came out and got to meet the legend."

"Tell them it was an absolute fluke. My mom was in the audience, and I was so afraid to go home to her punishment if I lost. My superhuman powers were displayed that day because my mom's bite would have been worse. Otherwise, Ishikawa-san would still be undefeated." Susan translated, and they all laughed.

"Also tell them that Mom is over there on the beach watching so we should just celebrate." Everyone laughed, and we all became friends.

That evening Butch was grateful that we didn't get annihilated and told me, "If you ever needed anything, I owe you one." It was time to call in that chip.

I ran into Butch after 3rd period. "Butch, remember Maeda? Well, you probably heard this morning that I asked Susan to homecoming."

"Sam, I owe you big time for Maeda. And that was one crazy move you made this morning. What do you need?"

"Can we double date? I'll pay for gas."

"What... you need a chauffeur or something?"

"You got it, Butch!"

"Sam, Homecoming at our age isn't about the dance. It's about the after party. Susan's a nice girl, but she might take advantage of you. I'll chauffeur you around from dinner to the dance, but my services end at midnight. You are on your own after that and don't worry about the gas. You saved my ass!"

My slight OCD kicked in. I had 2 weeks to prepare. I monitored the blue line Bus schedule from Gate 1 to Gate 2 and timed it on Friday, Saturday and Sunday night. The taxi schedule from the USO to Susan's house near Gate 2 and back to the USO. The taxi schedule from Gate 2 to Sam's by the Sea, which was approx. 5.5 kilometers. On Friday, it was 2 hours and 23 minutes. On Saturday, 2 hours and 10 minutes, and on Sunday, 2 hours. I went with the worst-case scenario and added another 43 minutes or a 20 percent contingency to the time. And figured I was safe and ready for next week. I need to go over the budget next. It would be $100 for 2 amazing 1-lb fresh Maine lobsters, drinks, appetizers, and desserts; $40 for transportation; pictures, $20; after party, $50. I wasn't about to be embarrassed, so my target budget was $400. I checked my emergency stash; I was short $220. I needed to turn on the charm with Mom and convince her to make up the difference. That week, I was a model student. Mowed the lawn. Cleaned the dishes and made an extra $40. I had $180 left to go. I reduced my lunch money spending and only ate French fries for the 2 weeks. Sweet – another $40 saved. Still short $140. My modified Friday, Saturday and Sunday traffic tests cost me $100. I was now short $240. Order and pay for the corsage and flowers $15. Short $255. By Wednesday, I finally convinced Mom to cover $160. The difference was $85. Maybe I could order a modest meal and save. Jean knew I was sweating bullets by Thursday. After my tutoring lesson that afternoon, she said, "I don't know what I'm gonna do, Mom. My imbecile of a brother asks somebody to Homecoming without a car or enough money saved. Here is 35,000 yen. I've worked hard to earn that. I had to deal with someone who seriously taxed my brain. Spend it wisely. Mom, I'm sure he doesn't even know how much that is. God save us all."

"Jean, that's approximately $156, based on the current exchange rate of 225 yen to $1. You are a total lifesaver. I have the best sister in the world." I hugged her.

"What can I do… you are my kid brother. But I still think they adopted you. Mom, can we test his IQ? He's so far behind in physics and pre-calculus. I worry!"

I had to self-talk myself out of the room. *Shut up and be gracious and walk away. You have the cash and are totally ready for Homecoming. It's okay to lose today's battle since you've won the war.* Jean was the Vince Lombardi of academics. She relentlessly pursued perfection, knowing full well that she couldn't attain it but in the process would attain excellence. Good was never good enough. Jean got one B in her entire K-12 experience. I was a realist and very good with numbers. I knew Mom's tolerance level for B's, and I just needed to make sure to stay within the one B per report card window. How could Jean understand what it was like to be a guy in high school? First, you play sports, then you become noticed and popular, and then you get the girls. I had a date with destiny for Homecoming, and her name was Susan.

Chapter 35

2nd Base

I had on my 2-button Koza tailored suit with a gray-on-gray shirt/tie combination and corsage in hand. I headed for the bus stop at 4:18 precisely. I had been sitting there waiting for approximately 15 minutes when I heard a honk. Then another 4 honks. It was Jean.

"Sam, are you slow at everything you do? Hurry up and get in the car!"

"Aren't you going to Homecoming, Jean?"

"Yes, I'm meeting my friend at her place, which is near Susan's house. I can take you there and then have one of our dates take you kids to the restaurant because we'll need at least an hour to get ready. Upper-class folks don't eat dinner at 7:00 p.m. or rush the dance when the doors open. We move at our own pace and are always late. Seriously, who plans to catch a bus to Homecoming at 4:30? What am I gonna do with you, Sam?"

I ran the numbers in my head and figured that I had just saved 10 percent of my cash, $40, shaved 60 minutes off the time, and eliminated most of the uncertainties. I was grateful that Jean was worried about me but didn't want me to think she was. When we arrived at her friend's house, she handed me a sheet of paper. It was a checklist reminder.

1. Always open the car door for Susan. 2. Open all doors for her. 3. Ask her what she wants to drink first. 4. If you aren't sure what to order to drink, just get the same thing she orders. 5. Let her order first. 6. Same rule for food as drinks. 7. Wait for Susan to start eating before you eat. 8. Homecoming is at the Botanical Gardens.

"I made a checklist of only 8 items, simple enough for even you to understand. Oh! And have fun, Sam!"

Chris, my sister's date, drove me to Susan's house and waited in the car. I knocked on her door. When she opened it, I was blown away. She was a total knockout!

Her father interposed himself and said, "Excuse me, young man, but I need to talk to you." As he led the way into the living room and gestured for me to sit, he continued, "What's your name, young man? Tell me about yourself."

"Sir, my name is Sam Rivtoc. I'm the luckiest freshman at Kubasaki since I am accompanying your lovely daughter to Homecoming. Although my sister doesn't think I'm that bright, I must be relatively smart since Susan accepted my request over all others. What time would you like me to have your daughter home by?"

"Midnight!"

"Considering the dance ends at midnight, and I'm a freshman without a license or a car, I will be dependent on others and, or taxis to return my beautiful date safely home. Rather than tell you that I will have her back by midnight, knowing that that might be a challenge due to my transportation limitations, I would like to ask for your consideration."

"Go on, Sam."

"Under normal circumstances, and if I were in your shoes, I would think that midnight would be totally reasonable. Would you kindly allow for certain contingencies and uncertainties in light of my lack of transportation and stretch it to 1:30 am? I'm planning on having Susan home as close to midnight as possible, but I don't want to disappoint you if we are late. To be honest with you, sir, I'm

∞

slightly nervous. This is all new to me since I've only had one girlfriend in my entire 15 years on this planet."

"Sam, I like honest guys dating my daughter. Have fun and make sure she gets home by 2:00 a.m. and not a second later."

"Deal, sir!" We shook hands, and I was off with Susan. Chris said hello to Susan, turned up the music, and drove off.

"Wow, that's a first! Normally, I'm struggling and fighting to get my father to agree to midnight. I need you to negotiate all my deals with my dad. Where are you taking me, Sam?"

"I'm taking you to Sam's By the Sea. I trust you like seafood?"

"Haha. I love their seafood, especially their lobsters, Sam! I still can't believe the way you asked me out… I can't believe that I said *yes* to a freshman… I can't believe I'm out on a date with you… and I can't believe you negotiated with my dad. You have me until 2:00 a.m."

I was an expert on getting on base. Unfortunately, the 6-month relationship with Ann Marie only prepared me for first base.

"Relax, Susan, you're going to have a great evening," I said as I strategically reached to hold her hand.

We gazed into each other's eyes, and she leaned in and started to kiss me. I was in trouble. I had mastered 2 moves—holding hands and kissing—and I had used them both within 15 minutes of the date.

Susan placed my hands on her breasts. I didn't mind at all. Then her hands started wandering a little below the belt. My senses were stimulated, and my little guy was trying to salute. I had officially advanced to 2nd base! Chris, who was observing the whole PDA, said, "Y'all need to get a room and simmer down back there. I don't want any *Sam* stains on my back seat. Being that he's a freshman and all, he might not be able to control himself."

We all laughed, but I was a little embarrassed by the truth in his statement.

Ping! I woke up from my flashback and had an urgent need to take care of.

"Excuse me, Linda; I need to go to the restroom."

"Did you get all excited dreaming about me, Sam?" As I squeezed by her and into the aisle, she tapped me on my butt and said, "Hurry back, cowboy."

What an intense dream! Deep REM finally. It seemed so real. But I hate it women hit on me... Ooooooh... and that smell... I'm about to get sick! I felt the dry-heaves and relieved myself in the restroom. Threw water on my face. As I returned, I noticed an empty aisle seat, sat down and closed my eyes. I thought of Caroline and reread the last text.

Hi, Sam, I'm sorry, but I shouldn't go on this trip with you. Jules needs your undivided attention. Call me when you land in Florida. Travel safely! Take care.

Thinking of her had been easy. I thought of her all the time and had over the past 15 years. It was the pain of losing her back in high school that hurt. What if I lost her again? I closed my eyes and went back to la la land.

Homecoming with Susan was exciting, adventurous and stimulating, but within 2 weeks, I discovered that it wasn't going to work out. I was a tadpole trying to date a frog. A date with a freshman was cute, but she was way out of my social league, and quickly the negatives outweighed the positives. The lack of transportation was a huge complication. Relationships weren't just about physical attraction and good company. Other forces impacted, like money, cars and time. I didn't have lots of money. I didn't have a car. The writing was on the wall, and I had run out of time. Ann Marie and I broke up, but outside factors forced that. We never talked about it. It just happened. With Susan, I knew after a week, and by the 2nd Friday, it was over. I approached her at lunchtime. It always seemed like the cafeteria was sacred ground and a place for communicating.

"Susan, first of all, I want to thank you for going out on a limb and agreeing to go with me to Homecoming. You made my day... You made my year. You made my high school!"

"Sam, I'm sensing that you are about to break up with me. Are you?"

"Susan, you are the IT girl. Every guy here would do anything... Say anything to go out with you. I just feel horrible that I can't treat you the way you deserve to be treated. I don't have a license or a car. I would rather see you be happy with someone else treating you properly than sad with me."

"Sam, you are breaking up with me in the sweetest way."

"No, you have a reputation to maintain. I'm just a freshman chasing a dream. So you broke up with me today. Okay?"

She smiled. "Got it. Thanks, Sam. You are the best, and I'm going to miss your sweet kisses. Oh, and Sam, I might ask *you* for a favor in the future."

"No worries, Susan. What?"

"My dad thinks the world of you, so when I want to stay out beyond midnight, can you come over and negotiate for me?" We both laughed.

Before I knew it, freshman year was over. Jean was graduating and heading off to Emory University in Atlanta. Before she left, she said, "Sam, I've been tutoring and tormenting you for the past 6 years so that you would someday turn out to be a *somebody*. It is time for you to fly on your own. I love you, and if you ever need anything I'll be there to pick you up!"

∞

Chapter 36

Sweet Southern Caroline

I transferred to Kadena High School after Jean graduated. Sophomore year was a blur. I felt like a traitor leaving all of my friends behind at Kubasaki, but a few classmates transferred too. I felt equally like a traitor to my friends at Kadena because of feeling like a traitor to my Kubasaki classmates. I still performed at a high level in Varsity football and wrestling to maintain the coveted *cool crowd* status.

Things had changed drastically by my junior year. A new girl, Caroline, had caught my eye. She was a year younger than yours truly and beyond cute. I couldn't focus on my classes or sports. The spotlight was on her. I needed more data. Ahem, covertly of course. I conducted *Operation Secretly* in the most top-secret way. Who were her friends? Any mutual ones? What classes was she taking? Any window of opportunity? She was enrolled in art class. I could drop a "harder" elective and add that "easy" art class. For a month, I noted her entire schedule. The probable path she would take from class to class. Where she ate lunch. What she ordered. Her choice of music. All her friends, especially this new girl, Randi. I had to eliminate any and all uncertainties. By September, I had devised a "Sam in distress" plan to engage her more directly than admiring her from afar. So I approached her friend, Randi.

"Hi, Randi."

"Are you talking to me, Sam Rivtoc?

"Yes."

"Why is Mr. Football Player, Wrestler, Smart and Popular Sam talking to me… the newbie?"

"I'm really embarrassed to tell anyone, but I need help. Yes, even Sam needs help now and then. Do you know anyone that is good at art? I'm taking an art class because I thought it would be an easy A. Floundering badly would be an understatement. I'm drowning."

"Sam, I might know some artists. Let me think about it and get back to you."

I tilted my head to the side and asked, "Randi, don't you know that girl? I'm not sure what her name is. She's in my art class. She's like the teacher's pet. Sounds like Clair, Carol, or maybe Caroline?"

Randi looked down and then looked at me directly. "Caroline? Yes, I know Caroline. Yes, she's very sweet. I do believe that she is in your art class!"

My recon seemed to be paying off, but I needed to contain my excitement and act like I knew nothing. "Are you sure she's in my art class? How do you know?"

"Sam, I'm not sure if I'm supposed to talk about it. But I'm 100 percent sure that Caroline is in your class," reported Randi.

"Excellent! Can you do me a huge favor and see if *Sweet* Caroline would mind helping me with my final project? I would owe you big time."

"Yeah, sure, Sam, I'll ask her."

Operation Secretly was turning into Operation Sweet Caroline. I was smitten because she knew who I was. My instincts told me that I was about to finally get to know her better. By lunchtime, Randi came by the table and said in a singsong, "Your Caroline wants to talk. You have your art tutor, Sam!"

"Randi, this is John. He's also part of the 'Pop-U-Lar' varsity crowd. John, Randi. She's a newbie in town with an attitude. Excuse me while I go 'reach out and touch' my tutor!"

∞

I walked over to Caroline's table and introduced myself.

"Hello, Caroline, I'm Sam Rivtoc. Thanks for agreeing to help me with my art project."

She brushed back a wisp of hair that had fallen into her face and smiled demurely. "Hi, Sam."

I caught my breath and refocused on the task at hand. "Do you mind if I join you for lunch?"

I recognized the nervous look and the way she had said my name earlier. Looking back, I knew I had her at "hello." With a nervous laugh, she answered, "Okay."

"Have you ordered, or can I get you something?"

"I was about to get in line when Randi told me about your art class issues."

"Caroline, you stay here and let me get us some food. Let me guess... I sense you are a salad with ranch dressing person. Right?"

"Ummmm, right. But I would also like?"

"Wait... small order of fries with soda... Probably orange soda!"

She nodded her head in confusion. "Yes, is it that noticeable, Sam?"

"No, just a good guess on my part!" Of course, I knew what she wanted. I'd been observing and taking mental notes for over a month.

We ate lunch together every day and talked about my final project. It was a Mona Lisa, which she had inspired me to paint. She was beautiful, classy and intelligent. There was an emotional connection. We were getting to know each other without even a single date. By mid-October, it was time for me to escalate.

I seized the moment during lunchtime. "Caroline, I have something important to talk about."

∞

"What is it? What's wrong?"

"My Mona Lisa. It's not coming out so well. I need lots of help, or I'm likely to get a B in Art, or worse, a C. That would not be good. I'll end up on restriction for the rest of the school year."

"Sam, I have time after school and on the weekends to help out. Your art skills are not good at all. Why did you enroll in art class?"

"I thought it was going to be an easy A and it's turning into a nightmare C. You are just too kind, Caroline. I have another problem, but I'm just too embarrassed to mention it."

"What, Sam?"

"Well. You've been so helpful with art, and I just think I might be overreaching. Would it be asking too much if.... You see, I have a huge favor to ask you.... Oh, never mind. I can't ask you for any more favors."

"Sam just ask me and I'll say yes."

"Anything?"

"Yes." She thought about it and then added, "Anything legal, Sam, and within reason."

"Pinky promise?"

"If you don't ask now, I'm going to reconsider helping you with the Mona Lisa."

"K. Caroline, I don't have a Homecoming date. Was wondering, if you don't have any plans... would you be so kind as to go with me?"

"Are you asking me out to Homecoming, Sam?"

"It's legal to go to Homecoming and within reason. You pinky promised that you'd say yes."

She smiled and said, "I'll go to Homecoming with you, Sam."

After school, Randi, John and the rest of my inner circle surrounded me to ask about my Homecoming date.

John said, "I heard that you asked Caroline to Homecoming."

Randi quickly chimed in, "If you call that *asking*? That was weak…Real weak. It was like a charity case. It's not a date; it's a pity date."

John edged Randi out, "Sam, Caroline is a nice girl…. We are talking total virgin nun… with chastity belt and 2 feet of body armor. Who in their right mind spends all that money and doesn't get laid? Sam, you are book smart but horrible at selecting women."

"That coming from the KozaVu expert." As I said that, I knew I shouldn't have in present company. Randi quickly looked at John in a new way. So to change the focus back to me, I quickly added, "What can I say? She's starting to grow on me, in a special way. It's more than physical attraction, John. And by the way, who are you going to go with?" I looked at Randi and smiled. "… Randi?"

Randi stated, "I don't have a chastity belt or body armor, but I'm not about to go with John and get laid. Sorry, John, but I'm a nice girl, too."

"Damn it, Sam! Why do you make me talk so freely around people I like?"

We all laughed.

Randi quipped, "I'm a girl, Sam, and that was the weakest, most unromantic ask-out in the history of ask-outs. You need to suck it up and ask her out on a real date before Homecoming."

"Randi, you are right. Maybe I'll invite her to watch *Top Gun* with me. That has action and romance. I'll test the waters, and if things progress, we can all go dancing next weekend at Kona Gardens."

Randi said, "Excuse me. By WE are you including John and me?"

"Yes, Randi. Remember the crazy 24-hour Panther Run Relay. Your team lost."

"Your team lost, too, Sam. The freshman team won it all that year, right? "

"Yeah, my ego was bruised when we lost to the freshman team. My body was sore for a week. But I had that one tiny consolation prize. We beat your team, and the bet was whatever I asked that was legal and within reason. So I'm collecting. A double date. A date with John is legal. Morally wrong, but still legal."

"Borderline unreasonable but okay; you won fair and square."

I devised a plan to ask Caroline out. Friday, I would head over to the bowling alley and "accidentally" run into Randi and John at 5:30. Order pizza and then head to the movies by 7:30. I asked Randi to pick up a rose for me and leave it in her car. That Thursday at lunch I approached Caroline.

"Hey, Caroline, any plans for this weekend?"

"No plans yet, why? Do you need help with the Mona Lisa?"

"Yes. After school Friday. Saturday all day and even into the evening. Maybe Sunday too."

"Sam, do you have OCD? I need to talk to my dad about the evenings. How late on Friday and Saturday?"

"Friday 9:30-10 ish and Saturday probably later but I'll know better after Friday night."

"Okay, Sam. I'll let you know tomorrow."

∞

The next day, Caroline smiled and said, "I can't believe it's your lucky weekend. You have me until 10 p.m. tonight and midnight on Saturday. I told my dad how much help you needed, so he agreed."

School ended at 3:00, and we headed to the art room. Time flew by. I noticed her hands, her smile... the mannerisms and knew I had fallen... hard. At 5:15, I looked up and said "Caroline, I'm starving. Wanna grab pizza at the bowling alley?"

"I'm not that hungry but, sure, I'll go with you, Sam. Let me make sure I have the key to the classroom to get back in."

We drove to the bowling alley and "ran into" Randi, John and the rest of the gang.

Randi yelled, "Hey! What are you doing tonight, Sam?"

"I'm painting my Mona Lisa with my favorite artist."

"What! Mr. Social Night Life is staying in on a Friday night to paint? It must be love."

Caroline responded, "No, it's not a date. He needs lots of help with art."

"Yeah, that's what they all say. We are grabbing pizza. Want to join us?"

"Sure, Randi!" Caroline and I both spoke at the same time. We laughed and sat down.

We ate and talked about football and the usual high school gossip.

Suddenly, Randi's father walked in. He sat down in his Navy uniform and asked what we were up to.

"Hi, Dad, just sitting around having some pizza."

Intrigued, I asked, staring at his freshly starched jacket, "Hi, Mr. Cruz, what branch of the service are you with?"

He looked at me and smiled. "I am involved in AWACS."

"What is AWACS?" I asked.

Randi stared at me in disbelief as her father explained, "It involves sonars, subs, and 'Pings.' And that, son, is all you need to know."

I looked at him with a confused expression on my face.

Randi waved her hands in front of my face. I refocused on her as she said, "It is like you flying around PINGING and following the girl of your dreams for 30 days."

I quickly changed the subject and asked, "What are you guys doing next, Randi?"

"They are going to go watch *Top Gun*, but I'm going to see Tom Cruise and the other hot guys on the screen. Wanna come, Caroline?"

"I'd love to go with you guys.... But Sam needs help."

"Caroline, I need a mental break. Let's go watch *Top Gun* with them!"

I paid for the 2 tickets, ordered a large popcorn and 2 sodas. The national anthem played... everyone in the theater stood at attention, then the lights dimmed, we all sat down, and the movie started. Twenty minutes into the movie... I made my move. I had tons of experience holding hands in movie theaters with Ann Marie. I looked over, and Caroline just smiled. It was kismet, meant to be because she smiled sweetly back at me.

After the movie, I ran to Randi's car, grabbed the rose and handed it to Caroline. "It's 9:30. I better get you home before your curfew." Caroline nodded.

As I drove her home, I said, "Thanks for a wonderful evening, Caroline!"

"Sam, I had fun tonight, but that wasn't a date." I looked puzzled, and she said, "If you want to date me, Sam, you have to ask me out properly.""

I parked the car and got out to open her door.

"Caroline. I'm going to be completely honest with you. I've liked you ever since I laid eyes on you back when school started. I'm only taking art class because I found out you were in it. I'm a lovestruck Romeo." I got down on one knee and said, "I take thee at thy word... go dancing with me tomorrow on a date, and I'll be newly baptized."

She smiled and said, "Okay. I'll go on a date with you tomorrow but don't think I'm going to kiss you tonight."

"So tomorrow is a date! And tonight, I wasn't planning on kissing you, that is, unless you wanted to... I would let you kiss me if you wanted. I still need help with my Mona Lisa. What time can I pick up you to get started?'

"Let's say 10:00 a.m., Sam. Good night! Thanks for a wonderful evening. And I've liked you ever since you walked into art class. I'm looking forward to our date... dancing tomorrow night!"

Ping! The fasten seat belt light had come on. I can't believe they woke me up! I wanted to go back in time for the next night. The night I kissed Caroline. The night she cast her spell on me. The night I tripped over the bushes. I closed my eyes and was taken to Christmas break. I knew I was getting five A's and one B. I wasn't sure what my art class grade would be. We had 2 weeks of Christmas vacation. I was getting either a C or a B. The 3 & 7 lashes kept haunting me, so I approached the art teacher and asked if I could work through the vacation on my Mona Lisa. By then, Caroline and I had been officially dating for a month. I spent the entire 2 weeks painting. My Mona Lisa was Caroline, and I wanted to make sure that it wasn't a C or B Caroline but an A Caroline.

By the 10th day, Mom came by the classroom and said, "Sam, it's okay. You aren't an artist. I'm worried you are going to get sick. Whatever grade it is, I won't be mad."

Caroline came by every day and said, "Sam, I worry. It's good enough. Not everyone is an artist." But I plugged away.

Finally, the art teacher came in on the 11th day. "Sam, I love your effort. You just aren't an artist. You look exhausted, and I admire your determination and dedication. Let's make a deal because I'm feeling really horrible knowing that you've been living in my classroom for the past 11 days. I'll give you an A-, but you promise never to take another art class with me again."

"I accept your deal, but I'm not done yet. I still have 3 more days to finish my Mona Lisa. I'll know that I could have improved my Mona Lisa but stopped short for the letter grade. And I wouldn't be able to live with that, considering what she represents. I plan to continue, ma'am."

When school started on the 15th day, I was exhausted but so proud to see my completed Mona Lisa. We had to present our drawings in class.

"This is my Mona Lisa. I took this class solely because I saw a beautiful girl at the beginning of the year. She had taken this art class. So I enrolled in this class to be able to see her smiling face each morning. I thought it would be an easy elective," I glanced at my art teacher and chuckled. I looked back at the class and continued, "But in all seriousness, it has turned out to be the most challenging class in the history of my education. My Mona Lisa represents all the females in my life that I loved so far. Her smile reflects all the fond memories I've shared. I've spent 18 hours a day, for the past 2 weeks, forgoing the vacation to finish this... Was this class worth it? Were my efforts worth it? You bet. My Mona Lisa is dedicated to my mom, my sister and my Caroline."

After class, Caroline approached me and gazed into my eyes.

"That was the sweetest thing anyone's ever said about me. I've been saving myself for the right guy, Sam. I can't wait for my 16th birthday in April." She leaned in and kissed me, and I melted.

I was on top of the world. I gave Mom the Mona Lisa and showed her my report card, six A's and one B. I was dating Caroline. For Christmas, I bought her a special gift. I had saved all summer and was hoping to invest in a used car. Instead, I purchased a special Tiffany Infinity necklace. I wanted her to know that I would love her forever.

I got my Varsity letters in football and wrestling. Caroline and I had amazing friends, and we went to the best parties and clubs. There was easy access to the clubs just outside Gate 2: Manhattans, 8-Beat and NY/NY. We danced every weekend. Access to alcohol in high school was just as easy: vending machines, Class VI stores on base, bars off base. There were random parties at the SeaWall, Maeda Point, and the Cave. Life was great, but my world was about to come crashing down, and I didn't know it.

Chapter 37

Hell Night or Heaven

Ping! It was Hell Night. I had lettered in wrestling my freshman year and when I transferred to Kadena High School I also lettered in football and wrestling. By my junior year, I was the head of the Varsity Club. There were 20 of us in the club. Everyone had at least 3 varsity letters and had to endure a week of initiation culminating in Hell Night. Everyone that went through the initiation wanted to make sure that the next group of newcomers would receive similar hazing.

The weeks leading up to Hell Night, John had been planning his revenge. He would report to me about successfully collecting dog poop and placing it into 20 energy drink cans, buying 20 "Good News! shavers," 20 bottles of tabasco sauce and preparing the paddle. Last year, he was the first person to volunteer for the paddling, thinking leniency would be granted because he was first. Well, he got hit hard, and the paddle flew 10 yards and broke. He couldn't walk for a week. Now, he was ready for Hell Night.

There were 15 Jock Straps and 20 Lettermen. It was Saturday Night in March. We congregated at Kadena High School at 7:30 p.m. A group of 6 went off to purchase beer for the post-initiation party. John was telling everyone he was low on gas, so 4 of the guys went off to siphon gas from one of the military vehicles. We asked for volunteers, and they all agreed that if you got caught, you were on your own. The final rendezvous point was Luke's Beach past Gate 4 at 10:30 p.m. Twenty-five of us headed toward the golf course near Gate 1. We ordered the Jock Straps to grab all 18 flags from the golf course within 30 minutes. By 8:30 they had completed their mission. We waited until 9:00 p.m. and the other 10 folks had not returned. Because the judge advocate general's office was close by, we ran the possibility of the MPs stopping by to question us. Instead of hanging out in the open, we headed to McDonald's. John directed the 10 Jock Straps to form a single line and order a milkshake.

"You need to order a milkshake and say, 'Thank you, McDonald's' and then pour it over your head." Our antics caused so much commotion there, we headed out to Devil's Den near the Gate 1 exit. That put us at the Den at 10:30 p.m. sharp, but the other 10 were still MIA. I was getting nervous because the prior year, everyone got arrested for buying beer and breaking into the high school gymnasium. My fear was that something bad had happened to the other folks.

John was leading the initiation at Devil's Den. He blindfolded the 10 and split the lineup into 2 groups. I heard John yelling, "Time for the Energy Game. Put your hands out. You need to pass whatever's in this can. I have Good News for the losing team." I knew what he was going to do so I started to run far away. I could smell the stench of watered down 2-week-old dog shit!

I could hear, "I'm sorry, Sir, but I'm about to yack from the smell" to "Is that shit?" to "Don't drop this and hurry up."

The Lettermen were all laughing. It was funny, but I was feeling sorry for the Jock Straps. When the game ended, John told the losing team to strip down and tossed the pack of Good News! razors at them.

I heard one of Jock Straps protest, "I'm sorry, sir, but it has taken me 16 years to grow my pubic hair, and my girlfriend would kill me if I shaved it off tonight." I laughed loudly and pulled rank on John and told them that they didn't need to shave their private areas. John looked at me, upset, but agreed and then poured tobacco

∞

sauce on their privates instead. I could hear everyone screaming from the burn. They all jumped into the ocean, which only opened the pores and enhanced the burning. I knew because I had gone through this initiation myself. When they returned from the Ocean, John handed each group 2 dozen eggs and told them to have an egg fight. By midnight, I knew that something bad had happened to the other 10 folks. As the paddle ceremony was commencing, 2 undercover police officers blinded us with flashlights in our faces and asked us all for our ID cards.

The bad news was that on Kadena, or any military base, if a dependent got into trouble, the parents got in trouble too. The good news was that there were 35 of us and most of the 20 Lettermen parents were officers, including the base commander's son. How bad could it get?

The next day we were all called into the JAG office with the police and attorney. They took statements from all of us. I was the last one. The person questioning me was Col. Dean. The father of Caroline Dean. I wanted to die.

"Sam, my daughter tells me that you are smart, popular and a leader. She talks about you all the time. Based on this report, I'm not sure if she knows you well at all. I'm concerned about my precious Caroline. You have 2 choices. You and your friends get 60 days of community service and the parents all get a reprimand. Or you guys get 90 days community service without any punishment to your parents," he paused to let it soak in and added, "but you will no longer date my daughter nor see her ever again."

"Col. Dean, may I have 5 minutes to think about your offer."

"Yes, Sam."

I knew there was only one choice I could make. When my time was up, I said, "Colonel Dean, I don't see the relevance of all the parents being reprimanded and me dating Caroline. But I understand why you would be concerned. The punishment does not fit the crime, but I have no leverage. So I will take one for the team and sacrifice the 1 person that I really care about for the good of the group. I promise not to date your daughter again. In exchange, can you reduce our community service to 60 days while still abiding by not reprimanding the parents?"

"Deal, Sam."

I broke up with Caroline the next day. She was hurt, and I was devastated. April came and with it Caroline's birthday. I ordered a dozen roses and signed the card with an Infinity mark. I was out drinking, drowning my sorrows so that I could forget my Caroline. I don't remember who I went to prom with, but I do remember sending Caroline a dozen roses and signing the card with the Infinity mark. Senior year, Randi and I were Homecoming King and Queen. My thoughts gravitated towards Caroline. I would see her wander the halls at Kadena High School. Jealousy would shroud me if she was talking to any other guy. I was the Far East wrestling champion. I was admitted to Georgetown on a full scholarship, but my thoughts were on Caroline. Suddenly, I was off to college. It was supposed to be the best time of my life. In actuality, art class and dating Caroline were the best times of my life.

I returned home when my spring semester ended and ran into Randi.

"Sam, I have good news and bad news."

"What? Well, good news first, of course."

"Good news, Caroline is single. Bad news, she needs a date for Prom and is planning on asking you. I know how you hate it when girls ask you..."

"What? How do you know?"

"Well, shortly after you left for Georgetown, Caroline found out the deal you made with her dad during that junior year fiasco. She had wondered why you broke up with her and never talked to her again but would send her flowers on her birthday, Homecoming and Prom. The whole school knew that you sacrificed your love for everyone else. I'm about to cry, Sam! Okay, maybe not. But that was an extremely COOL thing to do!"

"Let's go to Kadena High School. I've missed her smiling face."

As we entered the cafeteria doors, I could hear the chants of "Sam!" but I was focused on my Mona Lisa smiling.

Ping! The captain had turned on the seat belt sign. We were about 15 minutes away from landing.

I closed my eyes and went back to the cafeteria moment. I just needed 15 more minutes with my Caroline.

"Sam, I have a huge favor to ask of you."

"Caroline, you know that you can ask me anything so long as its legal and within reason. Let me guess; you are thinking of asking me out. Well, you can't ask me out. I need to talk to someone. Give me 3 hours."

"If you are talking about my dad, I wouldn't worry about it. I'm so mad at him."

"Caroline, please. Just give until 3 p.m. I'll meet you here at 3 p.m."

I got in my car and drove to the staff judge advocate's office and entered the building.

"Young man, who are you here to see?"

"I don't have an appointment but can you please let Col. Dean know that Sam Rivtoc would like to meet with him."

Col. Dean walked out immediately.

"Sam, how are you doing? Why are you here?"

"Col. Dean, Sir, I'm here because I made a promise to you more than 2 years ago. I vowed never to go out with Caroline again. She needs a date for prom, and I can't let her go by herself, and I refuse to let her ask me out. So, I'm asking you to allow me to ask your daughter out to prom. If you say no, I will honor our deal but I think that would be a grave mistake, sir."

"Sam, Caroline's been very upset at me for the past year. She blames me for losing you. My wife hasn't really spoken to me either. Do you know what it's like when you have 2 women whom you love angry at you? You are granted a reprieve and a stay of hostilities. Ask her out so that I may have some peace in my household again."

"I have a lot of catching up to do, Sir. Will you agree to an 8 a.m. curfew?"

"I can do a 6 a.m."

"No, no, no. Nothing good ever comes of 6 a.m. How about I flip you for it? 8 a.m. if I win, 12 a.m. if you win."

Col. Dean reached in his pocket to pull out a quarter, but I grabbed my lucky 1888 Morgan silver dollar and said, "I need a little luck on my side. Do you mind if I use my silver dollar? Heads, I win. Tails, you win." I flipped the coin, and it was heads.

The Colonel looked up and said, "Can I trust you with my daughter, Sam?"

"I'm here keeping my promise with you. She's my Mona Lisa, sir; you can trust me."

"Deal."

I was in love... My dopamine, serotonin, and oxytocin were at an all-time extreme high. I raced over to the florist and grabbed a card and wrote...

∞

Prom, holding your hand and kissing your lips are things I would like to do. Signed with the Infinity mark.

I showed up early for our 3 p.m. appointment, but Caroline was already there. I approached with a spring in my step, but it felt like I was walking in heaven, looking at my sweet, sweet angel, Caroline. She smiled, and all wrongs were righted. As I handed her the flowers, I got down on 1 knee.

"I take thee at thy word, go to prom with me, and I'll be newly baptized."

Caroline's smile brightened, and she said with a chuckle, "Sam, are you asking me out on a date?"

Ping! The flight attendant stated, "The captain has indicated that we are landing in San Francisco in 5 minutes. Please fasten your seatbelts."

I snapped back into reality that it was Caroline. It had always been Caroline. I should have known from high school that all the achievements didn't matter. Caroline was the missing dot to my "i" and the cross to my "t". I should have connected with her sooner.

Chapter 38
December 15 @ 22:05

 Ping! I received a text from Jean: *Let me know when you land. Is Caroline with you?*

I responded with *I just landed. Caroline had other plans and could not make it.*

I felt guilty knowing that Mom was anxiously waiting for me to introduce her to Caroline. I knew that it wouldn't happen on this visit.

 Ping! A text from Caroline. *Hope you landed in SF safely!*

I texted back *Yes, Heading towards baggage claim now. Been thinking of you.*

 Ping! As I continued down the escalator, I received a text from Caroline at 22:05: *Me too! Look down, Sam. Can't wait to see the Golden Gate, Napa and your family. The best is yet to come.*

Ping! Ping! Ping! It was Caroline!... Sweet, Sweet Caroline... My most important number. The Number 1... The one that got away... here... at the bottom of the escalator. I dropped my bag and opened my arms and was elated to see my Mona Lisa smiling in person! It is true that only Caroline could heal me! Of course, the "V" was for "viable." I am so glad I was "vigilant." It was December 15 at 22:05. Converting the sequential numbers in my head 12 (L), 15 (O) at 22 (V) 05 (E). I'm a Numbers Guy, and the numbers never lie. I was going to Get It Done because Caroline was the one... the one that got away, but my LOVE was found again.

ABOUT THE AUTHOR

The Ping Ha Chi nom de plume was born from a desire to share the author's story about the girl who got away. In Chinese, Ping refers to a duckweed, a flower without any roots. The protagonist, Sam, blooms in the business world, but lacks meaningful personal roots. Ha Chi refers to laughter and it's connection to life force energy. Coincidentally, hachi in Japanese refers to the number 8.

The author is a former lawyer and transactional partner, advising early-stage tech companies to global Fortune 500 companies. A senior executive for both a leading food manufacturing and a renewable energy company, he received his B.S. from Georgetown University and a J.D. from Emory University. His favorite flavor of ice cream is Dulce de Leche.

Visit him at www.pinghachi888.com

Made in the USA
Middletown, DE
12 December 2016